JUSTICE RETURNS

Rayven T. Hill

Ray of Joy Publishing
Toronto

Books by Rayven T. Hill

Blood and Justice
Cold Justice
Justice for Hire
Captive Justice
Justice Overdue
Justice Returns
Personal Justice
Silent Justice
Web of Justice
Fugitive Justice

Visit rayventhill.com for more information on these and future releases.

This book is a work of fiction. Names, characters, places, businesses, organizations, events and incidents either are the product of the author's imagination or are used fictitiously. Any resemblance to actual persons, living or dead, events or locales is entirely coincidental.

Published by Ray of Joy Publishing
Toronto

ISBN-13: 978-0-9938625-5-7

JUSTICE RETURNS

CHAPTER 1

Monday, 3:12 p.m.

JEREMY SPENCER GLANCED over as two prisoners sitting across from him got up and scurried away. He dropped his book on the high-pressure laminate table and spun around. Hindle was headed across the dayroom, aiming to punish him with a world of hurt. Again.

Hindle was an agitator who started fights with weaker prisoners just for the enjoyment his sick mind got from it. One of his usual targets was Jeremy, and today was one of those days.

He jumped to his feet as the tyrant cruised toward him, bent forward as if on a mission, flanked by a pair of lookouts. Jeremy could make out the scar running from Hindle's one good eye almost to his chin. That scar hadn't taught Hindle any sense, but it had earned him a good deal of deference among the weak.

Hindle was new meat who hadn't called out the wrong prisoner yet. When he did, he would be forced to learn some respect, or die. At five feet, three inches tall, Jeremy didn't feel qualified to teach Hindle that respect, but he stood his ground and waited.

Jeremy had learned quickly that punking out wasn't an option. Inmates who showed cowardice were marked, beaten, and abused, and though his throat constricted at the sight of Hindle, he was no coward.

"Heard you been bad-mouthing me, Spencer."

Normally, Jeremy would've laughed at the big goon's high-pitched voice, but right now things were too serious. He looked up at the freak towering over him by a foot and tried to control the quiver in his voice. "I never said anything about you, Hindle. No. I never said anything."

A deep rumble came from Hindle's throat as he reached out with two beefy fingers and poked at Jeremy's chest, spinning him halfway around. Jeremy wrapped his fist around the fingers, twisted them backwards, and kicked his tormentor in the groin.

Hindle groaned, his eyes widened, and he bent over, his hands cupping the injured area. Then he howled as his clenched fist came up, catching his opponent on the side of the head.

Jeremy wavered, his mind spun, and he connected with the concrete floor. The back of his head felt like it had been hit with a battering ram, and his eyesight went black for a few moments. He heard voices, sounding like nothing more than a mumble, and then his mind cleared. He blinked several times as his sight slowly returned.

He could barely make out Hindle's voice. "You're a dead man, Spencer." Then a canvas sneaker connected with his forehead. Jeremy brought his arms up to protect himself from further punishment as Hindle knelt on one knee, a fist cocked and ready to mash him into a pulp.

He rolled to one side as the massive bundle of flesh and bone descended. Hindle howled with pain as his fist hit the floor, clipping Jeremy's ear on the way down.

The goon cursed and a shank appeared in his hand. Jeremy lay on his back, staring up at Hindle's ugly face, now twisted into rage. "Like I said, Spencer. You're a dead man."

As the homemade weapon descended toward Jeremy's chest, he heard a sickening crack and a huge foot connected with Hindle's arm, driving it upwards and smashing it into his attacker's face. The shank flew through the air and clattered on the painted concrete. Hindle hit the floor beside it, flat on his back.

Blood poured from Hindle's nose; it was probably broken again. His arm was twisted at a grotesque angle, almost certainly broken as well. He would be spending some time in the prison infirmary.

Jeremy shook his head and blinked a couple of times. That was the closest call yet. "Thanks, Moe," he said in a hoarse voice as a hand grabbed his and pulled him roughly to his feet.

Moe looked down at Jeremy with a grin that threatened to take over his face, his tiny eyes, tucked deep into their sockets, almost disappearing. "Hindle won't try that again for a while."

The lookouts wandered away with the rest of the prisoners, the show over. Moe and Jeremy stepped away and slouched backward at the table as a pair of hacks rushed over, batons in their hand, glaring at the onlookers. They knew better than to ask who was responsible. Throwdowns took place regularly, and even in the crowded dayroom, nobody ever saw what happened. Snitches would be rewarded with swift, violent retribution.

"You saved my life that time, Moe," Jeremy said, worry in his voice. It wasn't the first time he'd thanked his friend for being there when he needed him.

Moe grunted. "Long as I'm around you'll be okay."

"That's what I'm worried about," Jeremy said. "What am I gonna do after you're gone?"

"I got friends here who owe me." Moe glanced around the room. "I'll speak to them."

An alarm sounded. "Lock it down," one of the hacks screamed.

As the prisoners ambled to their cells, Jeremy glanced back at the injured man on the floor, rolling and moaning in pain. Moe had saved his butt again, but it might be just a matter of time.

Before Jeremy had met Moe he'd hated tier time. He'd been a house mouse, rarely wandering from his cell to the dayroom. But even there, his dignity, privacy, and control were given up to hacks, and the simplest necessities were luxuries.

Though Jeremy knew he wasn't psychotic, his occasional trips to the ding wing to see the prison shrink were his only reprieve from the isolation and boredom of this place. But he wasn't crazy and he knew it. He was pretty sure they knew it too, but he played along with their little game. It was a break that got him away from the real nuts for a while.

He didn't mind the shrink's idle chatter and her wild fantasies about what made him tick. Most of the time. Except when she started talking about his mother. His mother was a wonderful woman and it bothered him when the shrink mentioned her as if she'd caused some kind of problem in his life. He wasn't the problem; they were. And he had no problems except one. He was stuck in prison and he couldn't make them understand he didn't belong here.

Prison was killing him physically and psychologically—it was a living death, like being buried alive. And he had a mission.

He had tried to fulfill his mission here but it wasn't as easy as he'd thought. Everyone was bigger than he was, and if it hadn't been for Moe, he would've been mincemeat by now.

Fate played a hand in that. He firmly believed it.

The stupid shrink called him a serial killer at one point, and though Jeremy didn't often get angry—except for righteous anger—he almost lost it. He tried to explain and finally gave up. She didn't understand and he didn't feel like wasting more time trying to convince her.

Moe was the only one who understood him and the only person he could truly call a friend. Without Moe to watch his back, he was in danger—maybe as good as dead already.

His cellie took care of him and Jeremy was grateful, but fearful. Moe was getting out soon and then he would be vulnerable.

There was only one logical option. He had to get out of this place. Now.

CHAPTER 2

Monday, 5:42 p.m.

ANNIE SAT ON THE back deck sipping ice-cold lemonade as she watched her boys play a game of one-on-one soccer.

The smaller one, eight-year-old Matty, gave the ball a powerful kick, sending it into the net at an impossible angle. Her other boy, her six-foot-four husband, dove for the ball, skidding across the grass in a failed attempt to stop the goal.

A fist bump later, they rested on the grass, panting for breath, their laughter reaching Annie's ears.

She'd finished her work for the day, taking care of a few phone messages that had gone unanswered over the weekend, scheduling in client needs that were faxed or emailed in, and taking care of some online banking. Everything else could wait until tomorrow.

Annie and her husband called themselves private investigators. When Jake had been laid off due to cutbacks, they had expanded Annie's part-time research business into more than fact-finding, stakeouts, and background checks.

The newly formed company had stumbled into many of the more frightening aspects of investigation—taking down killers, con men, and kidnappers.

Lincoln Investigations had been born, and they'd never looked back.

The game now over, Jake and Matty wandered up to the deck and dropped into chairs. Annie poured a round of lemonade and the guys downed it eagerly.

Jake looked at his watch. "Our guests will be here soon. We'd better get ready."

"I've done my part," Annie said. "All you need to do is cook the burgers."

Jake glanced over at the barbecue and shrugged. "It won't take me long to fire that up. I'll wait until they get here."

As if on cue, the front doorbell rang. Matty jumped to his feet and dashed through the back door. He returned a few moments later followed by Hank and Amelia. Sixteen-year-old Jenny trailed behind.

Jake stood and shook hands with the cop. He slid some chairs over for the newcomers, and they sat down.

Jake and Hank had been friends for as long as Annie remembered. Hank had wanted to be a cop, but Jake had decided to go to University of Toronto, not coincidentally, as soon as Annie enrolled. Jake had ended up as a construction engineer, a job he'd stayed with until he'd been laid off.

Having a cop for a friend came in handy for many of their investigations. Of course, there was a limit to how much information the detective could share, but whenever their paths crossed during a case Hank didn't hesitate to help out. It gave the cop a few more notches in his belt and Captain Diego didn't argue as long as Hank got results.

Amelia sat and leaned toward Annie. "I heard you had quite a harrowing weekend."

Annie took a deep breath and her mouth twisted into a grimace. "That's an understatement. I don't think I want to go through that again."

Jake spoke up. "If the law would allow us to carry weapons, I'd feel an awful lot safer."

"Maybe you should've become a cop instead," Hank said.

"I like being self-employed," Jake said. "And working with Annie."

"I'm on Jake's side," Amelia said. "After Jenny was abducted, things may have worked out a lot more smoothly if you'd carried protection." She smiled gently at Annie. "Nonetheless, you got my daughter back safely and I'm grateful for that."

Annie turned to Jenny. "We haven't seen a lot of you since then. How're you making out—emotionally, I mean?"

Jenny gave a small sigh. "I'm actually doing well now. Everybody has been so supportive. Sometimes I have a bad dream, but rarely." She touched her mother's arm and laughed. "I don't think it's done any permanent damage to either one of us."

Jake slugged Hank on the shoulder. "Time to get the barbecue heated up. Want to give me a hand?"

Hank nodded and the guys went to the other end of the deck, where the Master Chef awaited. Soon, flames licked at the grill as it heated up and the smell of charcoal filled the air.

Matty grew bored with the talk and wandered out to the backyard. "I'm going to see Kyle," he called.

Kyle was the seven-year-old son of their next-door neighbor and Annie's best friend, Chrissy. Matty and Kyle had been fast friends since they were old enough to talk.

"Come back in ten minutes. We'll be eating soon," Annie called, then turned to Amelia. "So tell me, how're things between you and Hank?"

"Just fine," Amelia said.

Annie laughed. "You know what I mean. Is it getting serious?"

"Yes, it's getting serious," Jenny interrupted, and giggled. "They can't get enough of each other. You should see the two of them sometimes. All googly-eyed as if nobody else in the world exists."

Amelia slapped Jenny gently on the hand and said in mock indignation, "We're not quite that bad."

"Oh, yes, they are," Jenny said. "Don't let her fool you. She's worse than a teenager around that man."

Amelia looked sideways at Hank, a look of admiration on her face. "He's been good for me."

Jenny gave a lopsided smile and rolled her eyes. "My mother has such a way of understating things."

Annie laughed. "I think you're right, Jenny. I can see it in her eyes. She's smitten."

Hank called over, "What's the joke there?"

"You wouldn't understand," Annie called back.

Hank shrugged and dropped some burgers on the sizzling grill. Flames shot up and then died.

"I guess it's time we got the food on the table," Annie said. "The burgers will be done soon."

CHAPTER 3

Monday, 6:11 p.m.

JEREMY SAT ON HIS bunk, his back to the concrete wall, and drew his feet up. A stingy amount of early evening sun seeped through the small plexiglass window and dissipated on the painted floor.

He looked over at his friend slouched on the cot along the opposite wall of their eight-by-eight-foot cell. "You took a big chance for me today," he said.

Moe shrugged. "It had to be, little buddy."

"If they'd caught you in the middle of the throwdown, you wouldn't be getting out of here today. No, you surely wouldn't."

Moe grinned wide. "But they didn't catch me, and even if they did I couldn't let him take you out. He was going for you serious this time. And anyways, them hacks don't like Hindle. They wouldn't care so much if I killed him."

Jeremy sighed wearily. "They don't seem to like me either."

"They don't much like any of us. That's the way it is. Just the way the system works. You don't do what they say and they hate you. Even if you do what they say, they hate you still." Moe shrugged a long shrug and sighed. "I guess life's like that inside as well as outside, least by my experience. I can't recall any time, until I met you, anybody really cared for me. Leastways not after my granny died, and I don't even think she liked me much. Took care of me is all."

"Might be like that for everybody," Jeremy said. "I know I always tried to do the right thing before I came here, and still—look where I am." Jeremy paused. "I had a good mother, though, and a good father. But they both died on me, and my grandmother was probably as mean as yours. She died before my parents, but I remember her always being nasty to me."

"Doesn't seem to be fair somehow," Moe said.

"Nope. It sure doesn't."

"Only time I had a job is when somebody needed something done, like, beat a guy up and stuff like that. That's why I always end up in here again."

"Because when they hired you," Jeremy said, "they didn't care what happened to you. They were out for what they could get and that's all they cared about."

Moe nodded. "That's for sure. Shucks, I'm pushing forty years old and ain't never even had a girlfriend." His shoulders slumped and he laughed out of self-pity. "Even the kind of girls you have to pay for didn't ever wanna be with me." He forced a grin. "Guess I'm too ugly for them."

"Doesn't matter, Moe," Jeremy whispered in a hoarse voice. "I love you like you were my brother."

Moe's grin turned to a wide smile.

It was almost quiet in the cell for a few minutes. Outside the small room, the occasional cell door clanged. A ding at the other end of the block cried for his mother, but nobody cared. The overhead light hummed. Moe sniffed a time or two—probably catching a cold.

"I'm going to miss you, Moe," Jeremy said at last. "I'm surely going to miss you."

Moe sat forward. "I expect I'll be back afore long." He waved a hand across the cell. "This is my life it seems. I'll be back here soon enough. Ain't nobody gonna hire me, seein's I can't read or write or nothin' them business people need."

Jeremy observed his friend a moment. He felt sorry for the big lug who'd never had much chance in the world. Finally, he said, "Moe?"

"Yup."

"I'm getting out of here soon and I'll take care of you. Neither one of us will come back to this place."

Moe leaned forward. "Little buddy, you're in here for life. Ain't nothing gonna change that."

"I have a plan," Jeremy said.

Moe whistled. "A plan?"

"Yes, I surely do."

A wrinkle took over Moe's brow and his eyes all but disappeared. "You think it'll work?"

"I'm pretty sure. I think it's fate. Just how I came here and met you. I'm pretty sure fate did that."

Moe's eyes tightened a moment, then he said, "You might have something there with that fate stuff."

"We'll see," Jeremy said. "We'll surely see."

"If you get out of here, we can take care of each other," Moe said, and touched his forefinger to his temple. "You got the brains." He flexed a huge bicep. "And I got this."

Jeremy chuckled. "We'll work it out." He held up a finger. "Whatever you do, Moe, keep yourself from coming back here again. And make sure you don't steal from anybody. That's probably the worst thing—taking other people's stuff. And don't let anyone use you, Moe. Promise me that."

"I promise," Moe said, holding up his hand. "I expect I'll listen to you from now on 'cause you won't steer me the wrong way."

"You can count on that, Moe. You surely can."

Moe grinned foolishly for a moment, and then rolled off the cot. "Well, I best get dressed. They're coming to take me out soon."

Jeremy watched as Moe took off his orange jumpsuit and dressed in the street clothes the law had been nice enough to provide. The pants hung four inches too short, and he couldn't do up the top two buttons of his shirt.

Moe finished dressing, stood straight, and grinned. "How I look?"

Jeremy looked up at the huge man towering above him and smiled. "You look fine, Moe. Just fine."

Moe laughed and looked at himself in the tiny mirror above the sink. "They don't fit so well, but leastways, it's better than wearing orange all day."

"Moe?"

Moe turned to Jeremy. "Yup?"

"How am I going to find you—once I get out of here?"

Moe dug a finger in his ear. "Ain't never thought of that." He frowned and rubbed his big, round, bald head. "There's a guy I know might be able to get me a job. Not sure, though. His name's Uriah Hubert and he's in Richmond Hill. If you look him up, even if I'm not at his place, he should know where I'm at. I'm gonna go see him first."

"Open up six," came from outside the cell.

Jeremy's heart jumped. Six was their cell number.

The barred door hummed back and clanged, and a hack appeared in the doorway. "Let's go, Thacker. You're going home."

Jeremy sprang off the bunk. Moe leaned down and wrapped his big arms around his friend, almost lifting him off his feet. When he let him go, Moe held Jeremy at arm's length, still leaned over. "I talked to my friends. You'll be okay in here."

"Come on, Thacker. Move it."

Moe turned to the guard. "I'm ready," he said and lumbered from the cell.

Jeremy couldn't speak as the door hummed again, slid closed, and snapped in place. He clung to the bars of the cell and watched as the guard led Moe through a metal door and out of sight.

He returned to his bunk and lay down. He hadn't totally perfected his plan yet, but it had to work—for his sake, and for Moe's.

CHAPTER 4

Tuesday, 8:30 a.m.

JAKE FINISHED WITH the bench press, racked the weights, and wiped off with a towel. He'd spent the last half hour in the basement doing a workout routine he rarely missed. He always felt better after, ready to face anything.

After a quick shower, he dressed and went into the office off the living room, where Annie sat at her iMac. She looked up as he entered, gave him a wide smile, and said, "I've got enough here to keep me busy most of the day. Lots of research to do."

Jake dropped into the guest chair and stretched out his long legs. "Have anything for me?"

Annie spun in her chair. "Maybe. If you want to take this one on." She leafed through a stack of papers, removed a handwritten sheet, and studied it. "A man called yesterday afternoon and I completely forgot about it until now. His car has been stolen and he wants our help to recover it."

Jake frowned. "A stolen car? That doesn't really sound like our thing."

"It's not just any car," Annie said, smiling as she handed the paper to Jake.

Jake glanced at the paper and whistled. "A sixty-nine Cuda. Sweet car."

"And the guy's heartbroken," Annie said. "I thought he was going to break down on the phone."

"What about insurance?" Jake asked, scanning the sheet.

"It's all there. He has comprehensive coverage, so it's insured against theft, but he wants the car back."

"I don't blame him," Jake said. "What about the police?"

"The car was stolen more than a week ago. He contacted the police immediately, but as you know, it's pretty hard to track down a stolen car, and so far, the police haven't turned up anything."

Jake set the paper on the desk and looked at Annie. "And he wants us to find it. Sounds like an impossible task."

"I can tell him we're not interested."

"Hmm. Not yet. Let me see what I can come up with. I'll give him a call first."

"I'll leave it with you," Annie said and turned back to her computer.

Jake picked up the paper, stood, and went into the living room. He scanned the sheet for a name and phone number, and then pulled out his iPhone and dialed.

"Hello?"

"Is this Whitney Culpepper?"

"Yes."

Jake introduced himself. "Can I drop over and see you?"

The man sounded excited. "Thanks for getting back to me so quickly. I'm at the shop, and you can drop by any time."

Whitney and his wife owned a florist shop in the heart of the suburbs. Jake got the address and promised to drop by immediately.

He hung up and poked his head inside the office. "I'm going to see this guy. Not sure what I can do, but I'll talk to him anyway. It's not far away."

"Good luck," Annie said without looking his way. Her fingers continued to fly over the keyboard. Jake watched her a moment, wondering how anyone could possibly type so fast when the letters on the keyboard weren't even in any logical order.

He grabbed his keys, went through the kitchen to the garage, and climbed into the Firebird. He hit the fob for the garage door, started the engine, and listened to its delightful rumble. He knew how Culpepper must be feeling. His own 1986 Pontiac Firebird was his pride, and losing it would be devastating.

He made the trip to the shop in ten minutes, pulled into the strip plaza, and stopped in front of Culpepper Flowers.

When he entered the shop, he was greeted by a vast array of plants, gift baskets, bouquets, and coolers stuffed with roses, carnations, and lilies. Myriad scents mingled together and filled the air with a unique perfume.

A woman sat behind the counter—probably Culpepper's wife. She looked up as he entered. He approached the desk, handed her his card, and introduced himself.

She glanced at the card, then turned her head and called, "Whit?"

A man appeared in the doorway of a room that led into the back of the shop. He took the offered business card, glanced at it, and motioned for Jake to follow him into the back room. He led the way and swung a chair around for his guest.

Jake shook hands with Culpepper, a middle-aged man with a massive shock of dark hair. He wore a pleasant, but sad smile. "You can call me Whit," he said.

"How'd you hear about us, Whit?" Jake asked.

"A friend recommended you. Said you guys were making quite a name for yourself lately."

"Ah, word of mouth. The best advertising."

The florist motioned toward the chair. "I didn't know where else to turn. I don't think the police are going to be able to help me. They didn't give me a lot of hope."

They sat and Jake glanced around the room. There were even more flowers back here than in front. It appeared Whit was working on a funeral arrangement. Floral wreaths and stuffed vases lined a table a little further back.

Whit leaned forward. "I hope you can help me," he said. "I've had that car for more than twenty years. Keep it in top shape. It means a lot to me. It's not even about the insurance money. I want the car back."

Jake explained to Whit how he could relate, his own car meaning more to him than just any car. "Where was the Cuda when it was stolen?" Jake asked.

"It was a week ago last Sunday. My wife and I were at

Richmond Park enjoying the day and the weather. When we returned to the car … it was gone. I don't drive it often. I usually keep it in the garage."

"Somebody couldn't resist."

Whit shook his head. "It may be more than a sudden urge. I belong to the Richmond Classic Car Club and know a lot of the guys. A good friend of mine had his car stolen two weeks ago, and one of the other members, a week or so before that. Mine is the third muscle car taken this month, all in the same area."

Jake thought about that a moment and then asked, "Do you have any photos of your car?"

Whit grinned. "Of course. Some people take pictures of their kids. I take pictures of my car."

Jake laughed. "Yeah, I have a few shots of mine."

Whit pointed to the wall above his desk. An eight-by-ten photo of a magnificent machine was proudly displayed.

"She sure is beautiful," Jake said as he stood and gazed at the sleek, black Barracuda. "They don't make them like this anymore."

Whit pulled out the pins holding the photo and removed it from the wall. "Take it with you if it'll help."

Jake took the picture and looked at it a moment, and then back at the hopeful man. "It may not be all that easy to find. If it was targeted, it may've gone to a private collector."

Jake watched the hope drain from Whit's face. The man truly was heartbroken.

"I'll do what I can to find it," Jake said. "I can't promise anything, but I'll give it my best shot."

CHAPTER 5

Tuesday, 9:44 a.m.

JEREMY SPENCER EASED from his cell, fearful to wander into the dayroom without the protective hand of Moe. Other than Hindle, who was taken care of for now, the rest of the prisoners had known enough to leave him alone when Moe was around. But now?

He stood outside his cell on the upper level, his eyes roving over the rows of cubicles on either side of him. Across the dayroom were more—on the lower tiers, even more—an endless mass of imprisoned men, some full of hope, most filled with despair at their mundane existence.

This was the same place Father had been dumped fifteen years earlier. Jeremy was only ten at the time, and could barely remember the circumstances of Father's conviction, but Mother had given him the details later.

Father had accosted a thief in their home late one night and ended up shooting the young burglar, killing him. A public defender representing the poor farmer convinced him to plead on a lesser charge of manslaughter and agree to a ten-year sentence. And so he had been locked up in this very place.

Five years later the family had received stunning news—Quinton Spencer, Jeremy's father, had been killed in his cell in this godforsaken place. There were no witnesses, and no suspects. Jeremy had been devastated. Mother had taken it hard, of course, and though she was heartbroken, they managed to get by.

And then Mother had hung herself—or so the police had determined, but Jeremy was positive there was another reason for her death. He was sure his mother, Annette Spencer, had been murdered, fully convinced she would never end her own life.

At seventeen years of age he was all alone. Both sets of grandparents were long gone, and the last person he'd had in the world had left him. He was unable to maintain the farm, and other than a vegetable garden he kept in the summer months, the farm lay wasted. Any jobs he could find barely paid the taxes.

All this because a thief had invaded their home. A filthy burglar who deserved what he got. Many times Jeremy lay in bed, fantasizing—the thief was still alive, begging for his life, and Jeremy slit his throat, or gouged out his heart, or smothered him to death, over, and over, and over…

And now with Moe leaving, and Jeremy soon to get out of here himself, his life was about to change. For better or worse, he didn't know, but something had to be done.

There were two types of prisoners. There were those who were willing to use violence for any reason. These were the newer, younger prisoners with a chip on their shoulder, looking down on the rest, bitter, angry, and lacking in respect. Then there were the old-school convicts. Old-schoolers gave more respect to fellow prisoners and tried to get by each day with a live-and-let-live attitude.

Liam O'Connor was one of the old-schoolers. He'd been here most of his life, never causing any problems, and even the most violent of prisoners left him alone. Many said he controlled the prison with even the guards giving him some measure of respect—respect he had earned.

Jeremy turned his attention to O'Connor's usual spot. During tier time he always sat along the far wall with two or three other old-timers. He was there now, his hands clasped together and resting on the table in front of him.

Prisoners looked Jeremy's way, some sneering, others watching as he took the steps down to the dayroom. Nobody spoke to him. He walked cautiously over to O'Connor's table.

The old Irishman looked up curiously as Jeremy approached. The other two who sat opposite O'Connor paid him no attention.

"Mind if I sit here a moment?" Jeremy asked.

O'Connor wrinkled his brow, his eyes burrowing into Jeremy's. Finally, he barely moved his head in a nod and waved a finger toward an empty spot on the bench.

Jeremy watched as O'Connor rolled a cigarette, lit it, and inhaled the smoke deeply. Then his eyes turned to Jeremy. "What's on your mind, lad?" His voice was gravelly, without expression, but not unkind, and he still spoke with an Irish accent after all these years.

Jeremy looked down at his hands as he twisted them nervously. Finally, he looked at the Irishman and his voice came out, barely above a whisper. "I want to find out about my father."

O'Connor's eyes bored into his. "You're Spencer?"

Jeremy nodded, not surprised the lifer knew his name. He probably made it his business to be in the know.

"And who's your father?"

"His name was Quinton. Quinton Spencer. He was in here fifteen years ago. Murdered inside ten years ago."

O'Connor took a long breath and gazed across the room, his eyes narrowing in thought. "I remember him," he said at last, looking back at Jeremy. "What is it you want to know about him?"

"I want to know who killed him."

The old prisoner unclasped his hands and straightened his back, observing Jeremy closely. Finally, he looked at his companions and nodded for them to leave.

When the others were gone, Jeremy slid down the bench until he was opposite O'Connor and waited eagerly.

The elderly criminal leaned forward. "No good can come of digging into the past, lad."

"I need to know, sir."

A hint of a smile appeared on O'Connor's face. "Call me Conny. Nobody gets the name 'sir' in here. Not me, and especially not the hacks."

Jeremy nodded. "Can you tell me who killed him, Conny?"

Conny shook his head. “I can’t tell you who, only why.”

Jeremy leaned in. “Why? Why was he killed?”

“You may not like to hear the truth.”

“I need the truth.”

Conny took a deep breath and stroked his mustache. Finally, he sighed lightly and said, “Your father was a snitch.”

Jeremy leaned back and frowned, raising his voice. “My father was no snitch.”

Conny’s face showed disapproval at Jeremy’s outburst. He pointed a finger. “I get that’s not what you want to hear, but don’t raise your voice to me.”

Jeremy was silent, twiddling with his fingers, his head lowered. Finally, he said, “Sorry, Conny. I’m not actually yelling at you. It’s upsetting news. My father was a good man, honorable, and if he was a snitch, then there’s more to the story. There’s a good reason.”

Conny took a breath and continued, “I knew your father a little bit. He didn’t belong here. He was a greener when he came in and stayed that way. Didn’t fit in.” He shrugged. “He certainly wasn’t a hardened criminal, and he didn’t learn the ways—the code.”

Jeremy raised his head. “Father was innocent. He killed a boy in self-defense, is all.”

“May be true. It happens.”

“But you don’t know who killed him?”

Conny shook his head. “Back then, I didn’t know everything that went on.” He took a deep breath. “There was a throwdown. Your father tried to interfere and ended up in the infirmary himself. He was in bad shape. The hacks got to him, I guess, and he snitched. The other two guys got the hole and, so the story goes, when they came out, one of them did your father with a shiv and vowed he would kill every member of his family when he got out of here."

Jeremy gasped. "My mother was killed two years later. I know she was. It wasn't suicide like the police said."

"If that's true," Conny said, "and he killed your mother, what about you?"

Jeremy shook his head. "I don't know. I was seventeen and nobody tried to kill me. At least, as far as I know nobody did."

Conny sat back and crossed his arms. "It might all be a load of bollocks. Stories grow."

"I believe it," Jeremy said. "Mother would never kill herself. She surely wouldn't."

"That's all I can tell you, lad. But a word of advice if you're listening—you might be best to leave it alone."

"I don't think I can do that, sir … Conny."

"It won't do you much good in here if the killer's outside."

"I'm not planning on staying in here. No, I'm surely not."

Conny laughed for the first time. "None of us are, lad. None of us are."

CHAPTER 6

Tuesday, 10:02 a.m.

JAKE SAT IN THE FIREBIRD in front of the flower shop, his head back, his eyes closed. He was working on a plan, slowly forming it in his mind.

He sat up suddenly, slapped the steering wheel, and said out loud, "I think it might work."

He got out of the vehicle, opened the trunk, and dug around in a small cardboard box. He removed a square metal case, about the size of a matchbox. He'd used this contraption once before, and it would fit his plan perfectly.

The device was a GPS tracker in a small waterproof magnetic container. It was motion-activated and only had to be switched on for its movements to be tracked in real time from a web-based satellite map on his cell phone.

Last time he'd killed the battery in his phone while using the tracker, so he checked the power level in his cell. Lots of juice, freshly charged overnight. He dug in the box again, found a new battery for the tracker, and slipped it in, just in case.

He called Annie. When she answered, he said, "I need you to meet me at Richmond Park, right away. Are you busy?"

"Nothing that can't wait," Annie answered. "What's this all about?"

"I'll tell you when you get here. I have an idea that might work. Park on the street at the east side of the park near the hot dog vendor if you can find a spot." He hung up the phone, hopped in the Firebird, and pulled from the lot.

The park was on the other side of town and Annie was already waiting, sitting in her car, when he arrived. He drove past her, circled the block three times at low speed, and then parked on the street, several spots from her vehicle. He flicked the switch on the GPS tracker, stuffed it under the passenger seat, and got out.

Annie was frowning when he climbed inside her car. "What's going on? Why the big show?"

"Trying to attract a little attention." He turned on his cell and opened the app for the tracker, and a small red dot appeared on a miniature map. He held the phone up for her to see. "That's my car, and we're going to wait for somebody to steal it."

Annie squinted at the red dot. "You want somebody to steal your car? You're very trusting."

"If, as I suspect, they're targeting muscle cars and then reselling them, I don't have much to worry about." Jake grinned. "I'm pretty sure they'll be careful with it."

"We may be in for a long wait."

"I don't think so. If they're going to steal it at all, it'll be right away. If it were spotted, why would they wait? Classic muscle cars are getting rare and they won't pass up an opportunity like this."

It took longer than Jake expected, but his assumption proved to be correct. Less than half an hour later, they watched as a man sauntered down the street from the corner. He stopped beside the Firebird, looked casually around, and then went to the driver-side door.

Jake kept a close eye through a small pair of binoculars as the would-be thief pulled a flat metal bar from under his jacket and wedged it between the car's window and the rubber seal.

"He's using a slim jim," Jake said.

"I'll never doubt you again."

Jake chuckled. "Yeah, until the next time."

Annie swatted him on the shoulder. "I'm serious."

"So am I."

Jake lowered the binoculars. "He's in now," he announced. "We'll wait until he's gone and follow him."

Less than a minute later, the Firebird moved from the curb, idled to the intersection, and turned right.

"Let's go," Jake said.

Annie started the Escort and pulled out while Jake followed the moving red dot on his cell. "Keep well back," he said. "Don't let him see you, and we'll use the tracker to keep tabs on him."

The route took several turns and a few minutes later they entered the industrial part of town.

"It stopped," Jake said, pointing ahead. "Take a right up there."

Annie turned where Jake indicated and drove slowly past warehouses and industrial units.

"It looks like he's in that building," Jake said, looking out his side window and pointing. "There must be a vehicle door around behind." He motioned toward the curb. "Pull over up there."

Annie spun the wheel and eased to the side of the street. "Are you going in there?" she asked, as Jake opened his door.

"Just to be sure we have the right place."

Jake stepped from the car and walked cautiously toward the building. He hugged the wall as he made his way along the side toward the back of the unit. When he reached the rear he stopped and peered around the corner. A couple of late-model cars occupied slots behind the building. There was a large overhead door dead center in the back of the unit.

He needed to see what was behind that door, but there were no windows.

The GPS unit wasn't entirely accurate, but his gut told him this was the right place. If he was a cop he could show his badge and he would have probable cause to enter the unit.

He wasn't a cop, but he knew one. Detective Hank Corning was head of the RHPD Robbery/Homicide unit, and car theft would fit nicely into that category.

He stepped back, pulled out his phone, and dialed. "Hank," he said when the detective answered. "I have a bust for you." He filled him in quickly with a short version of the story.

Ten minutes later two cruisers eased up the driveway and spun around behind the building, one at each end of the lot, cutting off access. Four uniformed cops hopped out and approached the building, their hands on their weapons.

Jake watched while an officer banged on the access door and shouted, "RHPD. Open the door."

There was no answer and the door didn't open.

Jake sprinted toward the front of the building. Hank's car was pulled up to the curb, and he now stood beside the front door of the unit, his weapon drawn. Jake stayed back and watched while the door burst open and two men ran out.

"Police! Stop," Hank ordered, stepping into view of the suspects, his weapon raised.

One man stopped short and put his hands up. The other looked around frantically then ran toward the street. Jake leaped forward. He was twenty feet from the runner and gaining. It was the guy who'd stolen his Firebird.

The man looked over his shoulder at Jake and spun across the street. The runner was no match for Jake's long, powerful legs, and as his quarry hopped a hedge, Jake grabbed his foot and held on. The man hit the ground hard, head first, and Jake dragged him back over the hedge, depositing him face down on the sidewalk.

"You're under arrest," Jake said.

The man attempted to rise but Jake's foot knocked him to his back. The thief scowled up at his captor.

Jake rolled him over, twisted his arms behind his back, and pulled him to his feet. Annie was out of the vehicle, approaching slowly. Jake waved at her and grinned as he prodded his captive across the street.

Hank's prisoner was already cuffed and was being loading into another cruiser that had pulled up in front. A uniformed cop stepped from the vehicle and took control of Jake's prisoner. He cuffed him, read him his rights, and bundled him into the backseat.

Hank was now entering the front door, his gun drawn. Jake followed behind and together they eased through the office area into a large room at the back of the unit.

There didn't appear to be any more suspects inside, and as Hank checked a couple of smaller cubicles off the main room, Jake stood and gazed around, his mouth open.

Along with his Firebird, there were three Mercedes, a BMW, and, at the far side of the room, a gorgeous black 1969 Plymouth Barracuda.

CHAPTER 7

Tuesday, 10:53 a.m.

JEREMY SPENCER WAS observant, always watching, always planning, and it finally paid off. His plan was perfected. Sure, there were a few unknowns, but he would tackle those when the time came.

Timing was important to his plan—timing and a bit of luck. The countdown was about to begin.

"Let's go, Spencer."

When the guard approached his opened cell door Jeremy knew the routine. He went to the doorway, held out his hands, and waited while the hack snapped the cuffs on him. They always cuffed him when they took him to the ding wing. That was an unfortunate routine, and it presented an obstacle he needed to overcome.

His earlier request for an extra session with the shrink had been granted. The dumb twit was eager to rehabilitate him, and Jeremy had the stupid fool believing her patient was making progress.

Oh, he was making progress all right. Progress that was starting now.

Jeremy led the way, the hack following, through clanging doors, down concrete hallways, until finally, at the other end of the building, he stopped in front of the final door.

A sign on the metal portal read, "Dr. Laurine Thicke, Prison Psychiatrist."

The hack tapped on the door, then opened it and prodded the prisoner inside. Jeremy glanced back as the guard stepped back out and closed the door. He would be keeping watch outside.

Dr. Thicke rose from her desk, her stern body a silhouette in front of the barred window. She moved out from behind her desk and motioned toward a stiff leather couch. Jeremy sat on the edge and watched the doctor sit, straight-backed, in an easy chair opposite him. She crossed her bony legs at the ankles and clasped her hands in her lap. Her dress was funeral black, well below her knees, and buttoned up to her throat. She stared at him through tight eyes, reminding him of a teacher he'd once known. He hadn't liked her either.

The shrink spoke in a husky, emotionless voice. "How're we today, Jeremy?"

We? Jeremy knew he was doing fine, excited, and eager to get started, but he didn't know how she was—except she was about to die.

He leaned forward and reached out his arms, his hands palms up, the chain hanging loosely between his wrists. "I'd be doing better without these handcuffs," he said. He didn't care about the cuffs and his comment was carefully calculated, every minute detail taken into account. His seemingly innocent action served to bring his hands that much closer to her throat.

She opened her mouth to speak and that was as far as she got. He sprang from the couch, leaped into her lap, and, in the same motion, wrapped the cuffs around her lily-white throat, cutting off her words and any screams she might attempt.

Her feet kicked uselessly and her hand struggled to reach the alarm button on the table beside her. He tugged the chain tighter, intertwined his fingers behind her head, and held on.

She soon stopped struggling, her once-flailing arms now hanging limp, the breath gone from her body, her windpipe crushed.

He removed the chain and stepped back. He didn't have time to admire his work. The session was scheduled to last an hour and he had more important things to do.

He tiptoed to the door. There was a lock on the inside, like the kind you find on a bathroom door. He spun the cylinder. It wasn't much but if the guard tried to come in when the hour passed, it would keep him busy a short while longer. Every second might count.

He hurried to the desk and pulled open the top drawer, removing a single key. He knew it was there because he'd seen her put it there on a previous occasion.

He spun around and tugged at the cord for the window blind, putting all of his weight into it. It finally snapped and he rolled up the cord, about five feet long, and stuffed it into his pocket.

He crossed to the side of the room and unlocked a door leading into an adjoining room. Several sessions ago, she hadn't been ready when he'd arrived, and she'd come from this room, locking the door behind her. He didn't know what was in there, but he knew where it went.

It was a storage room. Rows of file folders stuck out of upright slots, name tags visible. His file was likely in there somewhere—he didn't care. What he did care about was what else he knew was there.

The exercise yard ran along half the length of the outside of the building. From that yard, he'd previously explored, observed, and planned, and from this end of the area, though a good fifty feet away, he could make out the barred window behind dear Dr. Thicke's desk, twenty feet above the ground. What he also saw, ten feet further on, was another window, a window with no bars, facing the razor-wire fence. As close as he could estimate, the area below the window couldn't be seen from the guard tower.

He hurried to the far end of the storage room. It was Doctor Thicke's private washroom. He pulled open the door and there it was. Freedom. Well, not quite—there was still a small window in front of him, about fifteen by fifteen inches, that didn't open. He was expecting that.

He stood on the toilet and peeked through the window. There were two rows of fences encircling the prison, with twenty feet between them. This end of the building served as part of the barrier, making the first fence unnecessary. That meant there was only one obstacle between him and the outside world.

And a drop of twenty feet.

And a window.

But first, the part he was dreading most. He'd never attempted this before, but he knew it'd been done. He laid his left hand on the floor, its back downward, and curled in his thumb. Then he gritted his teeth and brought his foot down onto his thumb as hard as he could.

It only resulted in more pain than he thought possible and he bit his lip to keep from crying out. He took a deep breath and tried again. He felt a snap. His thumb was dislocated, and the pain was almost unbearable as he drew his left hand through the handcuff.

He forced the thumb back into the joint—more excruciating pain—but he could wiggle it. Barely. He knew it was damaged and would have to be taken care of soon, and though he was in a lot of pain, at least his hands were free.

He estimated he had at least forty minutes left.

He turned his gaze to the window. He couldn't break it; that would draw attention. He stood on the seat, gripped the free end of the handcuffs in his right hand, and worked at the caulking and rubber seal that held the window in place. He kept at his task diligently. His shoulder ached, his fingers were getting sore, and his left hand hurt like the dickens. Still, he persisted, and in ten minutes the pane had been loosened enough to work the glass out of place.

He lifted it out carefully and set it upright on the floor by the toilet, then dashed back to the outer room, pulled the two big cushions from the couch, and hurried back to the washroom.

He had to bend the cushions to squeeze them through the window, but one at a time, he got them through and dropped them carefully on the ground twenty feet below. Perfect.

He stood on the tank of the toilet and eased himself up, head first, into the window. It was a tight squeeze, and for once he was thankful for his small size.

He let go, aimed for the cushions, and dropped. He landed on a cushion with his right shoulder, bounced, and hit the hardened ground, banging his head.

His mind whirled, his senses dimmed, and blackness overtook him. Just twenty feet from freedom, he fell into an unconscious sleep.

CHAPTER 8

Tuesday, 11:29 a.m.

JEREMY AWOKE WITH A start. It took a few moments before his senses returned and he realized where he was.

His head hurt and he saw stars when he tried to stand. He lay still, staring upwards toward the opened window, waiting for his head to clear.

He didn't know how long he'd been out. He didn't have a watch, but as yet, he was undiscovered. His nasty fall was not something he'd anticipated, but it was one of the unforeseen circumstances that couldn't be avoided.

Assuming he hadn't been unconscious for more than a few minutes, he still might make it. He needed to hurry.

He kicked off his canvas shoes and stuffed them into the pockets of his orange jumpsuit. He unzipped the office cushions, removed the sturdy foam inside, folded the covers neatly, and waited.

Another of the unforeseen circumstances involved the

guards in the tower overlooking the yard. They couldn't see him from where he waited, but once he made a dash for the fence, he would be within their view.

He was depending on an unknown. It was yard time, and prisoners would be milling about. There was always a throwdown or two, without fail, and that always drew the guards' attention until the scuffle could be broken up. He'd watched the guards' actions and reactions many times.

He lay low and crept forward until he could see the yard but not the tower. His anxiety was deepening; he was running out of time, when finally, he heard shouting coming from the far end of the yard. It was a throwdown.

He grabbed one of the foam inserts and the leather covers and dashed toward the fence. This was the crucial part.

With the bulky foam under one arm, the leather under the other, he began to climb the fourteen-foot tall chain-link fence. His toes dug into the gaps in the links, his fingers into others. He disregarded the throbbing pain in his thumb and continued to climb.

The razor wire was sharp and a cut or two in the wrong place would bring him down, slashed and scarred for life, unable to continue. He had to be careful.

As he neared the top of the fence he clung on with one hand, tossed the leather onto the top, covering the razors, and then set the foam over that. It balanced precariously as he dug in his pocket for the cord from the window blinds. Holding one end of the cord, he tossed the other end over the cushion, drew it back through the links, and tied the ends together. It was hard to do with one hand, but he finally managed.

With his toes and both hands now free, he climbed up a few more inches and, with great difficulty, managed to pull his body onto the foam. The razor wire cut through the tough leather at one spot, and he felt a sharp pain in his side. He heaved again and he was over, landing on the hard ground on freedom's side of the fence.

The wind was knocked out of him. He landed on his back, unable to breathe for a while, but nothing seemed broken. He chanced a look toward the guard tower. He couldn't tell which way they were looking, so best not waste any time.

He was in pain all over—his hand, his thumb, his back, and his head still throbbed. But he was free.

He removed the shoes from his pocket, put them on, and dashed to the left, following the fence for fifty feet, keeping low. He was out of sight of the guard tower now, so he turned and raced across the open field surrounding the prison complex on all sides.

There was no doubt that once they discovered his escape the tracking dogs would be hot on his trail. Despite the pain, he ran without stopping for a good twenty minutes, always listening for the sound of the dogs' baying.

Finally, in the distance, a farmhouse came into view. Another unknown. He had to approach the house without being seen. The kitchen was probably in the back, the living room in front, and they were the most likely rooms where anyone might be. He circled around and approached the house from the side.

There was a garage at that end of the old farmhouse, a broken-down thing and, he assumed, not very secure. He was counting on that. He crept to the side door and smiled to himself as he pushed it open.

He stepped in and looked around. What farmer didn't have children at one point in his life? And what farm didn't have a bicycle in some shape or other? Hardly an unknown. A bit uncertain, perhaps, but he wasn't surprised to see one tucked at the end of the workbench, covered with an old blanket and a powdering of dust.

It probably hadn't been used for years, but it looked to be in good working order. They would never miss it—it had likely been discarded by an owner who'd outgrown it. The tires were in reasonable shape, but after years of disuse most of the air had seeped out. He scrounged around under the workbench, came up with an air pump, and filled the tires.

He rolled it to the door, pushed it outside, and hopped on, pedaling furiously across the front lawn, up the tree-lined driveway, and onto the gravel road. He glanced back. He hadn't roused any attention as far as he could tell.

It was vital he stay out of sight. His orange jumpsuit was a dead giveaway, and if seen, he would be as good as caught. He'd hoped to find some clothes hanging on a clothesline outside the farmhouse, but that was not to be, and he didn't want to take the time to sneak inside and see what he could find. Time was precious and short.

He started as he heard the baying of hounds, far in the distance, coming from the direction of the prison. They'd discovered his escape and the dogs had been let loose. The trail would stop at the garage, but he had to get moving.

He continued down the shoulder as the sound of the

hounds grew closer. They would be shutting down the roads soon, setting up roadblocks, and scouring houses in the area. But he wasn't going to take the roads. Five minutes later he saw what he was looking for. It was a pathway into a farmer's field, an entrance allowing the farmer access from the road.

He spun down the path and continued across the field. It was rough going with the bicycle, its large wheels bumping over clots of dirt and pitted areas as he made his way across the rough ground. The throbbing pain in his left hand and the cuffs still fastened to his right only added to the difficulty.

Soon there was a dip in the terrain. He spun down the grade, now out of sight of the dogs and their handlers, and had left no trail. He was going to make it—of that there was no doubt.

CHAPTER 9

Tuesday, 12:55 p.m.

ANNIE SAT AT HER DESK in the office finishing up some notes on the recovered automobiles, and preparing a report for the police. She was pleased to discover, for some of the vehicles, the insurance companies offered a reward for the safe return of the stolen property. They could always use the extra money.

"Annie, come in here. Quick." It was Jake calling from the living room.

Annie slid her chair back, stood, and went to the doorway. "What is it?"

Jake's eyes were on the television, and he motioned frantically with one hand.

She stepped into the room, dropped into her easy chair, and leaned forward. She watched the last half of a commercial and then the news anchor appeared on the screen, shuffling papers while a catchy staccato played, growing louder with each note, then fading to silence. The anchor spoke:

"This is Channel 7 Action News at One. Our top story: Richmond Hill is brought to full attention as a serial killer who held the town hostage a short while ago escapes from a maximum security prison.

"With the full story, here's Lisa Krunk."

A news reporter appeared on the screen, her long nose almost buried in the soft foam rubber of the mike, her overly made-up face sporting tight lips. She stood in front of an institution made of brick and concrete, surrounded by high chain-link fences, a guard tower visible in the background.

"I'm standing here in front of Haddleburg Maximum Security Penitentiary. Earlier today, twenty-five-year-old Jeremy Spencer, a serial killer the citizens of Richmond Hill will remember well, successfully escaped from this institution."

Annie saw behind Lisa's feigned concern to a smug interior. They'd had several run-ins with Lisa Krunk in the past, and the journalist considered herself in the running for a Pulitzer someday. Annie suspected the woman was secretly pleased with the escape; it could result in some sensational stories she would deem worthy of her attention.

The screen split, a photo of Jeremy on one side, Lisa on the other, her wide mouth flapping as she talked:

"The prison K-9 unit was immediately deployed to follow Spencer's trail but it ran cold at a farmhouse two miles from where I'm standing. Police have set up roadblocks in the area and the RCMP have been notified. At this point, there are no indications where the convict may be headed.

"Spencer escaped the building through an unbarred window and successfully scaled the fence surrounding the prison.

"Officials have expressed concern he may return to this city and citizens are warned to be on the lookout and to notify police immediately should they sight him or have any information as to the whereabouts of this dangerous killer."

Annie looked over toward Jake. He sat on the edge of the couch, his mouth hanging open.

Lisa concluded her newscast:

"As you know, during Spencer's murderous rampage, I followed the story relentlessly, and my own efforts helped to bring this killer to justice the first time. You can rest assured I'll again do all I can to assist the police in their manhunt.

"I'll bring you more on this breaking story as it unfolds. In an exclusive report, I'm Lisa Krunk for Channel 7 Action News."

Jake and Annie gazed at each other, speechless, as the news anchor moved on to the next story. Finally, Jake switched off the TV, sat back, and exhaled a long breath. Annie slouched back in her easy chair trying to digest the disturbing news.

She was stunned. The serial killer they'd risked their own lives to catch a short time ago was on the loose again. The news brought many questions to her mind. Would he resume his campaign of terror, or stay out of sight? Would the police be successful in tracking him down? And, would he return to Richmond Hill?

Finally, Jake said, "I wonder if Hank knows about this."

"I'm sure he would know immediately. And you can bet he'll be contacting Amelia and Jenny right away. He'll need to ensure their safety."

Jake nodded. "He'll probably put a twenty-four-hour watch on their home."

"It's not likely Jeremy would abduct her again," Annie said. "He never harmed her before, but still …"

Jake looked at Annie, a deep concern showing in his eyes. "I'm worried about you as well."

"And what about yourself? Don't forget, he tried to kill you."

In the wrong place at the wrong time, sixteen-year-old Jenny had been abducted by the serial killer when she saw his face. During the Lincolns' investigation, Annie had come too close to the truth and been taken captive as well. In an attempt to save them both, Jake had put his own life at risk.

Annie also felt concern for any possible future victims. Due to Jeremy's twisted sense of morality, anyone could be in danger.

Jake seemed to sense her unease and tried to put her mind at rest. "They'll catch him."

Annie wasn't so sure. Though Jeremy wasn't a

mastermind, he had a way of thinking through his plans that made him unpredictable, and extremely dangerous.

"I'll give Hank a call," Jake said, and reached for his cell phone.

Annie wandered back into the office and sat at her desk. She searched online for any other stories regarding Jeremy's whereabouts, perhaps more up to date than Lisa's broadcast, but nothing new had been reported.

She tried to get back to work in an attempt to brush the disturbing situation from her mind, but found it impossible to concentrate.

CHAPTER 10

Tuesday, 2:41 p.m.

JEREMY KEPT MAINLY TO the fields during his long journey, occasionally taking to the back roads for a short period when it appeared safe. It wasn't until he neared the suburbs, running out of farms and dirt roads, that he decided it was time to find some nondescript clothing.

He was reaching familiar territory. He had lived near Richmond Hill most of his life and he knew of a farm where an elderly couple had once lived. The old man had since passed on, and if things hadn't changed, the widow still lived there on her own.

He approached the house from a fallow field at one side, left his bicycle behind a hedge, and crept up to the front window. The old woman sat on a stuffed chair, her face glued to the television.

He went around behind the house and swung open the unlocked back door to the kitchen. The television blared in the other room. That was good; the old woman must be half-deaf and would never hear him.

He stole down the hallway, took the set of stairs leading up, and opened the first door. It was a bedroom. It appeared to be the one she used. A quick look through the dressers and closet didn't reveal what he wanted. The floor boards creaked as he moved down the hallway to the next room.

Stacks of cardboard boxes were piled in the corner, neatly labeled and filled with clothing. The packrat had kept everything. He selected a baggy pair of jeans, a checkered button-down shirt, and a faded baseball cap. All of the shoes were too big on him, so he decided to stick to the canvas sneakers the prison had so nicely provided him with.

He hurried back the way he came, wondering if it was okay to steal from the dead. He decided it was.

He changed into the clothes behind the hedge where he'd deposited the bicycle, dug a hole in the dirt and buried his old orange suit, and then hopped on his bike and headed away.

He was anxious to find Moe, but to find him he needed to locate Uriah Hubert. It was getting hard to find a phone booth these days; hence, finding a phone book was nearly impossible.

He assumed his face would be all over the news by now. As long as he kept it hidden, the baseball cap he wore, along with his small size and the bicycle he rode, would allow him to pass as a youth. It appeared school was out for the day and there were a lot of kids on bikes. He was just one of many.

Moe had said Uriah lived in the projects, the government housing north of town. The inhabitants were usually a close-knit bunch, and perhaps once he got there, the right question to the right person would suffice.

His hair had gotten longer since his last days of freedom, and his whiskers, though not long, were now coarse and black. He hoped it would disguise him for now, at least until he found a better way.

He kept his hat low over his eyes and needed to ask three separate people before anyone knew where Uriah Hubert lived. Nobody recognized him. Perhaps they hadn't heard yet, or didn't watch the news around here.

Uriah Hubert lived in an ancient tenement building, run-down and surrounded by castoffs of all kinds. Every square inch of the decaying brick wall, as high as could be reached, had been painted by graffiti artists and taggers.

A group of lounging hoods watched him curiously as he pushed open the creaky door of the building and rolled his bike inside. He hoped his transportation would still be there when he needed it again. There was no directory in what passed for a lobby, and no names on any of the apartments.

He tapped on the first door. "Is this where Uriah Hubert lives?" he asked a decrepit old man when the door opened.

The man raised a thumb. "Upstairs."

"Which apartment?"

"Upstairs." And the door closed.

Jeremy took the steps upward and knocked on the door at the top of the steps. It was eventually answered by a man wearing nothing but a pair of boxer shorts. His belly flopped over top of the waistline, his hair uncombed, an unlit cigarette drooping from his mouth.

"Uriah Hubert?"

The man glared. "Who's asking?"

"A friend of Moe's."

"Friend of Moe's, huh. What d'you want?"

Jeremy remained patient. "I'm here to see Moe."

"Not here right now. Come back later." The door began to close.

"My name's Jeremy. Did Moe mention me?"

Uriah grinned, his smoke-stained teeth lined in a crooked collection. He rubbed at his hair. "Why didn't you say so before?" He swung the door open and stepped back. "Moe said you might be comin'. Didn't know it would be so soon."

Jeremy thanked him and stepped into the apartment. He was hit immediately by the smell of human sweat and stale cigarette smoke. A half-empty pizza container lay on a wooden box passing as a coffee table. The cracked linoleum flooring needed a mop, or at least, a good sweeping. Two or three serviceable chairs were scattered around, a couch that bulged stuffing and springs was tucked under the grimy window, and in the corner sat a brand new sixty-inch television.

Uriah waved toward the couch. "Rest yourself."

Jeremy sat carefully on the edge of the couch and watched as Uriah perched on one of the wooden chairs, lit his cigarette, and looked at his visitor.

"How's everything at Haddleburg?" Uriah asked.

"Have you been there?"

"Long time ago. Fixed up my life now."

Jeremy shrugged. "I guess it's the same as it's always been. Things don't change much inside."

"Yeah. That's what Moe said." He pointed to the pizza. "You hungry?"

Jeremy looked at the dried-out food. He hesitated and then picked out a slice. "Thank you. I am rather hungry. I surely am." He hadn't eaten since the night before, and though the pizza didn't look especially inviting, he managed to down it while Uriah watched.

He wiped his mouth on his sleeve as the door burst open. Moe stood in the doorway. He blinked a couple of times and then ambled in, a huge grin on his homely face. "Hi, little buddy," he said.

Jeremy stood and subjected himself to a smothering hug. He related the story of his escape, his journey back to town, and his plans for the future, while Moe and Uriah listened intently.

"You can stay here till you get yourself some digs," Uriah said.

"You can sleep on the couch," Moe offered. "I can use the floor. There's only one bedroom, and that's Uriah's."

"That would be good," Jeremy said. "That would be really good."

"What're your plans?" Moe asked as he dropped heavily onto the couch beside Jeremy.

Jeremy looked at his friend, hesitated, then squinted at Uriah. "I have an errand. Would you have a gun I can borrow?"

Uriah frowned at the question. Finally, he spoke slowly. "I got a piece but I ain't used it for a long spell. Like I said, I changed my life." He sat back and scratched his chin. "Guess you could have it, but you can't say where you got it."

"I won't."

Uriah left the room and returned a minute later with a revolver, spinning the cylinder with the thumb of one hand, a box of cartridges in the other. He handed the weapon to Jeremy and set the ammunition beside the pizza box. He leaned over and frowned. "Your thumb looks pretty nasty. All swollen up like that. You better do something for it."

Jeremy tucked the pistol behind his belt and said, "Thank you for the gun. Do you have any ice?"

"Sure do. And I can wrap your thumb up for you or it ain't never gonna heal." He pointed. "If you wanna, I can get those cuffs off, too."

"Thank you," Jeremy said. "That would be very kind of you. Very kind, indeed."

CHAPTER 11

Tuesday, 4:49 p.m.

ANNIE WAS IN THE KITCHEN, putting together a garden salad to go along with the barbecued steak they planned for dinner. Jake had gone to Mortino's to pick up the meat, taking Matty with him.

She looked out the kitchen window. The sun was beginning to set, barely peeking over the tops of the towering maple trees lining the rear of their backyard, shades of red and orange coloring the patches of clouds in the late afternoon sky.

She gave the salad a final toss and covered it with a tea towel, then dug in the cupboard for some paper plates. The fewer dishes to wash, the better.

The doorbell rang and she hurried to the door and looked through the peephole. Seeing no one, she opened the door a few inches and peeked through the crack.

A boy wearing a baseball cap stepped out from beside the

door. Her mouth fell open as he raised a pistol in one hand and pushed on the door with the other.

She looked in horror when she realized it wasn't a boy—it was Jeremy Spencer.

She stepped back, attempting to close the door. His foot blocked the doorway, and he overpowered her, pushing it open enough to squeeze through.

He slammed the door closed with his foot, raised the pistol, and glared at her as she took another step back.

"Hello, Mrs. Lincoln," he said. His calm voice made her shiver, and she stood frozen. "May I come in?"

"What … what do you want?" Her voice was hoarse and it quivered when she spoke.

"I need to talk to you." He waved the weapon toward the front room. "In there, please."

Annie eyed the gun warily. Her heart pounded as she turned and walked into the room, then stopped and turned around to face him.

"Sit down, Mrs. Lincoln," he said, waving the gun toward her overstuffed chair.

She turned uneasily, sat where he indicated, and shrank into the soft cushion. She watched him back up toward the couch, the pistol never wavering in his hand, his eyes on hers. He sat on the edge and smiled.

"I don't mean to frighten you, Mrs. Lincoln. I'm not going to hurt you, but I need to talk to you. I surely do."

That didn't ease her mind. "What about?" she asked cautiously.

"About Mother."

"Your mother?"

"I want to hire you," he said. "I need you to find out who killed Mother. And Father."

Annie relaxed somewhat. Jeremy's mind was unstable, his manner unorthodox, but his reasoning was sound. She knew his father had been murdered in prison, and his mother's suicide had seemed out of character at the time.

"I know Mother was murdered," Jeremy continued. "I talked to someone in prison. He said Father was a snitch, but I know he wasn't."

"Did you get the name of the killer?" she asked.

He shook his head. "Nobody seems to remember, but according to prison rumor, whoever killed Father, killed Mother as well."

"I … I don't know if I can help."

"I'll pay you. I don't have any money right now, but I promise to pay. I surely will."

In his eagerness to get the words out, Jeremy's gun hand lowered. It lay almost on his lap, and she thought of making an attempt to overpower him. She quickly dismissed the idea. If he'd come for help, he had no intentions to harm her. At least, not right now, and any hostile action she made could result in a more dangerous situation.

"I'm sorry about the way I treated you before," Jeremy said. His head drooped as if in shame, but he quickly recovered and brought his eyes again toward hers. "I didn't want to chain you up but I had no choice."

"You tried to kill my husband." She spoke sternly.

Jeremy didn't react to her comment in a negative way. "He

was trespassing on my land," he said in an even voice. "I had a right to at the time, but I'm sorry. I truly am."

Annie moved her eyes toward the picture window over the couch. Jake should be back soon, and she was uncertain whether or not he or Matty could be in danger.

"Whatever you think of me doesn't matter," Jeremy continued. "Mother was a good woman and she was innocent." He paused and took a deep breath. "You're the only one I could turn to. The police don't care. They surely don't."

"You killed a lot of people, Jeremy," she said flatly.

His eyes narrowed and he spoke firmly. "They deserved it."

"Nobody deserves to be murdered," she said quickly, and then wondered why she tried to convince him. It was futile, of course.

He rested the gun on his knee, the barrel pointing away from her, as if to lessen the threat. "Will you help me?" He was pleading.

She glanced at the revolver. He caught her eye and looked down at the weapon in his lap. "I don't have this to convince you to help. It's only for my protection."

"Where're you staying, Jeremy?"

He gave a short laugh. "You know I can't tell you that."

"Then how'll I contact you?" Annie was digging for information, anything she could use against him.

"I'll contact you. I have the phone number for Lincoln Investigations," he said. "Will you help?"

She sat forward, almost completely relaxed, and looked

into his pleading eyes. "I can't promise right now. I have to discuss it with my husband."

"Jake's a fair man," Jeremy said. "He'll understand."

She almost laughed at his comment. Yes, Jake was fair, but she wasn't so sure he would have any inclination to help a serial killer. Especially one who'd come close to killing him.

She took a chance, gauging his reaction. "Jeremy, you know I have to report this conversation to the police."

"I don't care," he said. "They're already looking for me." He sighed. "You do what you think is right, and I'll do what I think is right. We don't happen to see eye to eye on everything, but you're a fair woman, and I think you'll agree with me, Mother and Father deserve to rest in peace."

"I can agree with you on that, yes," Annie said.

He leaned forward. "Then you'll help?"

"Call me tomorrow. I'll let you know."

He nodded his head up and down slowly several times, and then rose to his feet. Annie stood back and watched until he left. She closed the door behind him, put on the security chain, went back to the living room, and dropped into her chair, her mind whirling.

CHAPTER 12

Tuesday, 5:14 p.m.

JAKE UNLOCKED THE FRONT door of the house, but the security chain stopped it from opening. Annie must've put the chain on after he'd left.

He rang the bell and she came to the door, peeked past the chain, then opened it, a worried look on her face.

He stopped, one foot in the doorway, and frowned. "What is it?"

"I had a visitor. Jeremy."

His mouth fell open and it took a moment for the information to sink in. Finally, he asked, "Jeremy Spencer?"

She nodded.

Matty pushed past and darted upstairs. Jake stepped inside, never taking his eyes off his wife, a look of unbelief on his face. He followed her into the front room and they sat on the couch, facing each other.

"Why…? What … what did he want? Are you all right? Did you call the police?"

Annie forced a weak smile. "I'm all right and I called Hank. He said he'd drop right over."

"And?"

"And," she said, "Jeremy wants us to investigate the death of his mother and father."

"His mother killed herself."

"He's not so sure," Annie said. "And frankly, neither am I. He said he talked to someone in prison who remembers his father, and according to him, the same person who killed his father may have also killed his mother."

"Why?"

"Revenge, perhaps. But I don't know who. That's what we need to find out."

Jake looked at her in surprise. "You're not actually considering it, are you?"

She looked away. "I haven't decided yet."

"But he's a serial killer, and very dangerous."

"I know," Annie said, looking back at Jake. "But his mother wasn't."

Jake stood and paced. He wasn't surprised Jeremy had turned up in Richmond Hill, but he had no inclination to have a murderer for a client. He found it hard to have any sympathy for Jeremy or either one of his parents.

The doorbell rang and Jake glanced out the front window. Hank's car was parked at the curb. He went to the door and opened it.

Hank face was grim as he stepped in. His usual friendly greeting went forgotten as he followed Jake into the living room and sat in the armchair.

Jake dropped onto the couch and leaned forward. "This is a crazy situation."

Hank agreed. "It's certainly not normal." He looked at Annie. "The first priority, of course, is to catch Jeremy. Did he give you any indication where he was hiding out?"

"I couldn't get anything from him. I tried."

"I'm sure he would be careful about that," Hank said as he sat back. "You know the routine. I'm going to have to get a complete report from you. Everything you can remember. Times, what he wore, how he got here, etcetera."

"I'll get that done right away," Annie said.

"Did you see how he arrived? Cab, walking, car?"

Annie shook her head. "I was rather unnerved and I didn't watch him leave."

Hank bobbed his head. "That's understandable."

"He said he would call me."

"Oh?"

"Like I told you on the phone, he wants us to find out what happened to his parents."

Hank scratched his head, eyeing her closely. "That's not illegal if you want to pursue it."

"I don't like the idea," Jake said. "Jeremy Spencer is a nutcase."

Hank leaned forward. "I think you should look into it."

Jake frowned. "It could be dangerous."

Annie looked at Jake. "I really don't think there's any danger from Jeremy. He may be crazy, but I don't think he would harm us."

Jake let out a long breath and opened his mouth to speak.

Hank interrupted. "It may help us track him down. The

more contact you have with him, the better our chances. We can trace his call when he phones you." He raised his hands, palms out. "But it's entirely your choice."

"Unless we both agree," Annie said to Jake, "we won't go ahead with it."

Jake hesitated a moment, then shrugged. "If it'll help find that little creep, then we'll do it."

"I'll talk to Captain Diego," Hank said. "I'm sure we can take another look at the evidence."

"Do you remember the case, Hank?" Annie asked.

The cop looked up at the ceiling and squinted. Finally, he drew a deep breath and answered. "I barely remember it. It was quite some time ago. I'd just made detective at the time, but it wasn't my case. The ME ruled it as suicide, and Homicide never got a look at it. The case was closed and everybody moved on."

"Not everybody," Annie said.

"What?"

"Jeremy didn't move on. He's positive she didn't kill herself, and I think the death of his parents helped make him what he is today."

"Don't start feeling sorry for the lunatic," Jake said.

Annie frowned at Jake. "I'm not feeling sorry for him. I'm trying to understand him."

Hank agreed. "Understanding him is part of it. We know in his twisted mind, killing thieves is justifiable. That's been his MO thus far, and if he starts killing again, we know what kind of people he's targeting."

"Hank, that doesn't narrow it down much. This world is full of thieves and dishonest people."

"It's a start," Hank said. "We'll come up with something."

"Speaking of thieves," Annie said, "did you get anything from those car thieves?"

"Sure did. We separated them and made a deal with one of them, and he told us everything. Turns out they had a few spotters looking for valuable cars." He turned to Jake. "That's why you got so lucky. One of the spotters saw you driving around, and voila."

Jake chuckled. "It wasn't luck."

"Next you'll tell me it came from your extensive knowledge of the criminal mind," Hank said dryly.

"Something like that."

"What about Mr. Culpepper?" Annie asked Hank.

"Whitney Culpepper is over the moon, the insurance company is pleased, and we have enough info to track down the buyers, so Diego is happy too."

"And Diego owes me," Jake put in.

"Good luck collecting on that," Hank said with a chuckle. "He'll never admit it."

"Back to Jeremy," Annie said. "When can we take a look at the evidence?"

"There's not much, but I'll get at it right away and see what we have."

Jake wasn't overjoyed with the situation, but for the public's sake, and for Annie's safety, he would do what he could to find Jeremy. They were involved already, and there was no choice. Besides, he wanted to see that little creep back behind bars again.

CHAPTER 13

Tuesday, 5:51 p.m.

HANK FOLLOWED THE convoy of four cruisers into the driveway of the old Spencer residence on County Road 12. He didn't expect to find Jeremy. The killer was smart enough to know that would be too obvious, but they needed to be thorough.

Dead ahead, the old farmhouse stood dark. The windows were boarded up, weeds now taking over the front yard, and the old barn still stood to his right, a couple hundred feet away, further down the driveway. It was the place where Jeremy's mother had hanged herself many years ago.

Two cars continued on to the barn. The four cops would give it a thorough search, just in case.

Officers streamed from the cruisers and surrounded the house, their guns drawn. Hank drew his weapon and followed two officers to the front door. A cop pushed on the door and it yawned open.

The house was dark, boards covering the windows

keeping out the early evening sun. Maglites lit the way as the cops searched the building, clearing it room by room.

Jeremy wasn't there. No surprise.

Hank found a light switch and flicked it. No light. The power company would've turned off the hydro to the house and barn long ago.

Officers came in the back door, through the mudroom, then the kitchen, and converged in the large dining room.

"He's not here," a cop said.

Hank turned to the cop who had spoken. "I can see that, Yappy," he said.

Officer Spiegle, better known as Yappy, was a young officer that seemed destined to be a beat cop his whole career. He wasn't exactly dumb, he just never seemed to take any initiative. His father had been a well-respected sergeant who had been killed in the line of duty, so the amiable, unassuming cop was tolerated, and even well-liked by most who knew him.

Hank went out to the front porch, the cops following. The officers who went to the barn were on their way back.

"Nothing there, Hank," one of them called as they climbed from the vehicles.

"He may show up here eventually," Hank said, looking around the property. "He was very attached to this place. Never wanted to leave after his mother died, and he kept the place up as best he could. His parents, as well as his grandparents, are buried here."

"Do you want to post somebody here to watch the house?" Yappy asked.

"Not right now," Hank said. "Any officer would be a sitting duck, and I couldn't leave one staking out the place in a cruiser. That would be a dead giveaway, and Spencer would never show up." He paused. "I want to give him every opportunity to come back here. Let him feel like this is still his home." He pointed to two of the officers. "You guys stay here while I take another look around." He waved his hand. "The rest of you might as well go."

~*~

JEREMY SPENCER CAME through the trees and approached his property from the side. He stopped short at the tree line, more than annoyed to see a police car parked in his driveway. Another car sat behind it, and he assumed it was a cop's private vehicle.

He crouched down and watched, but no police were visible, at least not from his vantage point.

They had no right to be on his property. He might be a fugitive, but this was still his house, and they were trespassing on his land.

Right now wasn't the time to do anything about it. He knew how to use his pistol, but he would be outgunned and outmanned. No use taking a chance when he had things to do—a mission that couldn't wait.

As disturbing as the presence of strangers on his property was the look of the house. The windows were covered with boards—something he'd never authorized. They'd desecrated it, and he was fuming.

He crept to the side of the house and peered in the window through a crack between the boards. Two cops stood in his dining room, and by the light of their flashlights, he saw them talking and laughing. Someone else—someone he recognized—was snooping through everything. It was Detective Hank Corning, the cop who'd interrogated him after his arrest.

He knew why they were here, of course. Annie Lincoln had called them as soon as he'd left her, and they were looking for him. That was somewhat disturbing, not because she'd called the police, but because the police knew he would show up here. Did they know him that well? On the other hand, perhaps they would have come here looking for him anyway. He would have to double-think his actions from now on. Predictability could get him caught.

Jeremy watched for a while, disturbed about the invasion and fearful something might have happened to all of his possessions inside the house. He'd had an old faithful Hyundai, but the police had taken it from him long ago. He couldn't drive it now anyway, even if he had it. It was too dangerous. He was tired of riding that old bicycle everywhere he went, pushing it through the trees, and bumping across fields. Maybe he could borrow Uriah's motorcycle. That would surely do.

He rose to his feet, turned, and went back into the bush. He would go back the way he came, through the forest, retrieve his bike, then out to the next side road and back to the city.

He paused a moment where three tall trees made a perfect triangle. Right there, in the center of those three maples—that's where he'd buried Joey.

Joey was his first kill. Jeremy had been only sixteen years old at the time, Joey a year younger, but the bully had deserved it. The teasing and torture he'd taken from the lowlife delinquent and his friends was still a source of the occasional nightmare. He'd lured Joey into the woods and, with his father's old .22-caliber revolver, destroyed his tormentor. After he'd killed Joey, the torture had stopped, the other boys hopeless and helpless without their ringleader.

He could still remember that day as if it were yesterday, fond memories of the events still vivid in his mind—Joey on the ground, bleeding to death, dying, and begging. He'd stopped the boy's whining with a second bullet, right below the eye. He'd watched the blood as it pooled under the body, turning the orange and golden leaves to a bright red, and then he'd buried him deep, deep, deep. Fond memories, indeed.

He could still almost taste Joey's blood on his tongue. He remembered the pure, whole, and righteous feeling it had given him. What he'd done was a beautiful thing.

The world was a better place after that and he was pleased to have played a part in it. Even though the search for Joey had gone on for a long time, the bully was still right here, right where he belonged.

It took a few years after that happy event to finally find his calling—his mission, as it were—and he looked forward to getting back at it.

He turned from the scene and continued on through the woods. He wanted to visit the graves of his parents, but with the cops there, he didn't dare. He would have to come back another time. And anyway, he had plans to make.

CHAPTER 14

Tuesday, 6:26 p.m.

ANNIE STILL HAD DOUBTS about investigating the death of Annette Spencer. Jake wasn't so hot on the idea, and she had no clue if they would get paid for their time, but she decided to do some preliminary investigation. If it appeared there was anything to Jeremy's claim, then at that time, she could decide whether or not to pursue it further.

She went into the office, pulled up to her desk, and switched on her iMac. The Internet was her main source of information, and the digital version of the *Richmond Hill Times* was her online destination.

Past issues of the newspaper were fully digitized, and it didn't take long to bring up the only story the paper had run regarding the death of Annette Spencer. Annie printed the report, pulled it from the printer, and read it.

ME Rules Death of a Richmond Hill Woman a Suicide

The cause of death of Annette Spencer, 39, has officially been ruled as suicide, according to the medical examiner's report.

Last Thursday, July 12, she was found in the barn of their

County Road 12 home, a rope around her neck, and tied to an overhead beam several feet above her body.

According to the report, Spencer's body showed indications of asphyxiation. Spencer had a history of depression.

Friends of the family are surprised she would take her own life. Rebecca Woodruff, a lifelong friend of Spencer, claims the ruling is in error and has implored the police to investigate her death further. A police spokesperson said they understand the frustration, but that a thorough investigation was undertaken and the medical examiner's report is sound.

Two years ago, Spencer's husband, Quinton Spencer, was killed while incarcerated in Haddleburg Maximum Security Penitentiary. Five years prior to his demise, he was convicted of second-degree murder in the death of a young man who entered their home during an attempted robbery. The murder of Spencer was never solved.

The Spencers had one child, Jeremy, now 17 years old."

She searched for information on the murder of Quinton Spencer, but the only mention of him was in that story.

The section of the news report that caught Annie's attention was the comment from Rebecca Woodruff. Surely a close friend could shed some light on Mrs. Spencer's demeanor at the time. She needed to find Mrs. Woodruff.

Further research revealed that a Peter and Rebecca Woodruff had owned a farm close to the Spencer place, but had since sold out and moved into the city.

It didn't take long to find the phone number, and she dialed it immediately.

"Hello?" It was a man's voice.

She introduced herself and said, "I'm looking for a Mrs. Rebecca Woodruff?"

"Hold on."

It sounded like she had the right people. She drummed her fingers on the desk and waited.

"Yes, this is Rebecca."

"Mrs. Woodruff, I'm investigating the death of Annette Spencer, and I wonder if I might ask you a few questions?"

"Annette Spencer? My goodness, that was a long time ago."

Annie looked at her watch. "Would it be okay if I dropped by to see you this evening?"

"Well, I reckon it would be."

Annie promised to be there shortly, ended the call, and grabbed her keys from the kitchen. Jake and Matty were in the front room, and she gave Jake the short version of her findings and hurried out the door.

The Woodruffs lived in a small bungalow, a row of manicured hedges separating them from their neighbors, a profusion of flowers smothering the front of the house.

Annie clanked the knocker and the door was answered by a prim middle-aged woman, smile lines around her eyes, her long hair in a neat bun perched on the back of her head.

She introduced herself and was ushered in to a tidy front room, where she took an offered seat on the couch.

"Thanks for seeing me," Annie began.

Mrs. Woodruff sat on a stuffed straight-backed chair and crossed her legs, her hands in her lap. "Does this have anything to do with that Spencer boy escaping?"

Annie hesitated. She didn't know how much to mention about Jeremy, and being hired by a serial killer wasn't something she wanted to admit.

"It's a shame about that boy," Mrs. Woodruff continued. "He never had much chance in life." She sighed. "Still, a lot of people lose their parents and don't turn out bad."

Annie smiled, pleased the question had been avoided. "That's true, Mrs. Woodruff," she said. "I have recently found some information regarding the death of Mrs. Spencer, and I have reason to believe it may not have been suicide."

"My goodness, no. It certainly was not." Mrs. Woodruff shook her head adamantly. "Why, I knew that woman better than anyone, and she was the picture of health. The first five years were hard on her, with her husband in jail and all, and then with his death, she broke down, of course." She sighed. "Them was hard times for her, but if she was going to kill herself, that would be the time, not two years later."

"I have to ask, Mrs. Woodruff. The news report said she suffered from depression. Would you know anything about that?"

The woman shook her head again. "Goodness' sakes, no, she never complained of that to me. Never. I don't know where they got the idea from. I told that reporter a thing or two, and the police, but they never did anything about it. It was suicide, they said."

"There are unsubstantiated reports that the same person who killed her husband in prison also killed her. Would you have any idea who it may be?"

"She never had an enemy in the world. I'll go to my grave knowing she didn't kill herself, but for the life of me, I can't figure out who did."

Annie suppressed a smile. The woman was indignant and, even after all these years, still held the same firm beliefs.

"You're a private investigator?" Mrs. Woodruff asked. "Who'd you say hired you?"

Annie thought quickly. "We haven't actually gotten paid for this. It has only recently come to our attention, and my husband and I decided to look into it."

"Your husband, you say?" Mrs. Woodruff frowned. Her frown turned into a smile, and she held up a finger. "I know who you are now. You and your husband are the ones who captured the young Spencer lad awhile back."

Annie smiled. "We had a lot of help but, yes, that was us."

"Well, I wish you all the luck in the world finding Annette's killer." She stood and offered a hand. "I best be seeing about my husband. He's not doing too good and gets cranky if I don't take care of him."

Annie stood and shook the woman's hand. "Thank you for your time."

"If there's anything else I can do," Mrs. Woodruff said as she let Annie out the door, "give me a ring."

Annie promised she would, then went to her car and drove toward home, deep in thought. They still had no real proof of any wrongdoing, but if Mrs. Woodruff was to be believed, they were on the right track.

CHAPTER 15

Tuesday, 8:44 p.m.

JAKE TOOK THE EVIDENCE box from Hank and led him into the living room. The cop sat on the couch, laid his briefcase beside him, and flipped it open.

Jake pushed aside a potted plant on the coffee table, put the box on the table, and pulled off the lid. He looked inside.

"There's not much in here," he said and sat in the armchair across from Hank.

"There was only a cursory investigation," Hank said. "So there's not much to go on." He waved toward the box. "Some of the stuff in there relates to Quinton Spencer, his murder in prison, and the death of the boy he killed."

The front door opened and Annie came into the room. Jake looked up. "How'd it go?"

Annie leaned over, peeked in the evidence box, and then sat on the couch. "Mrs. Woodruff is adamant Annette Spencer never would have taken her own life. Other than that, not much was gained."

"I assume you haven't heard from Jeremy yet?" Hank asked.

"Not yet," Annie said. "But when he calls, it's all set to record." She glanced at the box again. "The thing that strikes me as odd about Mrs. Spencer's death is that it was in the barn. It doesn't make a lot of sense that she would kill herself there. Why not in the house?"

"Agreed," Hank said. "And women don't often hang themselves. They almost always rely on a drug overdose or poisoning of some kind. Occasionally carbon monoxide poisoning, but that's unusual for women too." He shook his head. "It's rare to hear of a suicide where a woman hung or shot herself."

Jake pulled some reports from the box and laid them out on the table. He handed a stack to Annie and leafed through the rest before turning to Hank. "What about physical items—the rope, her clothes, things like that?"

"That's all there is," Hank said. "Either they were destroyed, or never kept."

"This is interesting," Annie said, frowning at one of the reports she held in her hand. "The father of the boy Quinton Spencer killed, a Mr. Aaron Starling, was somewhat of a jailbird. A petty thief, later convicted of voluntary manslaughter for killing a man during one of his robberies. Served eight years in Haddleburg."

"Like father, like son," Jake said. "It's no wonder the boy took to robbing houses." He held up the report he was studying. "Apparently, when Quinton Spencer was killed in prison, there were no witnesses."

"There never are," Hank said dryly.

"I did research on that case as well," Annie said. "It was never solved."

Hank sat back. "Not that I'm going soft or anything, but even if you're a serial killer, it must be hard not knowing what happened to your parents."

"He doesn't deserve to know," Jake said. "I have no sympathy for Jeremy at all."

Annie gave a short laugh. "We noticed that," she said and then added, "Frankly, I don't either, but I think the public has a right to know what happened. And her friends do, too."

"The public has forgotten."

"Her friends haven't," Annie said and dropped her stack of papers on the table. "I think I'd like to have another look in the barn."

"After what happened to you in there, I didn't think you'd ever want to go back again," Hank said.

"I admit, it was a frightening situation, but it turned out well."

Jake set his papers in his lap and spoke to Annie. "We can go there tomorrow if you want." He looked at Hank. "There's no problem with that, is there?"

Hank shrugged. "None at all. It's not like there's any evidence left there."

"How's Amelia taking all this?" Annie asked Hank.

"She didn't say much," Hank answered. "Naturally, she wants to see him caught, but I don't think she has a lot of fear for Jenny. Just to be safe though, she's keeping Jenny out of school until this is over."

"Is someone watching the house?" Annie asked.

Hank grinned. "Of course. You think I'd want anything to happen to her? It took me a long time to find the right woman."

"Oh," Annie said. "That's the first time you've admitted she's the right woman."

Jake looked at Annie and chuckled. "He's the last one to know."

"I wonder if he's told her that yet," Annie said.

"Come on, guys," Hank said with a lopsided smile. "Let's get back to business." He leaned forward and picked up a file folder Annie had laid on the table.

Jake winked at Annie and buried himself back in the reports.

"What we're missing here is the motive," Hank said. "There's always a motive."

"According to Jeremy," Annie said, "someone in prison told him his father was killed for being a snitch."

Hank shrugged. "Could be, or perhaps that was the excuse to cover up the real motive."

"Aaron Starling has a real motive," Jake said, waving a report. "Quinton Spencer killed his son, and look at this." He turned the paper around and poked at it with a finger. "Starling was in prison at the same time Spencer was there. The only problem is, Starling was in Haddleburg's medium security wing, and Quinton in maximum."

"They would never see each other," Hank said. "The two don't mix."

"And what about Mrs. Spencer? Where was Starling when she died?" Annie asked.

Jake browsed the report and announced, "He was out by then."

Annie sat back. "Interesting. I wonder where he is now."

"I'll look into that," Hank said.

"Any other motives?" Annie asked.

"What about Jeremy?" Jake asked. "The creep might've killed his own mother."

"What about his father?"

"Maybe not related. Somebody killed his father, and then Jeremy killed his own mother?"

"Why?"

"Because he's crazy. That's the only reason he needs."

"I know his sense of morality is messed up," Annie said. "But I don't think he killed her. If so, why would he be so intent on getting us to investigate?"

Jake shrugged. "It's just an idea. I wouldn't dismiss it too quickly."

"One thing I know for sure," Annie said. "Annette Spencer didn't kill herself."

"And neither did Quinton Spencer," Jake said. "But I'm fresh out of ideas."

CHAPTER 16

Wednesday, 8:02 a.m.

JEREMY SPENCER HAD gotten up early. He hadn't slept very well, excited to get going again, dreams of his mission flitting about his head most of the night. The uncomfortable couch hadn't helped his sleep either.

Uriah was still in bed, so Jeremy borrowed his shaving equipment and smoothed off his face, then grabbed his cap and went out for the morning paper, leaving Moe asleep on the floor.

Uriah had been kind enough to lend him a few dollars the evening before, and Jeremy kept his head down, his hat almost covering his eyes, as he hurried to the newspaper box at the corner. The bustling pedestrians paid no attention to him as he dropped some change into the slot and removed a newspaper. He hurried back to the dingy apartment, laid the paper on the kitchen table, made himself a cup of coffee, and then sat down.

The television and newspaper were his best source of information, a vital link between him and those who needed his attention, and he was eager to get started.

He flattened out the paper and gazed at the first page. His own picture was front and center, along with a story of how he'd escaped, and a plea for the public to be on the lookout for him.

Further down, an interesting story caught his attention. According to the report, a gang of car thieves had been busted and several arrests made. The person responsible for their capture was none other than his old friend, Jake Lincoln.

Unfortunately, all the perpetrators were in jail, and he wouldn't have access to them. He would keep an eye on this story, and if any of them were released on bail, he could take care of it.

He turned the page and scanned a bunch of human interest stories—nothing there for him.

A short item on page four caught his eye and he chuckled. A Richmond Hill man had been released on bail after being charged with eight counts of break, enter, and theft. The man's name was given—Jackson Badger. Not a common name; he should be able to find him. And the best part was, Badger was on house arrest. That would make locating him a snap, especially with the photo of the thief displayed prominently beside the story.

He ripped out the article, retrieved Uriah's phone book from the bottom shelf of the kitchen cupboard, brought it to the table, and searched for Jackson Badger. He couldn't find it, but there was only one house with that last name in the book. It wasn't far away, a few blocks, at the other end of the government housing area. He memorized the address, closed the book, and folded up the paper.

He looked across the room as Moe stirred, raised his head, and grinned. "Morning, little buddy."

"Morning, Moe." Jeremy took the last swallow of his coffee. "I have to go out this morning."

"Where to?"

"You know. My mission."

Moe sat up and rubbed his eyes before lumbering over to the table. "You want me to come with you?"

"I can handle this one, Moe. Maybe next time."

Moe pulled back a chair and sat down. It creaked under his massive weight, but held. "You gotta be careful. Somebody might recognize you." He looked closer at Jeremy and blinked. "Where'd you get them new clothes?"

Jeremy stood so Moe could see his shirt—blue checkered, with cartoon pictures of racing cars on it. "Uriah lent me some money and I went to Goodwill yesterday before I got home. I found some great stuff and it fit me perfectly."

Moe's eyes disappeared as he grinned. "You sure look swell. Like a little kid."

"And that's why they won't recognize me, Moe." He laughed. "Just a kid on a bike."

Jeremy had started bringing his bicycle up to the apartment. He didn't want to take a chance on someone stealing it. You never knew who you could trust.

He retrieved the gun from under a couch cushion, tucked

it under his shirt at his back, grabbed his hat from a coat hook, and pulled it on. "I'll be back soon," he said as he opened the door and wheeled the bike into the hallway. He carried it down the stairs, out to the sidewalk, and jumped on.

He left the bicycle in an alleyway a block from his destination, looked carefully up and down the street, and then walked boldly to what he hoped was Jackson Badger's house.

He covered the tip of his finger with the sleeve of his shirt, rang the doorbell, and put his hands behind his back, one hand gripping the butt of the pistol. He waited patiently.

Nobody answered. He knocked on the door.

Badger opened the door and scowled down at Jeremy. "Shouldn't you be in school? What d'you want?"

"Are you Jackson Badger?" Jeremy asked.

Badger didn't answer, but it didn't matter; this was the guy in the newspaper photo. Jeremy pulled out the pistol and swung it forward.

Badger reacted fast. He turned and raced away, leaving the door open. Jeremy sprang inside. Badger was going for the back door; he couldn't let him get away.

As Badger struggled to unlock the door, Jeremy made it to the kitchen and leveled the gun. He pulled the trigger, but Badger ducked, and the window in the door shattered.

Badger dove across the room, behind the table. "What do you want?" he screamed.

Jeremy rounded the table carefully. "I want you," he said.

The thief was on his knees, caught in a corner, his hands in front of him as if to stop the attack. "Why?" he whined. "What did I do to you?"

Jeremy stayed back five feet and sighted carefully. A shot to the head could miss and then there might be trouble. The sensible thing would be to select the larger target, wound first, disabling his opponent, and then finish the job.

"It's not what you did to me," Jeremy said as he tightened his finger on the trigger. "It's who you are that's the problem."

Badger looked confused.

Jeremy pulled the trigger, the sound of the shot filling the room, almost deafening him. The bullet hit Badger in the chest. Blood sprayed, stopping short of where Jeremy stood.

The thief's eyes closed as he wobbled, then fell forward into a puddle of blood. One more shot in the back of the head ensured the job was done. Jeremy stood back, examining his handiwork.

He put the gun behind his belt, took the back door out, avoiding the broken glass, and went up the side of the house to the street.

He found his bike where he'd left it and, seeing no one on the sidewalk, he jumped on and pedaled away.

Thus far, it had been a wonderful day.

~*~

MRS. EDITH BADGER pulled her car into the driveway, squinted through the windshield toward the front door of her house, and frowned. Her worthless son had left the front door open again. He'd always been careless that way, and it was no wonder he got caught for his crimes. He was too inattentive and irresponsible.

She opened the back door of her car, retrieved a bag of groceries, and headed up the walkway to the front door. She stepped inside and called, "Jackson? You here?"

There was no answer.

She closed the door, set her bag on a small corner table, and raised her voice. "Jackson?"

Still no answer. She sighed, removed her jacket and scarf, and hung them on a hook behind the door. Retrieving her bag of groceries, she carried it into the kitchen, stopping once to call her son again, and dropped the bag on the kitchen counter.

Mrs. Badger looked down and frowned at a trickle of red liquid at her feet. Her eyes grew wide and she spun around, then advanced cautiously around the kitchen table, following the trickle of what she now realized was blood.

She froze for a moment, and then screamed again, the sound fading away as she collapsed to the floor and fainted. She lay still a few moments before opening her eyes, the realization of what she'd seen rushing back in.

She scrambled backwards, away from the sight, struggled to her feet, and then stumbled for the phone and dialed 9-1-1.

CHAPTER 17

Wednesday, 9:36 a.m.

HANK WAS AT HIS DESK in the precinct when RHPD dispatch was notified of the 9-1-1 call. They informed him immediately.

He glanced over toward the watercooler. King was wasting time as usual, chatting with a young female intern who didn't seem all that interested in talking to the unkempt cop.

Detective Simon King, recently transferred to RHPD and placed in the narcotics division, occasionally teamed up with Hank when not working a case. And right now was one of those times. Hank preferred to work alone and wasn't keen on being coupled with the stringy-haired cop—always with three days' growth of beard on his face, sloppy clothes, and an overall lazy attitude—but with the Spencer case, the had captain insisted on it.

Hank strode over to King. "We got a body."

King straightened up, winked at the intern, tossed his

paper cup into the wastebasket, and followed Hank from the precinct to the parking lot at the rear of the building.

They climbed in Hank's Chevy. "Who's the vic?" King asked.

Hank started the car and pulled out. He slipped a piece of paper from his pocket and handed it to his partner. "It's all there. A woman came home from shopping this morning. Found her son dead in the kitchen. Blood all over the place."

King studied the paper and whistled. "Jackson Badger. I know that name."

Hank glanced over at King. "A petty thief. Multiple break-ins. Released on bail yesterday."

"Yup."

Hank didn't want to make any presumptions, but the presence of Jeremy Spencer in the area and a victim who was a thief seemed to point in one direction.

"You think it's Spencer, don't you?" King asked, squinting at Hank.

Hank shrugged. "Maybe. Can't say yet."

First responders had cordoned off the entire property by the time they arrived. Three cruisers were parked on the street, one cop directing traffic. Hank pulled in behind the forensic van and shut off the engine, and they got out.

They ducked under the yellow tape and made their way to the front door. A uniformed cop leaning against the brick wall greeted them. "Morning, Hank, King," the cop said, handing over two pair of booties.

"Morning, Yappy," Hank said, and King grunted. They slipped the shoe covers on and stepped inside.

Investigators were busy conducting a rigorous examination of the entire house. Lead crime scene investigator Rod Jameson approached him, a clipboard in his hand. "The action's in the kitchen, Hank," Jameson said, pointing down the hallway.

The detectives went into the kitchen, a hub of activity. The police photographer, having finished taking photos of the victim, left the room. Hank went around the table and approached the body. Jackson Badger lay face down in a pool of blood that trickled across the floor toward the counter, distinct footprints in a stream of blood near the sink.

Glass crunched under King's feet as he approached the back door. Hank frowned at the careless cop. "Watch the glass, King," he said. "Be careful of the evidence."

Hank pulled on a pair of rubber gloves, approached the door carefully, and pushed on it. "The door's unlocked. The killer might've entered this way."

Jameson had come into the room. "The front door was open when the first responders arrived," he said.

Hank stepped back and looked at the investigator. "So he might've entered through the back and left through the front, or the other way around."

Jameson stepped aside to allow Nancy Pietek, the chief medical examiner, to enter the room. "Nice to see you again, Hank," she said as she put on a pair of examination gloves.

Hank nodded hello and motioned toward the body. Nancy approached Badger, crouched down, and examined the back of the victim's head. She looked up at Hank. "Looks like a gunshot entry wound. I'll know for sure after I do a thorough examination."

"So I assume the manner of death is a gunshot wound?" Hank asked.

"It looks like it," Nancy replied. She motioned toward the side of the body. "Look at the blood here. That's not from his head. I expect when we get him turned over, we'll see a GSW in the chest as well."

"If I were to hazard a guess," Hank said, "he was shot in the chest, fell forward, and then took one more shot to the back of the head."

Nancy stood. "It looks that way, but I can't make a determination yet. We'll have to wait until forensics is done before we move him."

Hank thought he had a pretty good idea of what had happened. He turned to Jameson. "I suppose there were no witnesses?"

"Nope. None that came forward."

"And the victim's mother?" Hank asked. "Edith Badger?"

Jameson motioned behind him. "In the living room."

Hank looked at King. "I'll go talk to the mother. Try not to step on too much evidence."

King shrugged and brushed back his greasy hair. "Relax, Hank."

Hank said nothing as he turned and went into the living room. Mrs. Badger sat on the couch, leaned forward, her head down, hands folded in her lap, gripping a tissue. A uniformed cop sat opposite her, looking uneasy. Mrs. Badger glanced up as Hank approached.

Hank nodded for the cop to leave, then pulled the chair in closer to the woman and sat down. He leaned forward and put his hand on her arm. "Mrs. Badger. I'm Detective Hank Corning."

She smiled weakly, the few wrinkles in her midforties face exaggerated by the pain in her eyes.

"I'm very sorry about your son," he said.

She sighed lightly and dabbed at her tears. "He really was a good boy at heart. I know he got in some trouble lately." She stopped as a sob escaped her lips. "But he didn't deserve this."

"Nobody deserves this, Mrs. Badger," Hank said softly. "And I'll do whatever I can to find out who's responsible."

She looked at him earnestly. "He was only twenty-two."

Hank sat back and sighed deeply. He always hated this part—hated seeing the grief people went through, especially when it was a senseless death like this one. "I'm sorry I have to ask you," he said. "Do you know of anyone who might've wanted your son dead?"

Mrs. Badger shook her head. "Not that I know of."

King had come into the room, standing silently. He spoke up, "Your son was a nasty character, involved in a lot of criminal activity, and likely had a lot of nasty friends. Think, Mrs. Badger. Surely one of them may be responsible."

Hank cleared his throat and frowned at the insensitive cop.

Mrs. Badger looked up at King, pain evident on her face. "I didn't know them."

"We have an idea who it might be," King said.

She looked at him quizzically.

Hank spoke. "We have no suspects at this point, but we'll

be looking at everyone." He waved for King to leave and waited for the crass detective to wander away before saying, "We need to get a complete statement from you when you feel up to it."

She nodded and Hank rose to his feet. "One of the officers will stay with you awhile. Speak up if you need anything."

"Thank you, Detective."

King stood by the living room door. Hank motioned to him and King followed him from the house. Hank stopped, turned back, and glared at his tactless partner, his brows in a tight line. He raised his voice. "I told you before. When someone is grieving, leave the questions to me."

King glared back and then finally looked aside and sauntered to the car.

Hank sighed and followed him, at the moment feeling more like a babysitter than a cop.

CHAPTER 18

Wednesday, 10:12 a.m.

ANNIE FELT HER STOMACH doing somersaults when Jake pulled the Firebird off County Road 12 and onto the dusty lane leading up to the old Spencer house.

It was a while since she'd been here, and memories of the terrifying events flooded back into her mind like it was yesterday.

Jake stopped in front of the house and she peered through the windshield, up to the small second-story window where Jenny had been held, fearful for her life.

Down the lane, a couple of hundred feet away, the old barn, now faded and worn with age, sat as a reminder of her own captivity. She wasn't so sure she wanted to venture down the lane to the place where she had been imprisoned, but she summoned up her courage and stepped from the vehicle.

Jake climbed from behind the steering wheel and watched her as she came around the front of the car to join him. "Are you okay?" he asked.

She nodded. "I'll be all right. It's just creepy being here."

The front lawn, once so nicely kept, was completely overgrown with weeds. Wild grass pushed up between the cracks in the crumbling sidewalk leading to the front porch that covered most of the front of the old red-brick farmhouse.

The surrounding fields hadn't fared any better. No longer pushing up wheat, oats, and corn, the fertile soil fed a mixture of grass, weeds, and wildflowers.

Jake glanced around. "Jeremy still owns this place. I wonder why he never sold it. A bit of money can go a long way in prison."

"Perhaps he expected to come back here one day."

"He may still come back," Jake said. "I hope he does. Maybe then, they can catch the little creep."

Annie glanced apprehensively down the lane. "Shall we go to the barn?"

They went down the gravel driveway and stopped in front of the small, decaying door. It was hooked on the outside, so Jake lifted the hook, unlatched the door, and it creaked open.

Jake followed Annie in and they looked around the enormous room, lit only by strips of light that streamed through spaces between the boards and splayed across the straw-covered floor. Rusty farm implements lined one side of the space. Huge columns supporting massive beams still held the roof firmly in place.

Annie shivered and caught her breath. On the far side of the room, fastened to a pillar, the chain that was used to hold her captive still hung, now rusting into dust.

As she moved closer to the pillar, she could make out the dog collar, secured to the end of the chain—the collar that had once been locked around her neck, chaining her up like a mad dog.

She stopped under the beam where Annette Spencer had been found, hanging from a noose. She was glad she hadn't witnessed that sight, but she could picture it in her mind. The woman, who Annie now believed had been murdered, hanging helpless, gasping for air, as her killer watched.

She squinted upward. Strands of rope still clung to the beam. According to the police report, she'd hung thirty inches from the floor. The report concluded she'd climbed into the haymow, wrapped the noose around her neck, and jumped off.

Annie had her doubts.

"Did you bring the tape measure?" she asked.

Jake lifted his shirttail. It was fastened to his belt. He removed it and handed it to her.

Annie held up a hand. "That's your job." She pointed to a long wooden ladder hanging on the wall. "I need you to use that and measure the distance from the rope on the beam to the haymow."

Jake removed the ladder from the wall and stood it up. The end barely touched the beam. He tested the rungs. "I don't know if they'll hold me," he said.

"I'll do it," Annie said as she took the end of the tape and climbed the ladder carefully. The rungs bent under her weight, but held. Jake took the other end, climbed into the haymow, and measured the distance. "Twelve feet, three inches," he said and climbed back down.

Annie hung on with one hand, pulled the report from her back pocket, and studied it. "Mrs. Spencer was five feet, four inches tall, and she hung thirty inches from her feet to the floor of the barn. I want to know the distance from the beam to the floor."

She held the end of the tape while Jake measured. "Fifteen feet, seven inches."

Annie climbed down the ladder and did some quick calculations. Finally, she announced, "She couldn't have done it herself. It's impossible. The rope would've been almost two feet too short."

Jake looked up at the beam, then the haymow. "I'm pretty sure, if she'd jumped that far, her neck would've been broken as well. And it wasn't."

"Now we have to find out who killed her," Annie said.

"I wonder if we should talk to the detective who was in charge of this," Jake said as he took the report from Annie and browsed it.

"He retired years ago, shortly after this case. Apparently, he has Alzheimer's disease now, so I'm afraid all we have to go on are his sketchy accounts."

"That doesn't leave us with much, then," Jake said, waving the report. "If the conclusion was suicide, then how much can we trust anything else in here?"

"There's really nothing else in there," Annie said. "It looks like we're on our own."

"And there's absolutely no more evidence left," Jake added, glancing around the space. "Is there anything else in here you want to look at?"

Annie shook her head. "Nothing."

They left the barn, latched the door, and returned to the car. Annie was more certain than ever they were looking for a cold-blooded killer.

"We're still lacking a motive," she said to Jake as they drove away. "And somehow, it ties into the death of Quinton Spencer. That's what we need to find out."

"And with no witnesses to his murder, and no evidence," Jake said. "Where do we start?"

Annie couldn't answer that question right now, but she was determined to find those answers—one way or another.

CHAPTER 19

Wednesday, 10:59 a.m.

HANK SAT AT HIS DESK, filling out a preliminary report on their investigation of the murder of Jackson Badger. King was in his usual spot by the watercooler. Around him, officers went about their tasks, the warm air inside the building not making their job of controlling crime in this small city any easier.

There was some talk lately of building a new precinct, or perhaps a second one, to help reduce the crime rate that grew with the city. Maybe that's all it was—talk. With their budget grossly underfunded now, an increase in funds seemed unlikely to Hank. He'd be happy to get a new desk. The one he had now had seen much better days, used by many of his predecessors, and his chair rocked a little from side to side. If he didn't have to fill out so many reports, and could spend more time on the streets doing actual police work, he wouldn't care.

He glanced across the large room as Captain Alano Diego stepped from his office, beckoned Hank over, and then looked toward the watercooler and called, "King."

King sauntered over and joined Hank. "I wonder what the captain wants."

Hank looked at the sloppy cop. "Maybe he picked up some clothes from the thrift store for you. Something to improve your look."

King chuckled. "Don't mock my uniform. It helps me fit in."

"Not around here, it doesn't. Maybe out in the back alleys, but a detective should look more presentable." He led the way to Diego's office and tapped on the open door.

"Maybe I'll buy a tie," King said and followed Hank into the office. He leaned against the filing cabinet and crossed his arms.

Hank sat in the only guest chair, stretched out, and looked at the captain, who had a worried expression on his face.

Diego adjusted his cap and looked at Hank. "I'm a little concerned," he said. "With this Spencer guy at large again, the city's going to panic. It's all still fresh in their minds."

"We're going to get him, Captain," Hank said.

King spoke up. "Hey, look at the bright side. He's killing criminals and making our job a whole lot easier."

Diego frowned at the cop. "King, if you recall, this nut's criteria aren't the same as ours." He leaned forward in his chair and glared. "And we don't need a vigilante running around this city."

Diego continued to stare at King until the cop looked away, and then opened a file folder on his desk and leafed through its contents before continuing, "Granted, this Badger was some character, but he was going down for sure. For a long time." He tapped his fingers on the desk. "Do you really think this is Spencer's work?"

"It's too much of a coincidence not to be," Hank said.

Diego bobbed his head up and down a few times in agreement. He leaned back, dropped his elbows on the armrests, steepled his fingers under his chin, and looked intently at Hank for a few moments.

"What's on your mind, Captain?" Hank asked.

Diego's jowls jiggled as he adjusted his tie. He slapped the file folder closed with one hand, pushed it aside, and cleared his throat. "I want to run something past you two."

"Sure, Captain."

Diego looked at the scruffy cop. "King, you weren't around then, but the Lincolns were responsible for bringing Spencer in before." He held up a hand toward Hank. "I know you would've gotten him eventually, but who knows how many more bodies we would've had in the meantime."

Hank leaned in. "I give them a lot of credit," he said. "But then, they're friends of mine."

Diego gave King an extended look, then spoke to Hank. "I want to give them every opportunity to aid us in this."

King interrupted, "They're not cops."

Diego looked King up and down. Hank knew what was on his mind. King wasn't much of a cop either, and Hank was pretty sure if Diego had had a say in his transfer here, he would've turned it down flat. Diego didn't comment on King's remark.

"I've been considering the idea of swearing Jake in as an

auxiliary constable," Diego said. "That is, if he would go for it. Many forces are utilizing the services of auxiliary constables now. And a uniform similar to regular cops may help."

King uncrossed his arms, stood straight, and pointed toward the precinct floor. "There're a lot of cops that resent him and that wife of his. There's a lot of talk going around they're interfering in police matters."

"I haven't heard anything at all," Hank said. "The Lincolns have some friends here besides me."

King's lips tightened and he leaned back against the filing cabinet.

Hank looked at Diego. "He may go for it, but I would nix the uniform. That's for show, and they aren't showy people." He leaned in. "But if you're thinking about it, you should consider Annie as well."

King was huffing, and it appeared to Hank he was about to walk out.

Diego removed his cap, brushed back his dark hair, and replaced his cap. "Of course, Annie as well."

"What about a weapon?" Hank asked. "If you recall, you allowed Jake to carry one before, and since this is a serial killer …"

"Perhaps," Diego answered. "Let me think on that."

Hank held back a grin. That would be sure to send his partner off on a tangent. He couldn't understand what was wrong with King. He appeared to see Jake as a threat—perhaps competition, disregarding the fact they were all on the same side.

Diego brushed at his dark mustache. "Does Callaway have a trace set up on the Lincolns' phone?"

"All ready to go, Captain," Hank said. "The minute Spencer calls, we'll know exactly where he's calling from."

"Let's hope he calls, then," Diego said, then paused before adding, "I realize the Lincolns think there's something other than suicide involved in that Spencer woman's death, and that's all well and good." He pointed a finger at King, then at Hank. "But your top priority is finding Spencer. Is that understood?"

"Understood, Captain," Hank said, and King grunted.

Diego continued, "As far as we're concerned, the case is closed, but give them whatever they need. If we can clean up a cold case, so much the better."

Hank nodded.

"It's not a cold case, Captain," King said. "It's closed."

"The murder of Quinton Spencer is a cold case, King. If, like they say, the same guy killed both of them, then what do I care if Mrs. Spencer's case is reopened?"

King shrugged and crossed his arms.

Diego waved a hand, dismissing them. "Okay, get out of here. Go catch me a serial killer."

CHAPTER 20

Wednesday, 11:32 a.m.

JEREMY SPENCER WHEELED his bicycle into the apartment and leaned it against the wall. Moe was sunken into the couch, his feet on the coffee table, watching television. Uriah was in the kitchen cooking up something that smelled vaguely like greasy eggs.

Jeremy sat at the table, laid his cap down beside him, and watched Uriah a moment.

Uriah spoke without turning around. "You want eggs?"

"No, thanks. I already had something." Jeremy paused and then asked, "Uriah, can I borrow your motorcycle today?"

Uriah slid the eggs from the pan onto a plate, shut off the burner, and dropped the hot pan in the sink. It sizzled and sputtered. He set the plate on the table, sat down, and took a bite before answering. "You know how to ride a bike?"

"It can't be that hard," Jeremy said. "Father had an old one a long time ago and I did okay with it."

Uriah looked thoughtfully across the table at Jeremy, his lips smacking as he chewed. “I need it back by four. I gotta go to work.” He waved toward the front door. “Keys are hangin’ up there.”

“No problem,” Jeremy said. “I’ll have it back by four.”

Moe wandered over to the table and sat down. “Where you off to, little buddy?”

“I thought I might go to my house.” He’d been disappointed and angry at seeing the cops there the day before and was anxious to visit Mother and Father’s graves. If no one was around there today, he had plans to go inside the house to make sure his stuff was safe.

“Need some company?” Moe asked.

Jeremy eyed Moe’s two-hundred-and-fifty-pound body. “Might be a lot of weight on the bike?”

“She’ll hold,” Uriah said. “Be careful over bumps, and watch out for potholes.”

Moe’s face brightened. “Can I come?”

Jeremy smiled at his faithful friend. “Sure, Moe. We’ll go together.”

Uriah dropped his fork and sat back. “You know, I don’t mind you guys staying here awhile, but I can’t afford to feed your ugly mugs forever. You gotta find a place soon.”

“Gotta get a job first,” Moe said, appearing worried. “Maybe start looking tomorrow.”

Jeremy knew Moe would have a hard time finding employment. He was a con, fresh from prison and, though Jeremy didn’t like to say it, not very bright. He felt somehow responsible for the big lug’s well-being, but he was in no better position than Moe. He had no money, no way of getting any, and no other place to go.

He really wanted to return to his home and stay there, but of course, it would be too dangerous. The cops would come snooping around again, so that was out of the question.

A new idea began forming in his mind. Though he wasn't a thief, and he hated those who stole from others, he wondered to himself if it would be morally wrong to take from those who'd taken from others. Would that really be stealing? He would have to consider the idea a little longer before making a decision.

"We'll find a way, Moe," Jeremy said.

"Did you get done what you went to do this morning?" Moe asked.

"Yes, everything worked out great. It surely did."

Uriah frowned. "And that's another thing. I don't know what you're doin' with that piece I gave you, but if you're gonna bring the heat down on me … like I said before, I'm going straight now, and I can't afford no trouble. I ain't goin' back inside."

"None of us are going back there," Jeremy said. "I'll be careful."

Uriah looked uncertain. "I'll give you a couple more days." He leaned over and raised a brow. "How's your hand?"

"Much better," Jeremy said. "It still hurts a lot, but the swelling's going down. It seems to be healing slowly."

"Best be careful with it," Uriah said, then stood and wandered down the hallway.

Moe leaned forward and looked at Jeremy. "So tell me. What'd you do this morning?"

"I killed a man. A man who deserved it."

Moe whistled. "Wish I was there."

"Maybe next time, Moe."

Moe grinned. "I ain't afraid."

Jeremy grabbed his cap and stuffed it into his back pocket, then stood and headed for the door. "Let's go now."

He got the keys from a hook by the door, then crouched down and picked up a pair of helmets. He handed one to Moe and put the other one on, tightening the strap. Moe was having a hard time getting it over his big head, but finally managed.

Jeremy removed the revolver from behind his belt, put in three more rounds to replace the ones he'd used, then tucked the weapon behind his back.

Moe followed Jeremy out, down the steps, and to the rear of the building. The dingy area was all asphalt, high wooden fences lining the back of the property. A nauseating odor emanated from a big blue dumpster, overflowing with a week's worth of refuse. Half a dozen cars that had outlived their usefulness occupied designated spots.

An old Suzuki was chained to a post by the fire escape door. Jeremy unlocked it, hopped on, and kickstarted it. It sputtered and died. The second attempt caught and he revved it a few times and turned off the choke, and the engine idled.

He spun around the lot a couple of times to reacquaint himself, then stopped beside Moe. "Get on."

Moe jumped on the back. The springs did their job, holding Moe's weight, and Jeremy eased away.

He stopped at the street as a police cruiser idled by. The

cop in the passenger seat glanced their way but the vehicle kept on moving. Jeremy pulled the motorcycle onto the street, followed the cruiser for a couple of blocks, staying well back, and then turned, being careful to signal.

In five minutes, they entered the outskirts of the city, with County Road 12 and his house a few minutes away.

He hoped there were no cops around this time, but if there were, he was prepared to deal with them.

CHAPTER 21

Wednesday, 11:47 a.m.

JAKE OPENED THE FRONT door and Hank stepped inside. "Where's your sidekick?" Jake asked.

Hank rolled his eyes and chuckled. "I snuck away without him." He shrugged. "He's not too hot on you guys anyway."

Jake had had some unfriendly words with Detective King in the past, and though Jake wasn't one to hold a grudge, he found it a lot easier to think without the crass detective around.

Hank followed Jake into the front room, and each sat on an end of the couch. Hank put his briefcase on the floor beside him and greeted Annie, who came into the room and snuggled up in her armchair, her feet tucked underneath her.

"We had a murder this morning," Hank announced.

Jake dropped his arm across the back of the couch and turned toward the detective. "And the reason you're here to tell us this is because…?"

"Could be Jeremy's work."

"Let me guess," Annie said. "The victim was a thief?"

Hank nodded and then explained the particulars of the case. "We have no proof yet, only a presumption. And at this point, there's no evidence that points to Spencer, or anyone else for that matter. I have officers canvassing the neighborhood, but so far, nothing."

"I wonder what he's using for transportation," Annie said.

"Only a guess right now," Hank said. "But either he's walking, which seems like a risky thing to do, or he's hooked up with someone else who has a vehicle."

"As far as we know, he has no close friends," Jake said. "Maybe no friends at all."

"Again," Hank said, "we're assuming it's Jeremy. Until I get a complete forensics report, and unless that report points directly to Spencer, we can't rule out the possibility that it may be someone else."

"It was Jeremy," Annie said.

Hank grinned. "I expect you're right, but cops have to go on facts. You're not bound by that."

"And that's why I don't want to be a cop," Jake said. He'd considered it as a career at one point—when Hank had announced his intentions—but it was an idea that had been short-lived and never revived. Being a private investigator was as close as he wanted to come to the demanding career of a police detective.

Hank cleared his throat. "Speaking of being a cop, Diego came up with the bright idea of swearing you two in as auxiliary constables. He said you have some expertise in this case and might be able to help."

Jake laughed and looked at Annie. "I really don't think either one of us is interested."

"It comes with a uniform."

"Great. Just what we need." Jake said. "You're forgetting, most of what we do is undercover. I don't think a uniform would help us with that."

Hank looked quizzically at Annie.

She shook her head. "I don't see the point."

The detective sported a crooked grin. "I had a feeling you guys might say that." He paused. "I believe Diego was hoping you would make catching Spencer a top priority."

"It is a top priority," Annie said. "I think we can work both cases at the same time, especially since they're related."

"Diego said to give you whatever you need. Whether it be in finding Annette Spencer's killer, or in apprehending Jeremy, he's behind you."

Annie laughed. "You would've given us that information anyway."

"Likely," Hank said. "But he warned King and me to make Spencer our only goal. And I agree. He needs to be on the top of our list. We have to catch him before he kills again." He snapped open his briefcase, removed a file folder, and handed it to Jake. "Mrs. Spencer is up to you two."

"What's this?" Jake asked, as he opened the folder.

"It's about Aaron Starling, the father of the boy Quinton Spencer killed."

Jake perused the single sheet of paper in the folder. "After Starling got out of prison, he found out his wife had left him and moved away. He left the city as well. Last known to be in

Alberta, but that dates back a few years. His current whereabouts are unknown."

"So that doesn't let him off the hook for Mrs. Spencer's murder," Annie said.

"What about Mrs. Starling? She could've killed Annette Spencer," Jake said. "She had a motive as much as her husband did."

"Hanging doesn't sound like the way a woman would commit murder," Hank said. "I'd wager you're looking for a man."

"I agree," Annie said. "It's unlikely a woman would have the strength to do it the way it was done." She filled Hank in on her findings in the barn.

"If your measurements are correct, and of course, I believe they are," Hank said, "then that seems to cinch it. Mrs. Spencer was murdered."

"It's at least enough evidence to open the case again," Jake said. "Assuming we catch Jeremy before his mother's killer is found, Diego would really have no choice."

"The captain's going to want some kind of report from you two as you go along. It's not mandatory, of course."

"That depends," Jake said. "Are we working for him, or are we working for Jeremy the scumbag?"

Annie laughed. "Either way, I doubt if we'll get paid for this."

"You'll get paid by getting on Diego's good side," Hank said. "Look at it as an investment for the future."

"You can tell Diego not to worry," Annie said. "We'll give him our findings. I don't see how that's going to hamper our investigations, especially since we have his blessing to start with."

"I'll tell him he has your full cooperation," Hank said with a smile. He closed his briefcase, picked it up, and stood. "In the meantime, I have some work to do before Jeremy kills again."

Jake stood and saw Hank to the door. He watched the detective drive away before returning to the living room, where Annie browsed the folder with the information on Aaron Starling. "What's our next move?" he asked.

Annie looked at him and shook her head slowly. "I'm not sure, but whatever it is, we need to come up with something quick. If this murder was the work of Jeremy, then it appears he couldn't wait to get back at it. That means he's not going to sit around much longer before he strikes again."

Jake sat on the couch and nodded. "That's probably why he was so intent on breaking out of prison. For some reason, he has a compulsion to kill."

CHAPTER 22

Wednesday, 12:42 p.m.

LISA KRUNK HAD GONE through a dry spell. Lately, there had been no news stories worthy of her attention, but now things were looking up.

First, with the escape of Jeremy Spencer, and now, with a murder taking place that seemed like Jeremy's MO, she was raring to go.

She wasn't exactly sure how to proceed with this one. Certainly, sensational stories were ideal for commanding the public's attention, resulting in increased ratings for her, but with her aspirations of a future job as a newspaper journalist, and the Pulitzer she felt destined someday to receive in mind, she was inclined to spin this into a human interest story.

There wasn't a lot to use right now. She could interview Edith Badger, but that wouldn't make much of a headline. And with this murder still fresh, the police didn't have enough to keep the viewers riveted. She would have to get some interesting footage, and then make up the rest.

She spun her head and looked at the driver of the Channel 7 Action News van. "Don, stop the van."

Don touched the brakes, pulled to the curb, and looked at her.

"Turn around. We're going to the Spencer house."

Don twisted the wheel and touched the gas, and they sped back the way they'd come. Fifteen minutes later, he wheeled the van up the dusty gravel drive and stopped in front of the old farmhouse.

"Get your stuff," Lisa demanded. Don jumped from the van, opened the side door, and removed his camera equipment.

Lisa gave him instructions while he worked. "I want some shots of the house—close up, at a distance, through the window, whatever you can think of. I can do the voiceovers later."

Don slung the camera over his shoulder and began shooting. He'd been with her a long time, and he would know exactly what she wanted.

She had plans to tie the story in with Jeremy's prior killing spree, include the current murder and the death of his mother, and show how Jeremy had been forced on this path through a series of unfortunate circumstances.

Maybe she could make him look like a sympathetic character—make the people feel sorry for him. Perhaps bring some tears to a few eyes. That would always be good. She could start with a few sensational short stories to whet their appetite, and if she did it right, she might be able to expand it into a one-hour special. Maybe go nationwide. This dumpy town was too small for her anyway.

Don had finished shooting the outside of the house. He turned off the camera and looked at her for further instructions.

"We're going inside," she said. Don looked skeptical, but dutifully followed her as she strode up the pathway to the veranda.

She twisted the knob. The door was unlocked, and she pushed at it with one finger. It creaked open and she peered inside. It was dark, but Don had a great lighting setup that would help.

She stepped inside the front room and sniffed with her long nose. The room smelled stale, stuffy, and rather unpleasant. No matter. She'd been in worse places before in pursuit of a story. This was old hat.

Don had gone back to the van and returned with some portable lighting. The room glowed in the dazzling beam, lighting up the dull antique furniture, turning the painted walls into gloss, and reflecting off the dark hardwood floors.

"I want shots of the whole house," she said. "The kitchen, upstairs, the basement." She knew what went on in this place before, and she was going to use every shot and piece it all together into a masterpiece.

She spun around at the sound of a familiar voice. "What're you doing here?" the voice said.

It was Jeremy Spencer. He stood five feet away, pointing a pistol at her. Don stood with his mouth open, his camera inactive, staring at the little man.

Then a huge goon, with a foolish grin on his ugly face, came into the room from the kitchen and stood behind Jeremy as he waited for an answer.

She looked at the gun, then at Don, then back at Jeremy, and then finally, at the halfwit looming over them all.

"I know you," Jeremy said, his brow wrinkled. "You're Lisa Krunk."

Lisa considered how to approach these unusual, and somewhat frightening, circumstances. The last thing she wanted was to get shot—and the first thing she wanted was a story. And here was a story, dying to be told.

"I hoped to find you here," she lied. "I'm very glad to see you."

"You're trespassing," he said, waving the pistol. "You truly are."

Lisa thought quickly. "We're visiting. We'll leave if you tell us to, but I wanted to talk to you."

"Why?"

"I want to do a story on you. To tell your side of things."

He pushed up his cap, scratched his head, and squinted at her.

She had him. He was interested.

"Did anyone else come with you?" he asked.

She shook her head. "Just the two of us."

Jeremy looked Don up and down. Her cameraman looked terrified, and she knew he was no threat to them. Besides, the huge thug Don stared at seemed to be as frightening as the little man with the gun.

"What do you want to know?" Jeremy asked.

"I want to know about your life, about your mother, and your father. You don't have to answer any questions you don't like, and we won't turn the camera on until you're ready. Everything is off the record unless you tell me otherwise."

Jeremy aimed the pistol toward her head and squinted across the sights. "I'm an honorable man, Ms. Krunk, but if I go ahead with this, and you betray me…" He left the sentence unfinished, but the meaning was crystal clear—and deadly serious.

She felt a shiver down her spine but spoke with courage. "I won't betray you. You have my word as a journalist."

He seemed to be considering that for a few moments. Finally, he said, "The interview will be only with me and not my friend." He turned to his dopey acquaintance. "Moe, you go out the front and watch for anyone coming, especially the police. Let me know if you see anything suspicious."

The floorboards creaked as the big dunce ambled across the room, grinning at her as he walked by. He went out the front door, closing it behind him.

Lisa was virtually alone with a madman, but she was bursting with excitement and anticipation. This was so much more than she'd ever hoped for. This was the story of the century, and she was right in the middle of it.

"I'll sit over there," Jeremy said, motioning toward an old stuffed armchair. "That was Mother's chair."

Lisa pushed a straight-backed wooden chair over, three feet from his. "You have to trust me Jeremy. You'll need to put the gun away."

"I'll keep the gun," he said. "I don't trust you, but this pistol will make sure I can." He sat in the chair and leaned back, his feet barely touching the floor. "Let's get started. I have things to do."

Lisa sat down, waited until Don was ready with the camera, and then switched on the microphone.

CHAPTER 23

Wednesday, 1:16 p.m.

ANNIE SAT IN HER SWIVEL chair, pulled it up to the desk, and switched on her computer. She had done some research earlier, attempting to find the whereabouts of Aaron Starling, but had been unsuccessful. His trail ended in Alberta. Nor had she been able to locate Starling's ex-wife, Sophie, and the parents of the boy Quinton had killed were nowhere to be found.

She checked her Rolodex, called the RHPD precinct, and was put through to Officer Callaway. Since Diego was giving them all the help they needed on this case, she might as well take advantage of it—the honeymoon might not last.

Officer Callaway was the brains behind RHPD when it came to research and all things technical, and he had access to resources she could only dream about.

The phone rang three or four times before he answered. "Callaway," he said, sounding out of breath.

"Officer Callaway," Annie said after she informed him who it was calling. "I need your expertise."

"Sure, Annie, whatever I can do to help." She heard him take a sip of something, probably coffee.

"I've been trying to track down the Starlings but came up blank. I was hoping you could dig something up for me."

"No problem. I'm familiar with the case. I went over it this morning with Hank. He said Diego authorized me to give you all the help I can."

She heard him tapping the computer keys, and she waited in silence a couple of minutes. This was about the only lead she had at the moment and she hoped it would take her somewhere.

"Aaron Starling is a dead end," Callaway finally said. "But Sophie Starling lives in Toronto. Remarried, now Sophie Burnham. Two stepkids. You want her phone number?"

"Yes, please," she said and wrote the number down as the officer dictated it. "Thanks, Callaway."

"What about her address?"

"The phone number is enough. Keep the address on file for now. I'm going to give her a call."

"Okay. Anything else, Annie?"

"That'll do for now. I appreciate your help."

"Any time."

She hung up and dialed Sophie Burnham immediately.

"Mrs. Burnham?" she asked when a woman answered.

"Yes?"

"Sophie Burnham?"

"Yes. Who is this?"

"My name is Annie Lincoln, and I've been … hired to look into the death of Quinton Spencer."

"Who?"

"The man who killed your son, Mrs. Burnham."

There was silence on the line. Finally, Mrs. Burnham spoke in a low voice. "That was a long time ago. I … I'd forgotten his name."

"Quinton Spencer died in prison. He was killed by another inmate."

Mrs. Burnham sighed. "Well, I guess he got what he deserved." She paused, then added, "I don't mean to sound harsh. I followed the case, and I don't think he was totally at fault. My son was turning out like his father, but still, he was my son. I miss him every day …" Her voice broke and she went silent.

"I'm sorry to bring it up again," Annie said. "But I was hoping you might know how I can contact your ex-husband, Aaron Starling."

"I have no idea. After our divorce, I had no desire to see him again. He may be dead for all I know, and if so, so much the better. He was a good-for-nothing man, a terrible husband, and an even worse father."

The woman sounded bitter, and rightly so. Annie hoped she was in a better situation now. "Mrs. Burnham, were you aware Mrs. Spencer was murdered shortly after her husband?"

Mrs. Burnham took a sharp breath. "Oh dear, I had no idea. I always felt sorry for that woman. She wasn't responsible for what her husband did, and I watched her in court, and I saw the toll the whole thing took on her. She was almost as much of an emotional mess as I was at the time."

"We're also looking into her death," Annie said. "The case was never solved."

"Dear, dear. I'd be glad to help if I could, but I was totally in the dark about the whole thing."

Annie paused, then asked carefully, "Mrs. Burnham, do you think it possible Aaron may be responsible for either murder?"

Annie heard her breathing. The woman seemed to be considering the question. Finally, she spoke. "He was in prison, you know, and I wouldn't put it past him. But all of his anger was directed toward Quinton Spencer. I doubt if he could've murdered poor Mrs. Spencer. He didn't seem to hold any animosity toward her."

"But perhaps Mr. Spencer?"

"It wouldn't surprise me."

"Thank you, Mrs. Burnham. You've been a big help."

They said goodbye and Annie hung up the phone thoughtfully. She was fairly certain Mrs. Burnham had told the whole truth. Annie didn't suspect the woman was responsible for either death, and in her mind, the phone call confirmed her position.

Mr. Starling, on the other hand, remained a possible suspect for the murder of Quinton Spencer—and perhaps, Mrs. Spencer as well.

She made some quick notes for her own reference. Later, she would transcribe everything she'd learned in more detail for Captain Diego.

Her cell phone rang and she looked at the caller ID; it was her mother. Phone calls with her mother usually amounted to a condemnation of her lifestyle, her job, and her husband. She didn't really want to talk to her right now, but she sighed and answered the call.

"Hello, Mother," she said, trying to be patient.

"Darling, I've been trying to call you."

"I was on the phone."

"I realize that. I heard about the Spencer boy on the news. It's such a terrible thing. I wanted to see if you were all right."

"We're fine," Annie said.

"They say he may be here in the city and the police haven't found him yet."

"No, Mother, they haven't. But they have some leads and I expect they'll get him soon."

"I hope you're staying away from the whole thing this time. You know he could've killed the lot of you before. I've been rather worried." Her voice had a note of disapproval in it. Annie wasn't about to tell her how involved they really were—that would only cause more problems.

Jake came into the office with two cups of coffee. He set one in front of her, pulled up the guest chair, and sat down. He sipped at his hot drink and looked at her inquisitively.

She covered the phone and whispered, "It's my mother."

He rolled his eyes, sat back, and continued to watch her, an amused look on his face.

"We'll be careful," she said into the phone. "I have to go now. I have some calls to make. Give my love to Dad and I'll talk to you again as soon as I can."

She hung up before her mother could protest, dropped the phone on her desk, and looked at Jake. "Mother's worried," she said with a short laugh. "She heard about Jeremy."

"The whole city has heard about him by now, and if he gets his way, they're going to be hearing a whole lot more."

"You're not worried?" Annie asked, taking a sip of coffee.

Jake shrugged. "We're the good guys. What do we have to be afraid of?"

CHAPTER 24

Wednesday, 1:49 p.m.

JEREMY SPENCER WAS beginning to think that maybe he could trust Lisa Krunk. She didn't ask him anything about where he stayed, what his next move was, or any subtle questions that might lead to him getting caught.

Though she'd just left, he thought it best to leave the house for now. He would be sure to keep an eye out in case the police came back. He knew they had their sly ways of doing things, and he had to be careful not to be caught off guard. He would have to be watchful over Moe as well. His friend seemed a little slow sometimes, and might do something that could lead to big trouble for both of them, just when he was getting started.

He turned as the front door crashed open and Moe rushed in. "Little buddy. The barn. It's burning down."

Jeremy stared at Moe for a long second before he realized what his friend had said. He scampered to the door behind

Moe. His heart dropped when he saw where the big guy pointed. Smoke could be seen rising high into the air, flames licking at one corner of the barn.

Jeremy stood frozen, unsure what to do. He had no telephone, Lisa Krunk was already gone, and his barn was ablaze. He stared at the horrific sight. Who could've done this terrible thing?

"We have to do something," he screamed at Moe, and raced toward the barn. The fire hadn't reached the main doors, still confined to one corner of the barn, but it was moving fast, licking at the dry boards and nearing the roof.

Jeremy pulled open the door and stepped inside. The far wall was smoke and flame, rising up from a large pile of hay. It hissed and crackled as it consumed.

"Grab that fire extinguisher," Jeremy said, pointing to the wall to his right. He ran to the left and pulled a second one down, yanking the safety pin as he ran toward the flame.

Moe had the extinguisher in his hand, struggling with it. "Pull the pin," Jeremy yelled. "Bring it here." The lug lumbered over and watched as Jeremy squeezed the lever of his.

"Aim for the base of the fire," Jeremy said, frantic as he attempted to extinguish the flame.

Moe copied his friend, but in half a minute, the tanks were empty. The flame still ate at the walls, emitting a dreadful low roar as it bit deeper and deeper.

Jeremy dropped the extinguisher to the floor and gazed at the fire consuming his precious barn. Smoke escaped through a hole now burned into the roof, the fire spreading in both directions.

Smoke in his lungs made him cough. Moe was choking too, rubbing his small eyes with his enormous fists, his face a rosy hue by the light of the fire.

Jeremy's heart sunk as he stepped back and watched. It was hopeless.

~*~

LISA KRUNK LEANED forward in the passenger seat of the van as it spun back into the driveway leading to the old Spencer house.

Though she was anxious to get some shots of the burning barn, a rare burst of morality forced her to call 9-1-1 first. It was fortunate they hadn't actually left the area yet, stopping at the end of the lane to get some additional footage. That was when she'd seen the rising smoke.

"Pull up closer," she said, pointing down the gravel lane toward the burning building.

Don did as directed and they jumped from the van and sprang into action.

Lisa stopped short and pointed. Jeremy and the goon were coming from the barn. Had he lit the fire himself?

"Get some shots," she screamed.

The red light glowed as the camera hummed. When she was finished editing, viewers would be able to see the escaped convict and his accomplice, coming through the smoke. She would let the people draw their own conclusions.

She charged forward, the microphone gripped tightly in her sweating palm. She thrust it into Jeremy's face. "Mr. Spencer, did you start this fire?"

Jeremy looked at her in horror, and then moved in close, glaring wildly into her eyes. He screamed, an unearthly sound like she'd never heard before. "I'll kill you if you accuse me of this." He screeched even louder, causing her to shrink back. "Do you hear me?"

She nodded, hoping Don had the camera on the raging little man and not on her face. She took a step back, still holding the mike in the air. She glanced at the big guy. He looked furious, mimicking Jeremy's anger. He clenched his fists and looked back and forth between Don and Lisa, baring his teeth, and growling like a mad dog.

Don seemed unfazed, always dedicated to his job, as he stepped back out of harm's way and continued to shoot.

This was good stuff. After Jeremy was back in prison, or perhaps dead, she already had plans for another special. And it wouldn't cast him in a favorable light. This footage was perfect to add to that future project.

Sirens screamed in the distance. The fire department was on its way, but they would never save the barn.

The smoke increased as the flames grew, snapping and popping. The entire side of the barn was on fire, one end of the roof completely engulfed.

Jeremy had calmed down, no longer angry with her, but the look of pain on his face as he gazed at the fire caused her to have second thoughts about her suspicion that he was the arsonist. She shuddered to think he might eventually suspect her, and if so, he would track her down. She would have to be careful, just in case.

Don stepped to one side, the camera now taking in Jeremy

and his friend, as they stood transfixed with horror, watching the barn go up in smoke.

A single fire truck spun into the yard and up the lane, grinding to a stop near the barn. Its siren died, and Lisa heard another one in the distance. Or was it a police car?

Jeremy and the goon were heading away. She watched them out of sight as they rounded the house. The police would be here soon, and he was a wanted man.

She turned her attention back to the fire. Men had streamed from the truck, hoses now being unfurled, and soon a cascade of water was trained on the raging fire.

The front of the building was now aflame. Long tangles of grass and wild shrubs near the door burst into flame and disappeared in a flash of smoke. Somewhere inside, an overhead beam let loose, taking half of one wall with it, the resulting crash shooting streams of sparks high into the air.

She knew it was too late to save any part of the old barn. The dedicated firemen could only expect to keep the flames from spreading, causing a grass fire, and taking out the surrounding copses of trees. Soon, the barn would be nothing but an old stone foundation, burning embers, and a piece of forgotten history.

She turned as a pair of police cruisers spun up the driveway. She would have a lot of questions to answer, but her reputation was beyond reproach, and as long as Don had space to record, it all made for great footage. Today was a very good day.

CHAPTER 25

Wednesday, 3:45 p.m.

JAKE LOOKED AT HIS SON with a mixture of pride and apprehension. Matty was taking a great interest in his parents' new vocation, and though every father wants his son to follow in his footsteps, Jake knew he would always be concerned if the boy eventually got into the often-dangerous profession he and his wife had chosen.

Annie, on the other hand, was determined Matty should learn whatever he took an interest in. She'd gone to Tech Mart earlier, a store that specialized in a wide range of security and surveillance equipment, along with Jake's favorite area to browse—a great selection of spy stuff. She'd returned with a fingerprint kit and presented it to Matty when he got home from school, and he was now at the kitchen table, a magnifying glass close to his eye, discovering the ins and outs of the entire family's prints.

Matty put the glass down and pushed the ink pad toward his father. "I want the rest of your fingers," he said.

Jake grinned, inked his fingers, and pressed them onto a clean white sheet of paper. "There you go." He stood and went to the sink, washed off the black, and then strolled into the living room.

"He's enjoying his kit," Jake said to Annie, who was curled up in her favorite chair reading a book—some kind of manual. She was always learning about something or other. Matty must have gotten it from her.

She set her book in her lap. "Maybe he'll be able to teach you a thing or two soon."

"It's okay," he said. "I've got you for that."

Jake's iPhone rang. He pulled it out and looked at the caller ID. "It's Hank," he said. He sat on the couch, put it on speaker, and answered the phone.

"Jake here."

"There's been an interesting development," Hank said.

"I'm all ears," Jake said, as Annie moved over to the couch and sat beside him.

"The Spencer barn is burning, probably nothing but smoke and embers by now. I'm just heading out there."

Jake and Annie looked at each other, neither one able to speak. Annie's mouth was open, but no words came out.

"You there?" Hank asked.

"We're here," Annie said. "Just struck dumb, that's all."

Hank chuckled. "I was too, when I first heard about it."

"I assume there're no suspects?" Jake asked.

"Not unless you include Jeremy."

"I don't think so," Annie said. "He's nuts, but he wouldn't burn down his own barn."

"I wonder why the barn, and not the house," Jake said. "There's no evidence left there to hide. Everything was destroyed years ago."

"If it's to hide evidence of any kind," Hank said, "then it's related to the death of Mrs. Spencer, and nothing to do with Jeremy's crimes before he went to prison. There's more evidence of those in the house than in the barn."

"And he would have no need to cover that anyway," Annie said. "It's a matter of public record." She paused, her brow wrinkled in thought. "I'm sure it wasn't Jeremy, but who, and how?"

"That's what we need to find out," Hank said. "It'll take the fire investigators awhile to determine the cause."

"Assuming it wasn't Jeremy, do you suspect arson?" Jake asked.

"I don't know what else it could be." Hank paused a moment, then added, "There's no electricity running to either of the buildings, so an electrical fire is out of the question."

"We never saw anyone around when we were there," Annie said. "But we never went into the lower level. It could be a homeless person has taken up residence there. Maybe careless smoking?"

"There're a lot of possibilities," Hank said. "But it's been vacated a long time, and it seems like too much of a coincidence for it to happen now."

"And we know how you feel about coincidence," Jake said.

"I'm pulling in the lane now," Hank said. "The barn's almost completely gone, but it looks like they have it under control." He paused. "And you'll never guess who beat me here. Your old friend, Lisa Krunk. She must've been monitoring the police band."

"She has a habit of showing up," Annie said. "But as much of a narcissist as she is, she's always interesting to watch."

Hank laughed. "Not when you're the subject of her attack, as the police department often is."

"Be sure to let us know if you find out anything interesting," Jake said.

"I will."

"Hank," Annie said. "Did you get the forensic report yet on the murder of Jackson Badger?"

"I checked in with them. They still have some evidence to go over, but so far, nothing. There were no fingerprints in the house other than Badger's and his mother's."

"And the officers who canvassed the neighborhood?" Jake asked.

"Nothing that sounds promising. They're checking out some vehicles seen in the area during the time of the shooting, but the information is pretty vague. No license plate numbers. The only ones we could identify were neighbors' vehicles. I don't expect that'll lead us anywhere."

"What about the cause and manner of death?" Annie asked.

"Just as I figured. Nancy determined he was shot once in the chest, fell forward, then was shot in the back of the head. Gunshot residue helped her come to that conclusion, as well as the trajectory of the bullet, etcetera. One bullet was found inside the body, the other in the floor under his head. The cause of death was the shot to the head."

"What caliber of firearm?" Annie asked.

"He used a thirty-eight. Ballistics ran the recovered bullets through our ballistic identification system to ascertain whether or not they came from a firearm that was previously used in a crime. No luck. That doesn't mean it wasn't used before, we just have no record of it."

"So a dead end all the way around."

"Not totally," Hank said. "I've been holding back one interesting tidbit of information. Nancy determined by the trajectory of the bullet in the chest that the firearm was discharged from a height of thirty-nine inches. Assuming the weapon was held at a comfortable height, our killer was around five foot two, maybe three."

Jake whistled.

"Jeremy is five foot three," Annie said. "That's a lot shorter than the average male, so unless it was a young boy who did the shooting, it seems to point to him."

"Exactly," Hank said. "And for anyone taller to have fired it, they would either have to be crouching somewhat, or holding it at an unnaturally low height. Not a normal thing to do."

"So we have something at least," Jake said. "Not real proof, but a good piece of evidence."

"It's more than we had before," Hank said. "Unless there's anything else you need to know, I gotta go. Looks like I'm needed here. I'll talk to you if I find out anything else."

Jake hung up, tucked his phone away, sat back, and looked at Annie. "I'll never doubt you again."

Annie laughed. "Where have I heard that before?"

"I have no idea," Jake said.

Annie laid her head back and closed her eyes. "As far as I'm concerned, we have lots of evidence Jeremy is the killer, but no leads on where he might be hiding out."

"I'd sure love to get him on the run," Jake said. "Otherwise, he's going to think he's safe, and someone else is going to die."

CHAPTER 26

Wednesday, 4:57 p.m.

JEREMY SPENCER WAS STEAMING mad and feeling helpless. Whoever had burned down his barn had to pay big-time, but he had no way of finding out who the culprit was.

The police were out of the question. Perhaps they would do some preliminary research into the fire, but he doubted very much if they would follow up, or even care who'd started it. After all, they had him in their sights, and it seemed like the police in this city were determined to make his life miserable.

To make matters worse, there was no insurance on the building or on the main dwelling. He now feared his beloved house would be next, and there was nothing he could do about it. He drew a deep breath, hyperventilating at the dreadful thought. That house was all he had left in the world.

He and Moe had barely made it back to the apartment in time for Uriah to go to work. Their roommate was angry, and

Jeremy felt like shooting him there on the spot. He decided against it. It probably wasn't a sensible thing to do, and besides, they needed Uriah.

He paced around the small apartment, Moe's head moving back and forth as he watched Jeremy from his spot on the couch.

"It's going to be all right, little buddy. You still have the house."

Jeremy stopped pacing and turned to Moe. "Sure, but I can't stay there."

Moe was out of ideas and stared back.

Jeremy's anger was building. He had to do something. "I have to go out, Moe," he said suddenly. Without waiting for an answer, Jeremy put his cap on and rushed out the door.

He kept his head turned away when he passed anyone on the street. Once, he stopped and turned around when a group of women, who took up most of the sidewalk, eased by. There was no sense in being recognized, especially this close to where he was staying.

He walked three or four blocks and took a turn down a side street, and before long, he stopped in front of a run-down two-story building. This had once been a prosperous neighborhood—likely many decades ago—but most of the structures in this area were now in a poor, neglected state.

He looked around. No one was in sight so he opened the front door, went through the small lobby, and continued on. He found what he was looking for—the door to the basement. It was unlocked, the lock probably long ago disabled through indifference and carelessness. Just what he expected.

He pulled the door open, found a light switch, and took the shaky flight of stairs down to a dingy basement. Along the far wall, there was a puddle of water, caused by a constant drip, drip from faulty plumbing no one cared to fix. The room was otherwise dry, with a stale smell, and the tang of something old and rotting filled his nostrils.

The inner wall contained a row of shelves, fastened precariously to the wall. All kinds of junk filled the shelves—clothes, rags, tools, and even a few children's toys. A washing machine stood at one end of the rickety shelves. It was old, but it looked like it still worked.

He gathered up the clothes and threw them in a heap against the wall, then tossed a pile of forgotten newspapers, books, and magazines on top of the pile. He found a can of something foul-smelling that bit his nostrils when he took the top off. It was turpentine, paint thinner, or something similar. He poured it onto the heap he'd made, along with a can of oil and another armload of clothes.

That would have to do.

He reached into his pocket and removed a cigarette lighter. He held it up, lit it, and stared into the brightness of the flame. He was struck by the power contained inside the tiny glowing light. It had the ability to turn itself from almost nothing, an insignificant spark, into a raging inferno.

Much like himself, when put to its proper use, it could change the world.

He crouched down, still holding the lighter, and touched it to the pile of clothes, chemicals, and castoffs. It ignited, the fire struggling to stay alive, then growing into something quite beautiful. He gazed at the red, orange, and blue light as it flourished, blooming up and up, casting its dancing glow across the floor, and lighting up the dingy walls surrounding him.

He stood back as the heat grew more intense. The shelves had caught fire, and the junk they still contained would soon be in flames.

He choked on the smoke and coughed it out, then turned and went to the foot of the stairs. He took one last look at his handiwork, satisfied it would thrive, and went slowly up the steps.

He was thankful there was a fire alarm inside the lobby. He didn't want anyone to get hurt. There was no reason for it; the people who lived here were innocent. He pulled the alarm and stood still a moment, listening to the shrill squeal and the jangling of bells sounding out the cry of danger.

He stepped into the street, kept his head low, and avoided the curious as he walked casually to the corner and crossed the street. Once on the other side, he moved back until he stood directly across from the building.

He watched as people streamed out the front door. Many would also be climbing down fire escapes at the side and back of the building. Unfortunately, personal possessions might be lost, but it was for the better. They could be replaced—lives couldn't. As well as the contented feeling this occasion gave him, he'd done a service to the neighborhood.

He stood among the gathered crowd and watched as fire trucks, police cars, and other emergency vehicles arrived, their sirens wailing, lights flashing. Men rushed from the machines, now about to earn their pay as they went about their task.

Through a pair of windows on the first floor, he saw the inside of the building, now glowing red as the fire climbed higher and higher, eating everything in its path. Soon, the second floor was ablaze. Firemen broke through the windows, streams of water blasting the building from every direction.

Policemen held back traffic, cutting off the area, directing drivers to a safer thoroughfare. More cops pushed back the curious onlookers, hustling them away, some officers aiding those who'd left the building, and others milling about, probably uncertain what to do.

They would never save the building and he didn't care. Though the people around him only had eyes for the hypnotic sight across the street, and would never recognize him, he turned and left the scene, wandering toward the place he called home. It wouldn't do for him to be recognized, especially since he'd come so far.

He felt so much better now. The burning building he'd left behind would never completely pay for the pain he'd felt as he watched his barn be consumed, but at least it gave him some measure of comfort.

He still needed to find out who the culprit was. It irked him that an unfeeling person destroyed his precious possessions. Someone changed his life in immeasurable ways to satisfy their own longing to be hurtful.

He finally reached Uriah's apartment and went slowly up the stairs. He had relieved his heavy heart and was feeling much better—for now.

CHAPTER 27

Wednesday, 5:58 p.m.

IT WAS TIME FOR THE Channel 7 Action News at Six. Lisa Krunk waited in the wings in nervous anticipation. She had rushed to get the editing done on time and was satisfied the short story about to air would be sufficient to whet the public's appetite.

She was going to milk this for all she could get.

She kept her eye on the monitor as the last few commercials ran, and then her heart pounded as teasers for upcoming stories rolled.

The anchor appeared on the screen and Lisa's masterpiece was introduced.

> *"Our top story: The serial killer who gripped this town with fear not so long ago reveals his side of the story. In an exclusive report, here's Lisa Krunk."*

Lisa stood in front of the Spencer farmhouse, a smug look on her face as she raised the microphone.

"As viewers well know, the convict, Jeremy Spencer, escaped from prison yesterday and has already made his presence felt in this city once again. In my never-ending effort to find the truth, and to bring you stories you need to hear, I was able to track down the man you'll all recognize, and conduct an exclusive interview with him.

"Today, we air the first installment of that interview."

While music played furiously in the background, a series of stills flashed across the screen—shots of victims, their families, the police, crime scenes, and lights flashing, until finally the scene dissolved into a close-up shot of Jeremy, zooming in slowly on his face as the music subsided.

Then there was a dramatic pause while the face faded away and Lisa appeared once again, this time sitting in a straight-backed chair, her hands in her lap, and she spoke.

"I'm here with Jeremy Spencer, currently the focus of a police manhunt, and the topic of discussion on the lips of everyone in this city."

The scene switched to a close-up of Jeremy's face, still and unsmiling. As the shot moved back, he could be seen sitting in a comfortable chair, a pistol gripped in one hand, resting in his lap. Lisa's voiceover began:

"'Mr. Spencer, tell us about the real Jeremy Spencer. Who are you, and what are your plans?"

Jeremy paused, and viewers could sense his mind in thought, then he spoke.

"As you know, I was arrested, convicted, and put in prison for something certain people believe was criminal. To me, and I'm sure to many who're watching this, what I did in the past, and will continue to do in the future, is very much justified.

"There're many types of people in this world. Most are law-abiding, good people, and my focus is not on them, and I've no desire to harm those who respect others."

Jeremy paused and looked down a moment. He drew a deep breath, looked back at Lisa, and continued.

"Father was one of those law-abiding people—a good man, and one murdered for his honesty. When a vile thief entered our home many years ago, and Father shot him, it set off a chain of events that resulted not only in the death of Father, but Mother as well. The actions of that despicable and disrespectful thief have changed my life dramatically, but they have opened my eyes in many ways. I'm sure the people will agree this type of behavior needs to be dealt with quickly, and severely, before more lives are destroyed."

Lisa's face appeared, a light frown on her brow.

"But surely, that's the job of the police?"

Jeremy leaned in, his nostrils flared, and his voice became lower, almost a growl.

"The police and the law have failed. They have failed Father, and Mother, and myself. Because of the incompetence of so-called authority, lives were destroyed. I feel responsible to rid the city I love of those deplorable creatures who have no respect for the property of others."

Lisa feigned surprise at his answer.

"Those victims of yours, did they not deserve a second chance? Could they not have been rehabilitated?"

Jeremy sat back, but his frown remained.

"The time I spent in prison was perhaps fate itself intervening. It opened my eyes to many things. These people can never be rehabilitated, but rather get worse and worse. Justice must be swift, concise, and final."

A faint smile touched Lisa's mouth as she asked,

"And that's what you intend to continue?"

Jeremy smiled, raised the gun, and pointed it toward the camera, his eyes piercing the viewers.

"As long as I have breath left in my body."

The picture faded and the close-up of Lisa in front of the Spencer farmhouse came back on the screen.

"There was much more to this interview and it will be aired on an ongoing basis, revealing a deeper look into Mr. Spencer's life, his goals, and his thoughts.

"In an exclusive report, I'm Lisa Krunk for Channel 7 Action News."

The story was over, and as the screen faded and the anchor reappeared, Lisa felt triumphant, sure the public would be clamoring for more.

~*~

HANK WAS FURIOUS. He'd been alerted to the upcoming story and raced into Diego's office where the captain stood at his desk, leaned forward, his eyes glued intently on the small television perched on a shelf in his office.

When the story was finished, Hank and the captain continued to stare at the screen in unbelief. Finally, they looked at each other, Hank dropped into a chair, and the captain blew out a long breath, his eyes flashing, and sat in his high-backed leather chair.

Hank spoke first. "I'm all for freedom of the press, Captain, and confidentiality of sources, and so on, but I think Lisa has gone too far this time."

Captain Diego leaned forward and slammed a fist down on his desk. He'd found his voice. "I want that footage, Corning. I want every scrap of it and I want that woman brought in for questioning. We need to catch that lunatic."

"I don't think we can do that, Captain."

"Why not? We already know the identity of the source; it's that scumbag Spencer. It's the *location* of the source that we want. And that footage can help with that."

Hank tried to remain calm. He wanted the footage as much as Diego, but it wasn't going to be easy to get. "We're entering into a gray area when it comes to whether or not we can legally compel her to give up her information. If she contests it, it would take time for a judge to rule on it. By then, it may be too late."

"We can still detain her for twenty-four hours. That'll cramp her style and make her think twice about whether or not she wants to help us."

"She's a stubborn woman, Captain. Detaining her won't do the trick. She'll hang tight and wait for the appeal, and with her connections, she's liable to get a hearing within twenty-four hours."

Diego sprang to his feet and paced his small office. Finally, he stopped, leaned over his desk, frowned at Hank, and spoke in a calmer voice. "You can find a way, Hank. You know what I want, and what we need." He straightened up and pointed toward the doorway. "Now, go get it."

CHAPTER 28

Wednesday, 6:18 p.m.

MOE SAT AT THE KITCHEN table, looking intently at his friend curled up on the couch, fast asleep. Jeremy had seemed exhausted when he'd returned from his walk, and had fallen asleep immediately, letting out soft snores and long, sighing breaths from time to time.

His little friend seemed to be carrying a lot of weight on his shoulders, both from the mission he had to carry out and from his financial burden. It didn't seem right to Moe that Jeremy should have to take care of him all the time. Moe knew he'd done his share in prison to protect his friend, but out here, he had to rely on Jeremy. It wasn't fair.

Moe had made a few phone calls earlier, stopped at some nearby businesses, and tried everything he could think of to find a job. It didn't look so good. Nobody seemed to want to hire him. He had no desire to return to prison again, but if worst came to worst, he would have to look up the guys he'd worked for before. But that's what had gotten him locked up last time, and he shunned the idea.

Jeremy had removed the pistol from his belt and laid it on the floor beside him when he went to sleep. Moe stared at the pistol, an idea starting to grow in his mind. He knew from past experience, the proper weapon often got you what you wanted. It had a power no amount of talk ever had. He knew that from prison too, because other prisoners boasted all the time about the things they were able to do with a weapon in their hand.

Moe pushed back his half-finished cup of coffee and crept toward the couch. He leaned down and picked up the pistol, the weapon dwarfed by his enormous fist.

Jeremy stirred and Moe held his breath. He didn't want to wake his friend, preferring to surprise him with some good news. Jeremy snored again and Moe stepped back carefully, stuffing the pistol behind his belt and pulling his shirt over top.

He left the apartment as quietly as possible, the door making a soft creak behind him as he eased it shut. He ambled down the hallway, took the flight of stairs down, and went out to the street. He stood on the sidewalk, looked both ways, finally decided on a direction, and shuffled away.

Two minutes later he stood in front of a small convenience store. He peeked in the window and, satisfied no customers were in the shop, he opened the door. An overhead bell jangled as he stepped inside and it startled him for a second. He grinned at his unease, and then walked casually inside and went to the back of the store.

The storekeeper, a little Chinese man, older than anyone Moe had ever seen before, gave him a quick glance and then buried his head back in a newspaper. Moe stood behind a display of candy bars and watched him a moment, summoning up enough courage to do what he knew he had to do.

He pulled out the pistol and held it behind his back, gritted his teeth, and stepped to the counter. The man looked up, right into the barrel of a shiny pistol, pointed toward his heart.

"Give me the money in your cash register," Moe said, the weapon never wavering.

The man stood straight, backed into the display behind him, and raised his hands. "I … I can't open."

Moe thrust his pistol arm forward. "Yes, you can."

The shop attendant looked at the register, then back at Moe. "Has a time lock."

Moe shook his head. "No, it don't. I know they don't have those things on registers. Just on safes." He squinted at the machine to be sure. "That's not a safe."

The man didn't move as he glared at Moe.

"I need the money," Moe said. "Please give it to me or I'll get angry." He hadn't expected the man to refuse. It didn't seem right to shoot him, but he was getting mad. Sometimes, bad things happened when he got too mad, and he wanted to avoid that.

"The police already coming," the man said.

Moe looked toward the front door. He didn't see anyone and he didn't hear any sirens. "I think you're lying."

The man shook his head. "No lie."

"Don't you have insurance?" Moe asked.

"No. No insurance."

Moe leaned over the counter and pushed his arm forward until the barrel of the weapon almost touched the man's nose. "Then I guess I have to kill you."

The man's arms shot straight up. "No kill. No kill. I give."

Moe stepped back and waited eagerly while the storekeeper pressed a button on the register and the drawer opened with a ding. He leaned over and looked at the stacks of bills—money he needed. "Put it in a bag."

The man slid out a plastic grocery bag and stuffed the bills inside.

"The coins too," Moe said, pointing toward the register.

The shop attendant emptied the register and held out the bag. "That everything."

"You sure? No more in the back?"

"No. That all."

"I'll shoot you if you have more you don't give me." Moe waved the pistol.

The man shook his head furiously. "That all."

Moe turned as a tiny woman stepped from the back of the store and approached them. She stopped short when she saw Moe and the weapon. Then she rushed toward the big lug, made a screaming, whining sound, and began pummeling him with her fists. "You thief. You bad man. Go away."

Moe stepped back, trying to protect himself from the furious woman. She advanced again, her fists flying as her husband stood behind the counter, calling for her to stop.

Moe reached in, grabbed the woman's flailing arms, spun her around, and picked her up off her feet. She kicked at him and continued to wail. Moe flexed his muscles and tossed her aside. She landed on the floor five feet away, still protesting, but didn't attempt to get up.

Moe pointed the gun at her. "I'll kill you. Stay there."

The shopkeeper kept his eye carefully on Moe as he came out from behind the counter and knelt down beside his wife. He looked at her, then back at Moe, waving frantically toward the door. "Go now. You have money. Go."

Moe tucked his pistol away, backed toward the door, then turned and left as fast as he possibly could. He bumped into a woman in his haste to leave, knocking her to the sidewalk. Her purse flew in one direction, a bag of groceries another.

"Sorry, lady," Moe said as he held out his hand to help her up. He retrieved her belongings and handed them to her, apologized again, and hurried up the street, leaving the bewildered woman staring after him.

He wasn't very good at this. Maybe that's why he always got caught, but he realized he'd done his best to help his little friend, and Jeremy would be proud he'd done something on his own.

Nobody had to tell him what to do for once, and everything had turned out all right. He was pleased.

CHAPTER 29

Wednesday, 6:34 p.m.

DETECTIVE HANK CORNING had very little usable evidence pertaining to the murder of Jackson Badger, and none that could lead them to the whereabouts of Jeremy Spencer. The footage obtained by Lisa Krunk could be his best bet yet.

Diego had practically demanded he get it, but he wasn't sure how to proceed on this delicate manner. Lisa could be obstinate when she wanted to be.

He went to his desk, picked up the phone, and dialed Lisa's number.

"Lisa Krunk?"

"Lisa, it's Detective Corning."

A chuckle on the line, then, "Hank, what took you so long? I've been expecting to hear from you for the last half hour."

Hank avoided her comment and got right to it. "Lisa, you know how I feel about withholding information."

"It's privileged information, Hank. You can't legally compel me to give it up."

"I want to talk to you. Where can we meet?"

A pause, then Lisa said, "I'm at the studio. I'll be here for the next hour or so."

Hank turned to see Detective King approach his desk and sit in the guest chair. King leaned forward and dropped his arms on the desk, watching Hank and listening to the conversation.

"I'll meet you there in ten minutes," Hank said into the phone.

"Very well," Lisa said. "I'll wait."

Hank hung up and looked at King as the unkempt detective spoke. "Where we going, Hank?"

Hank sat back. "To visit Lisa Krunk."

King rose from his chair. "Let's go."

Together they strode from the precinct, went to Hank's Chevy in the back parking lot, and got into the vehicle.

"Did you talk to Jake about being an auxiliary constable?" King asked, obviously trying to sound casual.

"They're not interested," Hank said, looking at his partner. King had a smug look on his face as he turned his head and looked out the side window. King said nothing, so Hank dropped it, started the vehicle, and pulled from the lot.

"We've finished canvassing the neighborhood where Badger was killed," King said and shrugged. "Nothing."

"Not so much as a lead?"

"Nope. Nothing that means anything. Even the next-door neighbors didn't hear a thing. No shots. Nothing unusual."

Hank peered through the windshield and frowned at a cloud of smoke taking over much of the skyline. Something was on fire a few blocks away. With one or two of the fire trucks still at the Spencer residence, he prayed there would be enough equipment to handle a city fire. He hoped there were no injuries.

The detectives discussed what little was known of the case during their ride to the Channel 7 studios, where Hank pulled into the lot and parked in a guest spot.

They entered the building, Hank showed his badge, and they were taken to the production control room, the technical hub of the broadcast operation. It was a high-tech television marvel. Hank took in the video wall, littered with monitors for programs and previews, graphics, and other video sources. Lisa Krunk stood from her seat at the control desk, grabbed a small handbag, flashed a surly smile, and led them to a break room down the hall.

Lisa sat up straight at a small round table and watched as Hank sat across from her.

King went to help himself at the coffee machine. "Anybody want coffee?" he asked.

Hank waved it off. Lisa avoided the question and spoke to Hank. "I'm sure you're here to get my footage."

"I can arrest you," Hank said.

Lisa smiled. "You won't."

"How can you be so sure?"

"Because you don't want to upset me, Hank. And you don't want to wait for a hearing. No judge is going to issue a warrant and risk setting precedent on such a touchy subject."

Hank sat up straight on the backless bench, a smile touching his lips. "Perhaps you're right. But what makes you think I care about upsetting you?"

"Because people listen to me, and I know you wouldn't want any of this to get negative press."

King sat beside Hank, set his coffee cup down, and glared at Lisa. "Are you threatening us?"

"Not at all," Lisa said. "But if you force me to give up the footage …" She shrugged. "It might make me unhappy, and that may tend to show, unintentionally of course, in my broadcasts."

Hank spoke flatly. "I want the footage, Lisa."

"What're you offering me?"

"My undying gratitude," Hank said.

"How about we offer her a night in a holding cell if she doesn't comply?" King said.

Lisa laughed out loud, throwing her head back. "What's this? Good cop, bad cop? You know that doesn't work on me."

King reached under his jacket and removed a pair of handcuffs. He dropped them on the table and pushed them toward Lisa. She looked at the cuffs and laughed again.

"If there's nothing else," she said. "I need to get back to work."

Hank leaned in. "What do you want?"

Lisa snapped open her handbag and removed a flash drive. She set it on the table and pushed it toward the center. King reached for it but Lisa snapped it back. "Not so fast." She twiddled the drive in her fingers, a faint smile touching her lips.

King glared at Lisa. Hank glared at King, and Lisa glared at them both, looking down her long nose.

Finally, Lisa spoke. "I'll give it to you on three conditions." She paused and Hank waited.

"What're the conditions?" Hank asked at last.

Lisa feigned surprise. "I thought you'd never ask." She leaned in. "I want you to promise not to release any of it to the public before I do. I don't want any stipulation on what I can and cannot do with it now, and …" She paused for emphasis. "I want another exclusive interview with Jeremy Spencer when you catch him, and also with the two of you."

"Not a chance," King said.

Hank looked at King. "Not so fast. That's not really an unreasonable request. It's nothing we can't do."

"She's threatening us."

"It's called making a deal," Lisa said to King. "I'm under no obligation to give it to you." She paused. "I'll tell you what I'll do. Forget about the interview with you, Detective King. Hank will be enough."

King rolled his eyes in disgust, got up and went back to the coffeepot, and dumped his cup in the trash can.

Lisa gave a short laugh, jerked a thumb toward King, and leaned in and whispered, "I didn't want him anyway."

Hank grinned. "That suits me even better." He held out his hand. "We have a deal."

Lisa shook the cop's hand and handed him the flash drive. "It's all on there. A good half-hour interview. I didn't include the shots from around the house, just the interview with Spencer."

"That's fine," Hank said, slipping the drive into his top pocket. He stood. "Thank you, Lisa."

"It's been a pleasure. Just don't forget our deal."

"I won't." Hank nodded goodbye and called for King, and the two cops left as Lisa watched them leave.

That was easier than he'd expected and Diego would be pleased. His only hope was there was something useful on the drive and this wasn't an exercise in futility.

CHAPTER 30

Wednesday, 7:21 p.m.

ANNIE, JAKE, AND THE two detectives huddled around Callaway's computer in the RHPD precinct. Hank sat in the swivel chair while the rest stood behind him. Hank had called Annie the moment he'd gotten the flash drive from Lisa Krunk, and she and Jake had met him at the precinct.

Annie glanced across the room. Her son, probably eager to learn some of the ins and outs of police work, had struck up a conversation with a patient female officer.

It seemed Annie was always taking advantage of Chrissy, and her friend's ongoing offer to watch Matty whenever they needed to go out, so rather than hustle Matty off next door, they'd brought him along this time; nowhere could be safer than the police station.

Callaway put the flash drive in his computer, touched a couple of keys, and stood back. Annie watched as a video of Jeremy, sitting in an easy chair, appeared on the screen. He held a revolver in one hand, lying across his knee. His left hand was bandaged, wrapped with gauze that was held in place with what appeared to be a piece of duct tape.

Lisa Krunk peppered him with questions, most of which he answered in one form or another, but some he refused. The newscast was but a small portion of the overall interview, the short, cohesive story she'd broadcast consisting of clips and sound bites picked out and pieced together.

Annie was making some notes, and when the video was finished, she turned to Callaway. "Can you start this at the seven-minute point?" Callaway leaned in and cued up the video, and it replayed from the point Annie indicated.

Lisa was speaking. "Mr. Spencer, why'd you come back to Richmond Hill and make your presence known here? Are you not afraid the police will apprehend you?"

Jeremy had answered, "I don't believe they'll ever catch us here. No, they surely won't."

Annie reached in and paused the video. "Did you hear that? He said, 'us.'"

Hank rubbed his chin. "He's hooked up with someone else. But we checked all his known associates." He looked at his watch and turned to King. "I want you to take another look at everyone he knew first thing tomorrow morning. Find out where this guy could be hiding out."

King shrugged and then pointed at the video. "See that pistol he's holding? It looks like a Smith & Wesson Thirty-Eight Special. The same caliber Badger was shot with. I'll bet that's the weapon right there."

"There's no way to be sure it's the actual gun," Hank said.

"But I won't take that bet. I'm sure Spencer is our killer." Hank pushed back his chair. "Did anyone else see anything on the video that could mean something?"

"What about his transportation?" Jake asked. "I think whoever he's hanging out with has either supplied him with a vehicle, or is driving him around."

"Must be," Hank said. "I doubt if Spencer could round up any other transportation in such a short period of time, and it hardly appears he's walking, or fool enough to take public transit."

"What about the barn?" Annie asked. "Did the fire investigator ascertain the cause of the fire?"

"Nothing conclusive," Hank said. "The fire began in one corner in a pile of hay. It could've been lit, but there's another possible explanation. Wet hay is the most common cause of hay fires. Mold can grow, chemical reactions take place, and it raises the heat to a point where the hay can burn."

"So, if water seeped in at the corner, the hay could be damp, heat up, and then finally combust," Jake said.

"Exactly," Hank said. "But the investigator still didn't rule out arson." He shrugged. "So nothing conclusive there, but they're still looking at it."

"Speaking of fire," King put in, "don't you think it's a coincidence there was another fire in town today? We don't get a lot of them, but in the space of two hours we get two."

"You think they may be connected?" Hank asked.

"Could be. Actually, I'd say they most likely are."

"Interesting idea, King. We need to look further into the tenants of the burned building." Hank turned to Callaway.

"Can you get me a background on all of them and cross-reference it with Spencer and everyone Spencer knows? Let's see if we can come up with a connection there."

"I'll get on it right away, Hank," Callaway said. "As soon as you guys are done here."

"And take a close look at the owners of the building as well."

"Will do."

Yappy approached the desk and handed Hank a report. "Hank, we got a call of a convenience store robbery a few minutes ago. Do you have time to look into it?"

"We're busy right now, Yappy," King said.

Yappy shrugged and glanced around the precinct. "It's evening. There's not really anyone to look at it right now. There're a couple uniforms on the scene taking the guy's statement, but he's pretty frantic. Apparently, the robber manhandled his wife and he's demanding we do something."

Hank looked at King. "We'll go as soon as we're done here, unless you have somewhere to be."

"Suits me," King said.

Hank turned back to Yappy. "We'll look into it within the hour."

Yappy nodded, then went back to the duty desk.

Annie had pulled up a chair and sat facing Hank. She leaned forward. "Hank, when Jeremy strikes again, we know what type of people his targets are."

"Yeah, thieves."

"So, how does he find his victims?"

"Television, newspaper," Jake said. "That seems like the most obvious way."

"Exactly," Annie said. "So, can't we follow the same procedure, and maybe determine where he might strike next, and who the target might be?"

"There're an awful lot of possibilities," King said.

Annie sat back and looked up at King. "The story on Jackson Badger was on the front page of the paper yesterday."

King laughed. "So you're suggesting we keep an eye on everyone who's a potential target."

"You have a better idea?" Jake asked. "I think it's pretty good, myself."

King sneered and said nothing.

"I like the idea," Hank said. "I'll check with the newspapers and TV stations and find out what stories they're running. If that's how Spencer finds his victims, then we may be able to get one step ahead of him."

"I don't know if we have enough cops around to cover them all," King said. "But I'll go along with it."

"Any more ideas before we get back on this?" Hank asked.

"Nothing from me," Jake said.

"Then let's go. King and I have to check out the robbery." He turned to Callaway. "I know you have a lot on your plate right now, but if you have time, can you take another look at this video and see if you come up with anything?"

"Sure, Hank. I'll work through the night if I have to."

"I wasn't expecting that, but see what you can do."

Annie stood. "We'll check in with you in the morning, Hank."

She rounded up Matty and they left the precinct. It seemed to her they might be making some progress on finding Jeremy, but she was no further ahead on discovering who'd killed his parents, or why.

CHAPTER 31

Wednesday, 7:33 p.m.

JEREMY WAS STARTLED awake by the sound of the door creaking open. He sat up, rubbed his eyes, and peered at Moe coming into the apartment. He squinted at the clock on the DVD player. He'd slept for more than an hour and he felt much better.

He sat up and stared at the big lunk who was grinning at him from across the room. He carried a grocery bag in one hand, and he dropped it on the kitchen table, pulled out a chair, and eased into it.

"Hello, little buddy," Moe said, a twinkle in his tiny eyes. "I have a surprise for you."

Jeremy yawned, made it to his feet, wandered over to the table, and sat down. "What's the surprise, Moe?"

"I brought you a present." Moe grinned a wide grin, his eyes almost disappearing.

Jeremy looked at the bag. "Where'd you get the money for a present? You don't have any money."

"Didn't need money." Moe leaned forward, excitement on his face. He grabbed the bag by the bottom and dumped its contents out. Bills fluttered and coins rattled across the table.

Jeremy looked at the pile of money a moment, and then turned his head slowly toward his friend, a frown gathering on his brow. "Where did you get that?"

"I borrowed your gun." Moe lifted his shirt, pulled out the revolver, and set it on the table.

Jeremy's mouth dropped open and he spun in his chair. "What did you do, Moe?"

"I got you some money. You said you need money and I know we have to pay Uriah for what he gave us yesterday."

Jeremy sprang to his feet, leaned in, and gripped Moe by the shoulders. "Did you rob a store?"

"I … I thought you'd be pleased." Moe shrank back and was silent, his beady eyes wide.

Jeremy repeated the question, his voice showing growing impatience. "Did you rob a store? Tell me."

Moe nodded. "I can't find a job and that's the only place I know where they have some money. Except maybe a bank, but that's not so easy to do."

Jeremy dropped into his chair, leaned back, and closed his eyes. This was almost unbelievable. After all the conversations he and Moe had had about right and wrong, about honoring the possessions of others, Moe had gone and done the unthinkable. He'd taken advantage of innocent people—probably hard-working people, trying to get by.

He opened his eyes, looked at his friend, took a deep breath, and tried to speak calmly. "Moe, please tell me this is all a joke."

"No joke, little buddy. You're not happy?"

Jeremy took a long breath and let it out slowly. "No, I'm not happy. I'm surely not."

"I'm sorry. I wanted to do something for you." Moe's shoulders slumped and he turned his downcast eyes away from Jeremy's glare.

"We have to give the money back," Jeremy said. "We surely do."

"We do?" Disappointment tinged Moe's voice.

"What else can we do? We can't keep it. It doesn't belong to us."

Moe raised his eyes and shook his head slowly. "I don't think that's a good idea."

"Why not?"

"'Cause I'll get caught."

Jeremy sighed. Moe had a point, but he would feel guilty about spending it on themselves. It was dishonest money, not earned, and it belonged to someone else.

"Leave it with me, Moe," Jeremy said. "I'll figure something out."

Moe's eyes brightened. "You not mad anymore?"

"No, Moe, I'm not mad anymore. I'm surely not." Jeremy leaned in and spoke sternly. "But you must never do anything like this again."

Moe's head bobbed up and down. "No more."

"And don't touch my gun again."

"I promise." Moe made an "X" on his chest with a stubby finger. "Cross my heart."

Jeremy held back a smile. It was hard to stay angry with

the big lug. Moe was only trying to help, but Jeremy had to keep him under control somehow. He valued Moe's friendship, and he knew Moe felt the same way toward him.

Jeremy scooped up the bills, stuffed them back into the bag along with the coins, and tied it shut. "What store did you rob, Moe?"

Moe pointed vaguely over his shoulder. "Down the street. A Chinese guy and his wife. A nice old man but the lady was kinda not so nice. She tried to hit me. I pushed her away. I think they're mad at me now."

Jeremy sighed. "They're mad at you because you robbed them, Moe." He paused a moment. "You can't go back in that store again. You surely can't."

"Okay."

Jeremy picked up the bag of money and the gun and went to the couch. He stuffed the revolver under the seat cushion and sat down. They were in a predicament and he had to figure out what to do. Finally, he grinned, jumped off the couch, and spoke to Moe, still sitting at the table, his head down, his hands clasped in front of him. "Moe, I have to go out." He raised a finger. "I want you to stay here."

Moe nodded.

Jeremy got the phone book, searched through it, wrote down an address on a scrap of paper, and tucked it into his shirt pocket.

"I'll be right back." He stuffed the bag under his shirt, pulled his hat low over his face, and left the apartment. He went down to the street, looking cautiously around, and then, keeping his head down, he walked a couple of blocks and turned into a drugstore. A postal outlet took up much of the back wall, and he scurried through the store and approached the counter.

He opened the bag and removed a bill, grabbed a large mailing envelope from the display, dumped the bag of money in the envelope, sealed and addressed it, and dropped it on the counter.

"I'd like to send a package."

He paid for next-day delivery and left the envelope. He felt reasonably good about his decision as he hurried back to the apartment.

CHAPTER 32

Wednesday, 7:47 p.m.

HANK PULLED THE CHEVY in behind a police cruiser, directly in front of Morningstar Convenience, and he and King climbed out. They were in an older part of the city—not completely run-down and half-empty like some of the streets further south, but an area vacated by the larger, more successful businesses, leaving this district to the lower middle class and the struggling entrepreneurs.

Crime was growing here as well, and Hank was beginning to know this area better and better because of it. Only three or four blocks away stood the remains of the building that had caught fire yesterday, and today's brazen robbery in broad daylight was more proof of the criminal element moving in.

A bell on the door buzzed as Hank opened it and followed King inside. A pair of uniformed officers, standing to one side of the entranceway, greeted them. The cops had finished their interviews and were seemingly standing guard.

"We waited for you, Hank," one of the officers said. He waved toward an old man behind the counter. "They're in a state, especially the woman, and we didn't want to leave until you got here."

"Thanks, guys. You might as well go home now. We'll take it from here."

Hank approached the old man who stood by the cash register, watching them carefully. Not far from the storekeeper, almost out of sight and facing sideways, a wooden chair was drawn up, and an old woman sat hunched forward, her hands clasped tightly in her lap.

"I'm Detective Corning," Hank said and motioned toward his partner. "Detective King."

Relief flickered over the old man's face. He glanced briefly at Hank, and then his eyes roved over King, taking in his sloppy clothes, dirty baseball cap, and stringy hair. "He rob us," he said at last, a fist clenched. His English was broken, and he spoke in a heavy Chinese accent.

The woman looked up, her wrinkled eyes drooped, her lips together into a thin unsmiling line. She nodded at them, almost imperceptibly.

"Can we sit down somewhere and talk?" Hank asked.

The man waved toward the back of the store. "Have customer."

Hank glanced back. A woman was bent over, examining some of the goods on a shelf, taking her time about making a selection.

Hank withdrew a notepad and a pen and jotted down

some preliminary information—their names, time of occurrence, etcetera. The old woman sat quietly, barely moving, but watching intently.

The customer made up her mind and she ambled to the counter with a jar of pickles. The detectives stood out of the way. The woman looked sideways at them as the proprietor rang in the purchase. She paid, gave them a last curious glance, and left the store.

King stepped back up to the counter, rested his elbow on the glass, and asked, "Can you tell us about the person who robbed you? What did he look like?"

The proprietor raised his hands, palms inward, and spread them wide. "Ugly. Big man. Big like mountain. No fat like sumo wrestler." He pointed to a skinny bicep. "Big here. He have gun."

"What kind of gun?"

The man looked blankly at King.

"Long gun, like a rifle? Small gun? A pistol?"

The man nodded vigorously. "Small. Small. In hand."

Hank pulled out his cell phone, did an image search, and came up with a variety of handguns. He scrolled through them as the storekeeper leaned in.

Finally, the man said, "That it."

"A Thirty-Eight Special," King said.

Hank frowned. "Like Spencer's weapon."

King nodded. "But there're a lot of them on the streets. It's pretty popular." He chuckled. "It wasn't Spencer. No one would ever mistake him for a mountain."

The front door buzzed and a couple of young boys came

in. The shopkeeper eyed them warily as they strode past and went to the rear of the store.

The woman beckoned toward her husband. He leaned and she whispered something in his ear. When he stood upright, his face brightened. "Want video?" he asked.

"You have a video recorder set up?" Hank asked.

The proprietor pointed to the back of the store above an entranceway into the rear. "Camera."

King rolled his eyes at Hank. Hank disregarded his partner and smiled at the storekeeper. "We would like to see the video."

"I get," the man said and scurried to the back of the room. Hank glanced at the woman, her emotionless eyes moving back and forth between King and Hank.

Finally, the man returned with a VHS tape and held it up. "Six hour. He on here somewhere." He handed the tape to Hank and smiled widely. "You catch?"

"We'll catch him if he's on there," King said.

"We'll do our best," Hank said.

The young boys came to the counter, paid for two cans of soda, and opened them on their way out the door.

"What time do you close up the store?" King asked.

"No close. Need money. Son come soon and we go." He paused and looked at Hank. "Can you leave policeman here?"

"We can't really do that," Hank replied. "But I'll make sure a car drives by the neighborhood and an officer will check in with you a few times throughout the night."

The storekeeper seemed satisfied with that. "Okay," he said. "You catch bad man and we happy."

After a final assurance they would do all they could, the detectives left the store and drove back to the precinct where he dropped King off at his vehicle.

Hank headed toward home. The robbery would have to wait until tomorrow. It was getting late and he was tired.

He had a murderer to catch—a serial killer on the loose—and didn't have a lot of time to chase down a hold-up man. Hopefully, the video would make quick work of this case and he could get back to what was most important—catching Jeremy Spencer.

CHAPTER 33

Thursday, 8:44 a.m.

JEREMY SPENCER PICKED up the newspaper he'd bought the day before, sat at the table, and spread it out in front of him. Moe slouched on the couch, his big feet on the coffee table, watching television. Uriah was still asleep, having worked until midnight the day before.

Jeremy glanced at the paper. He had found the Jackson Badger story on the front page; surely there must be more inside.

He stopped on page four, where a story caught his attention. A financial consultant, Mr. Wendell Hatfield, was accused by three different parties of fraud. According to the victims, Hatfield had taken their money, but they'd never received the promised portfolio, and he refused to answer their calls. Police were investigating the allegations, but no charges were laid as of yet.

The story filled Jeremy with righteous indignation—a

burning anger. This was a man who deserved his attention. The problem was, he would have to go downtown—something he was not keen on doing.

He leafed through the rest of the paper, but eventually returned to page four and studied the story further. The victims were all elderly, scammed out of their life savings. Worst of all, but something that suited Jeremy, the thief was still in business, likely even now in the process of stealing from other unsuspecting victims.

It wasn't hard to find the Hatfield Investments ad in the yellow pages, blatantly offering secure investments with a guaranteed return—something even Jeremy knew wasn't possible. He jotted down the address on a scrap of paper and stuffed it into his shirt pocket.

He dialed Hatfield's number and told the receptionist he'd inherited a large sum of money recently and would like Mr. Hatfield's advice. The eager receptionist made him an appointment for 9:30.

He folded up the paper neatly and turned to Moe. "I have to go out for a while. I want you to stay in the apartment. Do you understand?"

Moe glanced at Jeremy and nodded sheepishly. "Okay."

Jeremy felt certain Moe had learned his lesson the day before and the big lug would be fine without him.

He stood and went to the hallway closet, rummaged around, and found an old satchel—something to make it look like he meant business. He pulled the long strap over his neck, letting the bag hang at his side, and then returned to the living room and approached the couch.

Moe stood a moment to allow Jeremy to retrieve the pistol from under the cushion, and then sat back down, watching quietly as his friend checked the pistol, loaded in a couple of rounds, and put it carefully in the satchel.

Jeremy picked the motorcycle keys up off the counter, stuffed his hat in his back pocket, pulled the helmet on, and made his way downstairs and around to the back of the building.

The motorcycle started on the first kick. He checked the fuel gauge, then drove from the lot.

Hatfield's office was in a tiny storefront off the main street. He was in a relatively modern part of the downtown core, but far from the bustling financial district.

Jeremy drove by the building, and then parked the bike one street over and walked back, keeping his hat low, and his head turned away from the occasional pedestrian.

He stood in front of the store and looked up at a sign reading, "Hatfield Investments," with a notice underneath guaranteeing secure investment consulting. Jeremy chuckled, knowing that sign would soon be replaced by a "For Rent" sign.

He approached the front door, paused a moment, took a deep breath, and then went boldly in. The front area was barely big enough for a pair of chairs on one wall, and a desk on the other. Jeremy turned to the desk, where the receptionist had her head down, buried in a fashion magazine.

"I have an appointment with Mr. Hatfield," Jeremy said.

She glanced up briefly, brushed back a stray strand of straw-colored hair, dropped the magazine facedown on the desk, and then went to a door in the back of the room, opened it, and stuck her head in. Jeremy heard her say, "Mr. Black's here to see you."

She pulled her head back and beckoned to him. "You can go right in," she said and then returned to her desk and picked up her magazine again.

Jeremy pushed the half-opened door the rest of the way open and stepped into the room.

A man rose from behind a desk, leaned over, and held out his hand. "Welcome, Mr. Black," he said.

Jeremy shook the chubby hand and was waved toward a seat on the near side of the desk. He sat down, swung his satchel in front of him, holding it in his lap, and glared at Hatfield.

The thieving financial consultant was a little overweight and pushing fifty, most of his bulk hidden by an expensive suit, but rolls of fat showed where a snug red tie choked his neck. His short dark hair was slicked back like a wise guy, without a touch of gray, obviously colored.

Hatfield smiled, and Jeremy saw the evil in his face, his lying lips, and his deceitful eyes. If anyone ever needed killing, it was this slimeball in front of him. Jeremy couldn't wait to pull the trigger, ending his pathetic life.

"I understand you have some money to invest," the vile man said, obviously eager to sink his teeth into Mr. Black's inherited cash.

"Yes, a fair sum," Jeremy said politely.

"You're in luck," Hatfield said, reaching to one side of his desk and picking up a sheet of paper. "I have an exclusive investment opportunity that was handed to me this morning." He flipped the sheet over and squinted at it. "A guaranteed high yield."

"That's exactly what I'm looking for," Jeremy said.

"Excellent. How much money are we talking?" Jeremy saw a greedy gleam in the con man's eyes.

"It's all right here." Jeremy reached into his satchel and tightened his hand around the pistol. He stood to his feet and moved in against the desk, removed the weapon, and raised it, holding it twelve inches from the scumbag's face.

Hatfield took a sharp breath and raised his hands midway up, attempting to sink into the back of his cushy, leather chair. "I … I don't have any money," he whined.

"Neither do I," Jeremy said.

"Then what do you want?"

"I want you," Jeremy said as he pulled the trigger.

Hatfield slumped forward and his head hit the desk with a thump, his arms dangling to the side, a fresh hole through his skull above the right brow. The back of the shiny leather chair was spattered with blood and brains.

Immediately, a scream came from the doorway and Jeremy spun around. He'd expected the dizzy receptionist to do just that, and he was ready. His next shot hit Hatfield's accomplice in the chest and she crumpled to the floor, landing on her back inside the room, to one side of the door. One more shot in the face, and it was over. His job was done.

Time to go.

He shoved the weapon into his satchel and then ran through the reception area and out the front door, keeping his head turned away as he passed an old man on the sidewalk.

He hurried to the motorcycle, another job well done, but this time he was doubly pleased. He'd gotten two at once.

CHAPTER 34

Thursday, 9:35 a.m.

HANK DROPPED INTO HIS chair at the precinct and switched on his computer. He had a lot to do today, aching to make some headway on the Spencer case.

He had gotten up early, and as soon as his first cup of coffee wiped the drowsiness away, he was on the phone with the local television station, as well as the two daily newspapers.

Three stories of interest would be coming out in one morning paper, none in the other.

A young woman had been conditionally discharged after she was caught shoplifting some cosmetics. Her name and picture would be in the paper.

There was to be a story on a known burglar released from a two-year stint in prison, who swore he'd gone straight, and now put in time at the local mission.

The third story pertained to a mob boss who'd somehow managed to get off on a long list of charges. Hank disregarded that one. Jeremy would never get close to him anyway. Hank knew exactly who the crime lord was, and he was always flanked by a pair of burly bodyguards.

On the morning and noon news, the city's only television station would also be running the story on the organized crime case, as well as a lengthy interview with the reformed burglar.

None of the other stories involved thieves as far as he could tell.

He'd made a call to the precinct and arranged to have a pair of undercover cops watching each of the potential victims until further notice. If Spencer targeted either of them, they'd have him.

He'd also given Detective King a call to be sure he was on top of his assignment—to recheck Spencer's known associates to see if he could come up with something. Surprisingly, King was already on it.

And now, at the precinct, he sat in silence and watched his computer boot before getting up and going to Callaway's desk. The computer whiz just came in, and Hank was anxious to see what he'd learned.

"Morning, Callaway," he said, pulling up an empty chair and sitting down. "Please tell me you found something on Lisa Krunk's video."

Callaway looked up from his monitor. "Sorry Hank. I went over it meticulously, and came up with nothing."

Hank dropped his arms on the desk. "What about the tenants of the burned building? Any connection to Spencer there?"

"Again, nothing, Hank. I was here until two in the

morning. Dead ends all the way around." Callaway sat back and shrugged. "If there's any connection at all, I sure can't find it."

"That leaves King," Hank said. "He's doing some canvassing this morning, and if he comes up blank..." He paused and shrugged. "Then I don't know what our next move is."

Hank stood and went back to his desk. He still had the video tape from the convenience store robbery to go over. He'd better get on that this morning. Hopefully, they could ID the gunman and get the case wrapped up right away, but first, he had some calls to make.

He spent the next half hour contacting all the local clinics, as well as the emergency center at the hospital, to see if anyone had come in with a broken or sprained thumb. Another dead end. Hank hadn't expected a positive result. By the look of the duct tape on the wrapping, Spencer had probably wrapped it up himself.

~*~

MRS. DORA QUAKER pulled the black shawl over her head and tied it snugly at her throat. She was in no mood for this, vivid memories of her husband's funeral fresh in her head, but life went on.

Her husband had always managed the money in the family, and she'd never held much interest in it. It had taken her a long time to figure out what was left after the funeral and other related expenses. It was a tidy sum, but with her now seventy-one years old, it wouldn't be enough to last her forever.

She'd been excited when one of her friends had told her of an investment opportunity. The woman had recently committed her life savings to a guaranteed high-yield investment and was eager to share the news with Dora.

And with a prestigious name like Hatfield Investments, it had to be true, and she thanked her lucky stars.

She tucked her checkbook into her handbag beside her reading glasses, plucked her cane from the coat rack, and hurried to the door. Mr. Hatfield's lovely receptionist had set her up with an appointment for 10:30, and she didn't dare be late.

She struggled out the door and down the single flight of stairs to the sidewalk. It was slow going in her rheumatic condition, but she breathed in the fresh air, rested a few moments, and then hurried along as quickly as her painful joints would allow.

Ten minutes later, she reached her destination and tugged at the door, finally able to open it enough to push it back and allow her to step inside before it closed again on her heels.

No one was at the receptionist desk, so she took a seat, rested her cane on the chair beside her, and waited. After several minutes, she grew impatient, and called, "Hello?" She listened, then called again, "Hello? Is anyone here?"

There was no answer and she sighed, sat back, clasped her hands in her lap, and hoped she hadn't missed her opportunity.

Five minutes later, she grabbed her cane, struggled to her

feet, and hobbled to the open office door. She was indignant to see a man—surely it must be Mr. Hatfield—asleep at his desk. Dare she wake him? She'd come a long way.

She stepped inside the office and froze at the sight of a body, a woman's body, on the floor beside the doorway. And she wasn't asleep. That hole in her head, and that blood soaking into the floor, could only mean one thing.

She forgot the pain in her joints as she stumbled back to the receptionist desk, picked up the phone, and dialed 9-1-1.

CHAPTER 35

Thursday, 11:17 a.m.

A CALL CAME IN TO 9-1-1 at 10:38 and RHPD dispatch was notified immediately. First responders were on the scene within minutes and the area was secured.

Shortly later, the forensic van arrived and CSI began their painstaking job of examining the details at the scene—collecting, packaging, preserving, and logging forensic evidence.

A crime scene photographer snapped shots of the bodies, blood spatters, and trace evidence, documenting the entire scene.

The ME examined and detailed the state of the bodies and determined their identity.

One thing was clear. The shooting of Wendell Hatfield was close-up and personal.

Hank arrived at the office of Hatfield Investments and pulled up behind a police cruiser. A curious crowd was gathered outside the building, bombarding an officer who guarded the door with questions.

Hank greeted the cop and was let inside. He glanced around the outer office. It contained chairs, a desk, and not much else. An investigator was finishing up with some fingerprinting. He went into the inner office, took a quick glance around, and approached the ME, Nancy Pietek, crouched beside the body of a female inside the office doorway.

"Hey, Nancy," he said.

Nancy glanced up. "Morning, Hank." She stood and turned to face the detective. "I've finished my preliminary examination of the bodies. Both appear to have been shot by a small- or medium-caliber weapon, one shot in the female from a distance and one up close, the male shot from a few inches away."

"I assume the cause of death is a GSW in both cases," Hank said.

"It appears to be." Nancy motioned toward the body at her feet. "The female was shot in the chest as well as in the face, entering below the nose. From the gunshot residue, the second shot appears to be from a distance of perhaps eighteen to twenty-four inches. The shooter also appeared to be standing directly over the body when he pulled the trigger. The bullet pierced the skull and embedded itself in the floor."

Hank looked across the room and nodded toward the other body. "And the guy over there?"

Hank followed Nancy to the desk. "One shot in the face," she said. "The bullet entered above the right eye, also from a distance of eighteen to twenty-four inches."

Hank looked carefully at the position of the body, the arms dangling at the side, his face against the desk, blood drying on the laminate top, more spattered across papers and file folders.

Nancy continued, "The victim would've been sitting at the time, his head against the back of the chair, as indicated by the bodily tissue and blood pattern on the chair. Taking into account Hatfield's height and the position of the exit wound, the gunman would've held the weapon at a height of approximately forty to forty-five inches."

Hank looked at the position of the guest chair. "Considering the height of the shot, if the shooter was sitting, then he would've pushed the chair back later. But if he was standing at the time he took the shot, then he would've been fairly short."

"I'd say he was standing, Hank. Remember, the shot came from a distance of eighteen to twenty-four inches, and the victim's head was resting on the back of his chair. The killer appeared to have been leaning forward when he pulled the trigger."

"The killer had to be standing, then," Hank said. "And he was either crouched down, or he was leaning in and about the same height as Jeremy Spencer."

Hank looked thoughtfully at the body. "Hatfield was shot by a visitor, perhaps a client, or someone under the guise of a client, and then the receptionist came into the room, and the gunman shot her from a distance, then moved in and finished the job."

"It appears that way," Nancy said.

"It seems to me," Hank continued, "that if he shot the receptionist first, as he entered the room, then Hatfield wouldn't still be sitting at his desk. He would've tried to get away. Maybe behind, or under the desk, or behind the chair." Hank paused a moment. "I think Hatfield was caught totally unawares." He looked at Nancy and asked, "Time of death?"

"I'd say no less than one, perhaps two, hours ago."

Hank strode out to the reception area and glanced at the magazines on the desk, some papers at one end, a pen, a makeup bag. He opened the top drawer, removed a small booklet, and flipped it open. It was a schedule of appointments with only two listings for that morning. A Mr. Black at 9:30 and a Mrs. Dora Quaker at 10:30.

Mrs. Quaker had discovered the bodies, and Mr. Black sounded like an assumed name, taken on for the occasion.

Mr. Black was the killer, no doubt.

He went back into the office and approached the lead investigator, Rod Jameson. "Have anything for me? Fingerprints?"

"There's a variety of fingerprints on the near edge of the desk," Jameson said, pointing. "There're also other prints in the outer office, on the chairs, and on the entry door handle. We'll get all those checked out ASAP."

"What about the woman who called it in?"

"Mrs. Dora Quaker," Jameson said, glancing at a clipboard in his hand. "Officers have taken her home and will get her statement. I spoke to her for a moment. She didn't touch anything except the telephone in the outer office, and the chair she sat on."

"I assume she was checked for gunshot residue?"

"Yes, and we checked in her handbag. No weapon. I'd be very surprised if she was the perpetrator."

Hank nodded. "It's not a woman's preferred method of murder." He paused. "What about surveillance video?"

"Nope. Nothing in here. Nothing in the outer office, and there doesn't appear to be any type of surveillance set up anywhere along this street."

"Officers are canvassing the neighborhood," Jameson continued. "They already checked with the neighboring stores." He pointed with a thumb. "A dry cleaner next door. A beauty parlor on the other side. Nobody heard anything or saw anything. They'll check for video as well, but I wouldn't hold my breath on that one."

"Is there a back door here?" Hank asked, glancing around.

"No back door."

Hank was missing one integral piece of the puzzle—a motive. If the killer was Jeremy Spencer, then what did he know that Hank didn't? Was the killer a thief? He pulled out his phone, called the precinct, and was put through to Callaway.

"I need all the info you can get me on Wendell Hatfield and Hatfield Investments," he said when Callaway answered. "Everything. Especially if it relates to anything dishonest he may have been involved in."

"Right away," Callaway said.

"I'll check in with you later," Hank said and hung up.

This could've been a revenge killing, or something else, but whatever it was, it likely related to money. Hatfield

Investments was all about money—perhaps big money. But whatever it was, and whoever the perpetrator was, it seemed to be personal.

And if Spencer was involved, Hank had to find a way, not only to connect him to these murders, but to track him down once and for all.

CHAPTER 36

Thursday, 12:26 p.m.

JAKE MOPED AROUND THE house most of the morning and he and Annie hadn't come up with a plan of action. He was aching to get some results, but was at a loss on how to proceed.

Annie was doing some research on a variety of things—spontaneous fire and arson, potential future targets, and the psychology of serial killers. Jake wasn't sure what else she was looking into. His wife was always learning something new.

He was outside washing the Firebird when Hank parked at the curb and strode up the driveway carrying his briefcase. Jake shut off the washer, tossed the nozzle aside, and greeted him.

"Don't shine that up too much," Hank said with a chuckle, motioning toward the Firebird. "Someone may decide to steal it again."

"Let them try," Jake said. "I'll sic Jeremy Spencer on them."

"Speaking of Spencer, I just came from a very interesting crime scene."

"Oh? Another murder?"

"A double homicide," Hank said. "Is Annie around?"

Jake jerked a thumb toward the house. "Inside."

"She'll want to hear this too."

They went in the house and found Annie, still in the office, glaring at the computer monitor. She sat back and waited while they pulled up chairs and sat down.

Hank told them what took place at Hatfield Investments. When he was finished, he added, "I have Callaway checking into Wendell Hatfield now."

"That was yesterday," Annie said.

Hank was confused. "What was yesterday?"

"The story on Hatfield Investments was in yesterday's paper."

Hank leaned forward.

Annie left the room and came back with a newspaper. She opened it up and handed it to Hank, pointing to the bottom of page four.

Hank read the headline aloud. "Investment Consultant Under Investigation for Fraud." He scanned the story and then tossed the paper onto the desk. "This is Spencer's work. I can see his hand all over it."

"And this time he killed two," Jake put in.

"I think the receptionist was in the wrong place at the wrong time," Hank said.

"Normally, that creep doesn't kill innocent people," Jake added. "Maybe he assumed she was involved somehow."

"Perhaps she was," Annie put in. "Although the story doesn't name her as being under suspicion. Maybe Jeremy's upping his game and doesn't care who he hurts anymore." She paused, then asked, "What about the gun?"

"I think the ballistic evidence will show it was the same weapon Spencer has," Hank said. "A thirty-eight-caliber. And I'm betting it'll also show it was the same gun that killed Jackson Badger. Until we get the report back, I'm going under the presumption Spencer's responsible."

Hank gave Callaway a call and told him about the story on Hatfield in the paper. "Don't spend any more time digging into Hatfield Investments. See if King came up with something that'll help you find a lead."

When Hank finished with the call, Annie asked, "Did the fire investigator determine the cause of the fire in that building?"

Snapping his fingers, Hank picked up his briefcase and opened it. He removed a folder. "I got the investigator's report early this morning." He ran a finger over it. "Here it is. Arson suspected. The fire started in the basement in what was determined to be a combination of clothes, paper, and an unknown chemical."

"Different accelerant than the barn fire," Jake noted.

"If arson was involved in the barn fire, and the two are related, then it appears the arsonist used whatever was at hand," Hank said. "But we may be stretching the facts. There's no evidence they're related, other than coincidence."

"I think they are," Annie said. "But whether or not they're connected to Jeremy's killing spree, or to the murder of his parents, I don't know." She pulled a sheet of paper from a small pile on the corner of her desk, waved it, and handed it to Hank. "I've been working on a report for Diego, but there's not much here."

Hank took the paper and glanced at it.

Annie continued, "I spoke to Sophie Burnham yesterday. She's the mother of the boy Quinton Spencer killed—now remarried. She doesn't sound like a suspect and she has no idea where her ex is now. She said although her husband was distraught at the time his son was killed, he didn't appear to hold any special animosity toward Quinton Spencer."

"If all that is correct, then we're out of suspects," Jake said.

"And you're still firmly convinced Annette Spencer was murdered?" Hank asked.

Annie nodded. "I can't prove it now that the barn's burnt down, but I'm fully convinced my measurements are correct."

"They are," Jake added. "I double-checked her figures." He paused. "If that's the only evidence of a murder, then that may be a motive to burn the barn down."

"Perhaps," Hank said. "But why after all these years? Who, besides us, knew Annie came up with some evidence?"

"No one," Annie said. "Just us, King, and Callaway."

Hank handed the report back to Annie. "That doesn't point to arson, then. It may've been spontaneous combustion like the fire investigator suggested."

There was silence for a few moments, everyone with their own thoughts. Finally, Hank said, "I checked with the newspapers and the television station this morning and put undercover cops on two possibilities. I'll do the same for tomorrow, and every day, if necessary, until we get this guy."

"What if you held a press conference, Hank?" Annie asked.

"To what end?"

"This may sound like giving contrary advice, but perhaps you could explain who Jeremy's targets are, and warn them, if they fit the profile, to be extra vigilant."

Jake laughed. "Sort of like warning the bad guys not to get caught."

Hank rubbed his chin. "It wouldn't hurt and it may save a life. Even the bad guys don't deserve to be murdered."

"There's one thing to consider," Jake said. "Jeremy may see the press conference and be on his guard, resulting in a reverse effect to what we want. He may then turn to more obscure targets, and at the very least, be more careful."

"You make it sound like a lose-lose situation," Hank said with a chuckle.

Jake shrugged. "It may be. Either way, if that weasel strikes again, someone loses."

Hank leaned forward, rubbed at the back of his neck, and sighed deeply. "The problem is, we don't have a lot of time. We've had three murders in two days, and there's bound to be another one tomorrow if we don't get Spencer on the run."

"Anything we can do to help, Hank?" Jake asked.

"It doesn't seem like it, unless you can come up with an idea. We have officers on the streets, we're still going over everyone even remotely related, and investigators are studying the evidence from this morning's murder." Hank sat back, looked at Jake, and held up his hands, palms out. "What else is there?"

Jake grinned. "Annie'll come up with something. She always does."

"I appreciate your undying faith in me," Annie said. "But right now, I'm as stumped as you guys are."

Hank stood and picked up his briefcase. "Let me get back to the station, maybe toss some ideas past Diego, or talk to King. Give me any lead, no matter how small, and I'll run with it."

Jake walked to the door with Hank and watched the detective drive away. He rinsed off the Firebird, pulled it into the garage, and headed back into the house to see if, by any miracle, Annie had come up with an idea. He wasn't really expecting she had.

CHAPTER 37

Thursday, 12:54 p.m.

ANNIE HEARD THE DOORBELL ring and thought perhaps Hank had come back for some reason. Jake was in the kitchen and she heard him rummaging around, likely looking for something to eat.

"I'll get it," Jake called.

She heard the bell ring again and in a moment, Jake running down the hallway. The front door opened and closed. Then it opened and closed again, and Jake came into the office.

"Those delivery guys don't even give you a chance to get to the door anymore. I had to chase him halfway to his van." He tossed a padded envelope on the desk. "Package for you."

Annie pulled the envelope toward her and looked at the front. "No return address," she said. Her name and address were handwritten. She turned the package over. The back was blank.

She ripped the tab to open the package and peeked inside. Her eyes widened and she stared at Jake a moment, and then dumped out the contents of the envelope onto the desk. It was a stack of money—bills, bundled together with an elastic band. A single folded piece of paper fluttered out with the stack.

Jake had dropped into the chair and was leaning forward, resting his arms on the desk. He watched her intently as she unfolded the paper and read, "I promised to pay you. Here's a down payment. J.S."

"It's from Jeremy," she said.

"Don't touch the money. Fingerprints."

"You don't think we should keep it?"

Jake sat back and folded his arms. "I don't know. I really think we should turn it over to Hank."

Annie dropped the note she held as if it was on fire. "I shouldn't have touched that."

"How were you to know?"

"I think you're right. We'd better give it to Hank." Annie opened her desk drawer, found a pen, and used it to ease the note and the stack of bills back into the envelope.

Jake looked at his watch. "Let's go right now. It's only one o'clock, and Hank was headed for the precinct when he left here."

Annie picked up the package, went to the kitchen, and put it into a grocery bag. Jake grabbed his keys and they hurried out to the Firebird.

Jake avoided a speeding ticket as they raced to the precinct, parked in the back, and hurried inside.

They said a quick hello to Yappy as they passed the duty officer and went straight to Hank's desk, where the detective had his head buried in paperwork.

Hank glanced up when Annie sat in the guest chair. His eyes widened. "I just got back. How'd you get here so fast?"

"We brought the Firebird," Jake said. "It'll outrun your heap any day."

Hank chuckled. "And it drinks twice as much gas, too."

Annie dumped the envelope from the grocery bag onto the desk. "It's from Jeremy," she said.

Hank raised both brows, looked at the package, and then at Annie. "Did you open it?"

"It's money," Annie said. "A stack of bills with a handwritten note from Jeremy."

Hank leaned in, picked up the envelope by one corner, and dumped out the bills. "I wonder where he got that," he mused.

"No idea," Jake said.

Hank took a sharp breath, glared at the money a second, and then grabbed his briefcase. He snapped it open, reached in, and dropped a video tape on the desk. He slapped the top of his desk. "I've been so busy, this completely slipped my mind." He spun his chair around. "Callaway, do we have a VCR around here somewhere?"

"In the storage room," Callaway called back. "You want me to get it?"

"Yes, quickly, please," Hank said and then spun his chair back around. He picked up the tape and held it up. "This is a security video from a robbery that went down yesterday. A convenience store."

Annie saw the connection. "And you think the money may've come from the robbery?"

"Yup. Could be."

"But whatever that little piece of garbage is," Jake said, "he's not a thief."

"I got a description of the robber from the store owner. You're right, it wasn't Spencer, but it could still be the money."

"We'll soon find out," Annie said. "Here comes Callaway." The cop was lugging a VCR across the room.

Hank spun his chair over to Callaway's desk and Jake and Annie followed. They waited while the technical wizard plugged in some wires and then reached for the tape.

In a moment, they watched as the video played. The camera was ten feet from the cash register and they could plainly see a man standing behind the counter, watching over the store. A customer approached the register, paid for a package of something, and then left.

"How do we fast-forward this thing?" Hank asked.

Callaway showed him how and they continued to watch the video flash by at high speed. Soon, a huge man came into the store and Hank stopped the tape, rewound it a bit, and then hit the "Play" button.

They watched the robbery as it unfolded. There was no audio on the tape, a disappointment, but they had enough.

Hank paused the tape, leaned in, and pointed to the screen. "That looks like the same gun Jeremy had."

Callaway moved in for a closer look. "Hard to tell, Hank. But it could be."

Hank sat back and looked up at Callaway. "Can you compare it to the video from Lisa Krunk?"

"I'll try. This is a videotape, so we don't have very good resolution to work with, but I'll see what I can do."

"And run facial recognition on the robber. With a face like that, and a body that size, he shouldn't be too hard to nail down."

Callaway squinted at the screen. "I think I can do that, even with the poor resolution."

"You can do it," Hank said. "I've seen you do more with less."

They watched the rest of the video, until finally, the robber rushed from the store and the proprietor picked up the phone and called the police.

"He had a gun," Annie said. "But he didn't use it. Even when the woman attacked him."

"I don't think he's a killer," Hank said. "Just a big lug who used the gun to get what he wanted."

"What about the money?" Jake asked, explaining to Callaway about the money in the package they'd received. "This may be stretching it, but can you identify the bills the proprietor puts in the bag as being the same ones in the bundle?"

"Not exactly, but I can look at the stacks of denominations as he pulls them from the register and compare them to how many are in your stack of bills."

"That'll be close enough to give us a good idea," Hank said. He looked at Jake. "If it fits, what're the odds the money you got would be in similar amounts?"

"Nil," Annie said.

Hank stood and pushed his chair away from the desk. "We'll get out of Callaway's way and let him do his magic."

Annie turned to Jake and touched his hand. "I think we may be on to something now. I'd like to stay here and see what Callaway comes up with." She glanced at her watch. "We may be awhile. I'll call Mom and ask her to go to the house and wait for Matty to get home."

Jake frowned. "Why your mother? Why not Chrissy?"

"Because we take advantage of Chrissy's good nature too much. Besides, Mom likes to feel needed."

Jake shrugged, nodded his agreement, and sat down in front of Hank's desk. Even though her husband and her mother rarely saw eye to eye, Annie was glad Jake never put up much of an argument.

She called her mother and was assured the woman would be happy to watch for Matty, and why didn't her daughter call her more often? Annie chuckled, promised she would, and hung up.

She turned to Jake. "Dad needs the car this afternoon, but she'll get him to drop her off right away."

She smiled. For Jake's sake, she would be sure to hustle her mother from the house as soon as they got home.

CHAPTER 38

Thursday, 2:11 p.m.

JEREMY SPENCER DROVE slowly down the street, not worried about being recognized. The helmet hid his face quite well.

He pulled to the side of the street, tugged the motorcycle over the curb, leaned it against a signpost, wrapped the chain around it, and locked it up securely. He was in a good neighborhood and didn't expect anyone would touch it, but you could never be too careful.

He took off the helmet, fastened it to the back of the bike, and pulled his cap from his back pocket, tugging it down low over his eyes.

Strolling up the sidewalk, he approached the house with care and peeked in the small window in the garage. Perfect. Annie's car was there, but Jake was gone. He was here to see Annie anyway, and preferred Jake not to be around.

He went boldly to the front door and rang the bell,

keeping his head low so his face couldn't be seen through the peephole.

"Who is it?" came a muffled voice.

He gripped the pistol in his right hand. "It's the Boy Scouts." He hadn't planned what to say. Whatever would a Boy Scout be doing coming around this time of day?

His impromptu reply seemed to have worked. He heard the chain rattle and then the door opened.

He raised the weapon and looked up, straight into the face of … a stranger?

She gasped and tried to close the door, but he rammed into it with his shoulder. It popped open and he stepped inside, waving the pistol at the strange woman. "Where's Annie?" he asked.

The woman put her hand to her mouth, her eyes wide, glaring at the weapon in his hand.

"Stand back," he said.

She moved backward.

"I'm here to see Annie." He took a step forward and glanced down the hallway to the kitchen.

"She … she's not here."

Jeremy squinted closely at the strange woman. "Who're you?"

"I'm … I'm Annie's mother."

She might've been lying; he'd better make sure. He waved the pistol toward the living room. "In there."

The woman who claimed to be Annie's mother backed into the living room and sat carefully in a chair, never taking her eyes off him. He followed, keeping the weapon steady as he crossed the room and peeked into the office. It was empty.

He returned and sat on the edge of the couch. "Do you have a name?" he asked.

She paused and then said, "Alma."

Jeremy ran his eyes up and down her frame, stopping on her face. She looked somewhat like Annie, and not bad looking for her age. A little older than Annie, of course, but the same blond hair, the same blue eyes, good figure, but somehow with a meaner, colder look about her.

He decided she was telling the truth about who she was.

"When will Annie be back?"

"I … I'm not sure. She asked me to come over and wait until …"

He frowned. "Until what?"

"Never mind. She asked me to watch the house."

Jeremy sat back and laid the pistol in his lap. "I'm not here to kill Annie," he said. "But I wanted to talk to her. She's been doing some investigation for me."

Alma looked at him with contempt. "What kind of investigation would she be doing for you?"

"She's trying to find out who killed my parents. She surely is."

Alma watched him closely for a moment. "I heard about your mother. I never knew her, but I heard she killed herself."

"No. She did not kill herself." He spoke vehemently, almost in anger, and his hand moved to the pistol.

She watched his movement. "You won't shoot me," she said in a cool, defiant voice. "I know all about you."

He forced back a smile. She sounded a lot like Annie sometimes, too. He picked up the pistol and waved it. "Sometimes I kill people for fun, too."

She laughed—a mocking laugh. Disbelief. "Name one person you've killed for fun."

"Never mind," he said.

She laughed again, leaned back in her chair, laid her arms on the armrests, crossed her legs, and relaxed.

"I saw what you did on the news," Alma said. "Do you think that's going to bring back your parents?"

She was starting to sound like the shrink he'd seen in prison, and it annoyed him. He gritted his teeth. "I don't want to hear any of your psychobabble."

She persisted. "I don't know much about your father, but I remember when he killed that boy. It was a shame, but I don't think your father deserved to go to prison over it."

He cocked his head. "You remember that?"

She nodded. "Of course. It was big news at the time." She paused. "I'm sorry about your parents, but don't you think you're taking this too far?"

"It can never be too far." The sound of his voice almost surprised even him—angry, loud, through gritted teeth. He felt a growing rage and wanted to shoot her now. He raised the gun, his finger on the trigger, and his hand trembled as he repeated, "It surely can never be too far."

Alma's eyes widened and she raised her hands halfway up. "Annie can find out who killed your parents if anyone can," she said, her voice trembling. "Shooting me won't help you."

He glared at her for almost a minute, until finally, he

calmed down. He'd come close to pulling the trigger. Except for Joey, who hardly counted, that could've been the first time he killed an innocent person. She probably deserved it, but it wasn't his job.

He lowered the gun again, laid it in his lap, and crossed his arms.

She relaxed somewhat. "If you're planning on waiting until Annie gets home, it's going to be awhile."

He looked around the room, not sure what to do. Finally, he said, "I'll leave her a note."

Picking up his gun, he climbed off the couch and went into the office, keeping a careful eye on Alma through the open door. She was turned in her chair, watching him.

He found a sheet of paper in the printer and a pen in the top drawer. "I was here to see how you were proceeding with Mother's murder. I hope you got the money. J.S.," he wrote. He folded the note and propped it up against the monitor. She would be sure to see it there.

Alma turned back slowly, keeping an eye on him as he went back into the living room and stood in front of her. "I left a note," he said. "Don't touch it."

She said nothing.

"I should go now," he said. "I know you'll probably call the police, and that's all right." He stared at her a moment, and then turned abruptly and strode to the door. "Make sure you put the chain on when I leave. You can never be too safe."

With that he opened the door, closed it behind him, tucked the gun behind his belt, and hurried down the street to the motorcycle.

He was a little disappointed. He wanted to talk to Annie, but he didn't dare call her. He had no idea what was happening with her investigation and was anxious to see Mother and Father's killer brought to justice.

CHAPTER 39

Thursday, 2:33 p.m.

JAKE'S CELL PHONE RANG. He pulled it out and glanced at the caller ID, then frowned and looked at Annie. "It's your mother. That may be the first time she's ever called me."

Hank pushed back from his desk and grinned. "Even I know that's unusual."

The phone rang again and Jake answered the call.

"Jake, it's Alma." She sounded frantic.

"Yes, Alma."

He heard her take a deep breath. "Jeremy Spencer was here."

Jake sat up, hit the speaker icon, and whispered, "Jeremy was there." He spoke into the phone, "Are you all right?"

"Yes, yes, I'm fine. A little shaken, but he didn't try to harm me."

Annie leaned in. "What did he want, Mom?"

"He said he wanted to speak to you, dear. I put on a brave face, but I wasn't feeling so brave."

"Did he threaten you?" Jake asked.

Alma paused. "He got angry at one point and I was afraid he might do something, but he calmed down."

"I never thought he would dare show his face there again," Annie said.

"Again?"

Annie hesitated. "He was there once before. He said he would call, but he never did."

"Mrs. Roderick," Hank said. "It's Hank Corning. I'll send an officer right over to watch the house in case he comes back."

"Thank you, Hank," Alma said. "I really am quite shaken."

"Hang in there. Someone will take your statement as soon as you feel up to it. In the meantime, keep the door locked until the officer gets there."

Alma agreed and Jake hung up the phone.

Hank shook his head, berating himself as he stood. "I really should've expected this. With Spencer, you have to expect the unexpected." He crossed the room and spoke to the duty officer. When he returned, he sat down and said, "I've arranged for an officer to take the first shift. Be prepared for a cop to be at your house until we catch this guy."

"Sounds good to me," Jake said. "Whatever it takes."

"What about Matty?" Annie asked. "I think we should pick him up from school."

Hank jumped back up. "I'll arrange it." He went back to the duty desk and soon returned. "A cop will pick him up at school and take him home."

"Thank God for cops," Annie said.

"Hank, I got him." It was Callaway calling from his desk, triumph in his voice.

Hank spun around, got out of his chair, and Jake and Annie followed him to Callaway's desk.

Callaway was grinning. "I got an ID on the robber."

Hank leaned over, looked at Callaway's monitor, and said, "Moses Thacker. Goes by the name of Moe. Got out of prison this Monday and already he's back at it." He looked at Callaway. "Do you have an address for this guy?"

"Nope. No address."

"Get a BOLO out to everyone. Tell officers to bring him in, but use caution; assume he's armed and dangerous."

"Right away, Hank."

"Will you print his complete profile out for me?" Annie asked.

"Sure." Callaway clicked an icon and the printer hummed.

"What about the weapon he used in the robbery?" Hank asked.

Callaway dug through a pile of papers, pulled out two sheets, and arranged them side by side on his desk. They were close-up pictures of Smith & Wesson .38 Specials. He pointed to one. "This is from Lisa Krunk's interview with Spencer. I had good-quality footage to work with, so it's pretty crisp." He pointed to the other photo. "I couldn't get a quality shot from the surveillance videotape, so I can't swear to it, but they look the same."

Jake leaned in and inspected the printouts. He couldn't see any difference between the two.

"They're the same," Annie said, certainty in her voice.

Jake chuckled and looked at Annie. He didn't question her. She would likely be proven to be correct.

"We gotta get this guy," Hank said grimly. "If we get him, we get Spencer." He pulled out his cell phone. "I'll talk to King. He's got a lot of CIs and contacts on the streets. Maybe he can find out something." He called the detective, filled him in, hung up, and turned to the Lincolns. "He'll get right on it."

Callaway reached back into the stack of papers and pulled out some more printouts. "Here's the best part," he said as he laid out the papers. They were pictures of money. "I did an approximation of how many of each bill the storekeeper pulled out of the cash register, compared it to Annie's stack, and I came up with figures close enough to be identical."

Hank pumped a fist and grinned at Annie. "You're right."

"She always is," Jake said.

Annie disregarded the kudos. "Did you check the bills for prints?"

"Sure," Callaway said. "Every one of them was covered. The bills have been handled by a lot of people. We have a record of Thacker's prints, but forensics didn't find his on the bills, so there's no definite proof it's the same money. We found one of Spencer's thumbprints on a bill, but that doesn't prove a whole lot. We know it came from him."

"We don't need solid proof," Jake said. "We have enough evidence to connect him to Moses Thacker, and that's all we need. We'll get all the proof we want once they find him. It won't be too easy for a big, ugly lunk like him to hide out for long."

"There's one thing that confuses me about this," Annie said. Jake and Hank looked at her and she continued, "Jeremy hates thieves, and yet, this money came from a robbery, and it appears to be his gun that was used. Surely he knew where the money came from."

"Maybe he's branching out," Jake said. "I'll be sure to ask him before I knock his block off."

Hank scratched his head. "I'm confused about that too, but the evidence is right there, plain as day."

Yappy approached the desk. "Diego wants to see you," he said to Hank, and pointed two fingers at the Lincolns. "And he said you two might as well come in too."

"Thanks, Yappy," Hank said and then looked at Annie. "Are we done here?"

"I can't think of anything else right now."

"Then let's go see what the captain wants."

They went into Diego's office. Annie sat in the guest chair and crossed her legs while Jake leaned against a filing cabinet. Hank stood at the end of the desk and looked at the captain, sitting forward in his straight-backed chair. "What's up, Captain?"

"Fill me in," Diego said.

Hank gave Diego the rundown on their recent discoveries, and added, "We're getting close now."

"I want to hold a press conference a little later. Thought I'd give you some time to get ready."

"Anything special you want me to cover?"

"Whatever you think, Hank," Diego said. He straightened his tie and looked at Annie. "You making any headway with Spencer's parents?"

"Not a lot," Annie said. "This case is colder than cold. The only thing I know for sure is Annette Spencer didn't kill herself. But our proof burned up with the barn."

Diego thought about that a moment. "Somebody knows who killed her," he said slowly, as if it was a profound statement.

"Do you have any ideas for us, Captain Diego?" Annie asked.

Diego cleared his throat and sat back. "I wish I did."

"Anything else, Captain?" Hank asked.

"That's it. I just wanted to give you a heads-up about the press conference."

As they were leaving, Diego called to Jake.

Jake turned around.

"I understand you're not interested in being sworn in as an auxiliary constable?"

Jake shook his head. "No offense, Captain, but it's not our thing."

Diego shrugged one shoulder. "Keep it in mind," he said and dismissed him with a wave. "Good luck." Diego opened a file folder and Jake went back to Hank's desk.

"If we're done here," Annie said, "I have some research to take care of, and I'm sure my mother will want some company."

"I'll let you know if anything pops up," Hank said as the Lincolns left.

As Jake drove home, he reflected on the day's discoveries. They were finally getting somewhere, and he could almost see that little creep behind bars already.

CHAPTER 40

Thursday, 3:18 p.m.

BY THE TIME THE LINCOLNS arrived home, Matty was already there and an officer was in the entranceway. Matty rushed from the kitchen when he heard his mother's voice as she greeted the cop.

"Mom, what's going on?" he asked. "Why did a policeman pick me up at school?"

Annie crouched down, gave her son a hug, and then held him at arm's length. "I wanted you to be safe. There might be some danger from a case your father and I are working on."

Matty frowned. "Is this another killer you guys are trying to catch?" He crossed his arms. "Because if it is, you might need my help." He tried to keep a straight face, but Annie wasn't fooled.

Jake leaned down. "Matty, we're put on this earth to help other people."

"Oh?" Matty said. "What're the other people here for?"

Jake straightened and scratched his head as Matty scurried away, back to the kitchen.

"I think his brain is bigger than his body," Annie said.

"Don't let his size fool you," Jake said. "He's tougher than he looks." He put his arms around his wife. "And so are you."

The officer cleared his throat and wandered into the kitchen while Jake gave Annie an extended kiss.

Eventually, she had to push him away. "There's time for that later. Right now, I have to talk to Mom."

"It's a date," Jake called as she went toward the kitchen.

Annie's mother sat at the table, Matty beside her. She'd struck up a conversation with the officer—something to do with citizens carrying handguns. The discussion ceased when Annie came into the room. She went to the table, leaned down, and hugged her mother.

"Are you okay?" Annie asked.

"I'm all right. Sit down, dear," Alma said, waving toward a chair.

Annie sat and faced her mother. "I can take you home whenever you want."

She turned when she heard Jake from the doorway. "I can take her."

Alma didn't give her usual haughty look at Jake's presence, but rather forced a weak smile. "Thanks, Jake. I'll be ready in a minute."

Annie and Jake exchanged a look as Alma rose from the table. Her mother found her handbag in the living room and waited silently in the front hall.

"Drive slowly," Annie whispered to Jake.

He grinned. "I'll try." And then he left.

While Matty pestered the officer with questions, Annie went to the office. As she reached to switch on her iMac, she saw a folded piece of paper leaning against the monitor. She picked it up, opened it, and read its contents. It was signed J.S.

She pushed the note aside, not sure what to make of it, and booted her computer. She needed to make some notes while the information they'd discussed at the precinct was fresh in her mind.

Her concentration was interrupted a few minutes later when the phone on the desk rang. She swung around and picked up the receiver.

"Lincoln Investigations."

"Mrs. Lincoln, it's Jeremy."

Annie spun around. The red light on the recorder was blinking. The call would be recorded. "Yes, Jeremy."

"Did you get my note?"

"Yes. I just got home now and saw it."

"I'm sorry I missed you," he said.

"You frightened my mother. Please don't come around here anymore." She sounded like she was scolding him, and if it wasn't so deadly serious, it would almost be humorous. Who scolds a serial killer and expects them to listen?

"Please give her my apologies," he said. "I had no plans to hurt anyone. I only wanted to talk to you about my parents."

Annie didn't answer. She heard him breathing on the line.

"Did you find out anything?" he asked.

She paused, not sure how much to tell him. She would need to be careful not to put him on his guard, or give away anything they'd discovered.

"Did you get the money?" he asked.

She didn't want to mention the robbery and their evidence of his involvement. "Yes, I got the money," was all she said.

"I'm sorry it couldn't be more. I'll get as much as I can eventually, but I need to know if you've made any headway?"

"I've been looking into it but haven't come up with anything solid yet."

"Have you been trying?" His voice was louder, slightly frantic.

"I've talked to a few people and did some research," she said.

"I don't think you're trying hard enough." There was a pause on the line and Jeremy spoke more calmly. "If I tell you something, will you spend more time?"

"Tell me something? Like what?"

Another pause, then, "Where a body is buried."

Annie caught her breath. She thought before answering. "Yes, I'll spend a lot more time."

"His name was Joey Benitto," Jeremy said. "I killed him nine years ago. They never knew what happened to him."

She was stunned. The case had made headlines for many weeks as the search dragged on and on. She remembered it like it was yesterday—the news conferences, and the tearful pleas from the boy's mother, without a trace of Joey or a plausible reason for his disappearance.

"Where's he buried?" she asked at last, finding it hard to breathe.

"Near my house. In the forest."

"Will you show me where?"

"Mrs. Lincoln, I'm not going to show you in person. That would never do." He paused, then said, "But I can describe the exact location to you."

"I'm listening."

"You promise to find Mother's murderer—and Father's?"

"I'll do everything I possibly can. I'll give you my word, but there's not much to go on yet." She didn't want to promise anything, but she also didn't want to discourage him. "The research I've done so far leads me to believe your mother didn't kill herself. I'm convinced of that, and the police are convinced as well. They'll give me everything I need to continue the investigation."

She heard his breathing on the line. Finally, he took a long breath and said, "In the forest, about a quarter mile straight west of my house, there're three tall maple trees that make a perfect triangle. That's where Joey is. Right in the middle, buried deep."

"Why'd you kill him, Jeremy?" she asked.

"Because he was a bully and deserved to die." He paused, then added, "Just find my parents' killer."

"Jeremy, if you turn yourself over to the police, they'll help you. I'm sure you'll get extra consideration for telling us about Joey." She knew that wasn't accurate and it was a useless request, her feeble attempt to keep him on the line a little longer.

He must've known what she was trying to do. "I have to go now," he said. "I know the police are likely tracing this call. They won't find me, of course. I'm using a throwaway phone."

"Wait, Jeremy." But the line was dead and he was gone.

She dialed Hank's number immediately and filled him in on Jeremy's revelation.

He remembered the case well and was almost speechless at first. "I was still a beat cop," he said. "But I was involved in the search. I hope he's telling the truth."

"I believe he was. He seems desperate to find out who killed his parents, and he wouldn't send us off on a futile chase. That wouldn't help his cause."

"We'll soon find out," Hank said. "We also traced Spencer's call and police have been dispatched. They'll scour the entire area."

"He said he used a burner phone."

"I wouldn't doubt it, but I'll let you know if they find anything. In the meantime, I'm getting ready for the press conference, and then I'll organize a search for Joey Benitto's body."

Jake had returned, and he came into the office and sat down, watching Annie curiously.

"I'll talk to you soon," she said to Hank, then hung up.

"Is something up?" Jake asked.

"There certainly is. Jeremy called."

She played back the recorded call as Jake sat leaned forward, listening intently, his face clouding over with anger. When the call was finished, he sat back, took a deep breath, and glared at the phone, speechless.

CHAPTER 41

Thursday, 4:28 p.m.

HANK SCANNED HIS NOTES for the press conference, tucked them in a file folder, and went into Diego's office. The captain looked up, sat back in his chair, and brushed down his bristling mustache.

"We may have a conclusion to a cold case," Hank said.

The captain sat forward. "The Lincolns found out who killed Annette Spencer?"

"Better than that. Remember Joey Benitto? The boy who went missing a few years ago?"

Diego frowned. "I think so. We never found him, right?"

"Right. But Jeremy Spencer is claiming to have killed Joey and buried his body in the forest near his home."

Diego's eyes widened. "Spencer? He would've been a teenager at the time."

"Sixteen years old, I believe. And Joey was fifteen. Spencer called Annie a few minutes ago and, in return for her work on his mother's case, gave her the exact location. I'm going to organize a search right after the press conference."

"This is big news," Diego said. "No one was ever sure what happened to the boy."

"It sure is. I hope it pans out," Hank said as he turned to go. "All ready for the press conference? The crowd is waiting."

Diego stood. "I'm ready." Together they went to the front door of the precinct.

News vans and vehicles lined the street. Photographers and reporters bustled about, jockeying for the best spot at the podium. Passing cars were directed through the maze, and curious passersby stopped to see what all the commotion was.

Hank came from the precinct doors behind Captain Diego, followed by a pair of uniforms. They came down the steps, stopping at the makeshift podium set up at the bottom of the stairs.

Hank looked over the crowd of reporters. Lisa Krunk was at her usual spot, front row center, Don at her side with the camera ready. Other familiar faces waited eagerly as Hank removed his notes from the file folder, spread them out on the podium, and cleared his throat.

"Thank you all for coming." He paused. "As you all know, Jeremy Spencer escaped federal custody on Tuesday, and has made his presence felt in this city once again."

The crowd murmured.

"As with his original victims, he's again targeting those who've been less than honest. We have reason to believe he's responsible for three more recent murders, two today, and one yesterday.

"I can't go into detail on those specific cases as they're still under investigation, but suffice it to say, Spencer is a person of interest in all three murders, as well as wanted for being a fugitive who escaped federal custody."

Hank held up an eight-by-ten photo. "Spencer is suspected to be in the company of this man, Moses Thacker. Thacker was released from prison this Monday. Copies of this photo will be handed out to all of you after the conference. I urge you to broadcast or print this picture with a notice he's wanted for questioning.

"As always, I urge the public, if you see either of these men, call 9-1-1 immediately. Don't try to approach or apprehend them."

Hank paused, studied his notes, and then looked out over the crowd. "As I said before, Spencer targets those who've been less than honest. I urge you, if you fit this description, to be very careful."

Hank glanced briefly at Lisa and continued, "As noted by a recent broadcast, Spencer is a self-styled vigilante who feels it's his mission to eradicate from this city those individuals who have no respect for the property of others."

He paused again. "I'll take any questions now."

Lisa Krunk's loud voice could be heard over the shouts of others. Hank avoided her and pointed to a reporter in the second row.

"Detective Corning, you've indicated Spencer targets those who're less than honest. Does that description exclude anyone?"

Hank chuckled. "I guess we've all been less than honest in some ways, but Spencer specifically targets those who steal from others."

Hank pointed to another reporter.

"Detective, do you have any indication of Spencer's whereabouts?"

"We're currently following up on a number of leads and hope to make an arrest soon."

And again. "Do you know who burned down the barn at the Spencer residence?"

"The fire investigators are still looking into it. We have no evidence of arson."

Hank pointed to Lisa.

"Detective, I understand the Lincolns are involved in this case. Given their role in apprehending Spencer last time, can you tell me what part they're playing this time?"

Hank glanced at Diego. The captain gave an almost imperceptible nod. Hank said, "Their role in this case is strictly in an advisory capacity. As you indicated, they have certain expertise in this case, and we don't want to leave any stone unturned in our search."

Question after question came, some thought-provoking, most redundant, all sincere.

Hank held up a hand. "There'll be no more questions. We'll issue a press release when further information becomes available."

As the crowd pelted him with more, Hank closed the folder and leaned in to the mike. "I want to urge the citizens of this city to be cautious. None of us are exempt from danger, and until this vicious murderer has been caught, please be careful." He paused. "Especially anyone who suspects they may be among those he targets."

Hank picked up the folder and turned. The assembled group wanted more, but Hank climbed the steps behind Captain Diego and disappeared inside the building.

Diego pulled Hank aside. "I'll give you all the manpower you want in the search for Joey Benitto's body."

"I've already made a call to Toronto," Hank said. "They're sending out a GPR technician. Ground-penetrating radar will find that body quicker than anything else. If Spencer gave us the right instructions, we already have an approximate, perhaps a precise, location. Corpse-sniffing dogs or chemical analyses of air and soil won't do the trick accurately. That body has been there for almost ten years."

Diego slapped Hank on the back. "Get on it, Hank. And let me know the minute you find something."

Hank knew this would be good for the captain's career. Solving a high-profile cold case was not something done every day; at least, in this city it wasn't. It would be good for his own career as well, but he wasn't concerned about that. He was going to make sure Jake and Annie got their due credit.

He dropped the file folder into his drawer and then went to Callaway's desk. The cop had his nose buried in his monitor. "Did you get anything on Spencer's call?" Hank asked. "I assume he wasn't caught or the champagne would be flowing."

Callaway shook his head. "There was no trace of him

anywhere in the vicinity where the call was made. There was no GPS on the phone itself, but I was able to triangulate the phone's approximate location during the call. Spencer appeared to be on the move, and as the cell towers tracked the signals, I could compute his rough location. We had his exact position at one point, but the call was terminated and he was gone before officers got there."

"I expected as much," Hank said. "We'll get him yet."

He went back to his desk to arrange for the excavation of the remains of Joey Benitto.

CHAPTER 42

Thursday, 5:05 p.m.

JEREMY SPENCER TURNED off the television; he'd seen enough of the news. What made him chuckle was Detective Corning's warning to thieves to be careful. There was no end of those, and he would have his pick, but he would have to be cautious in who he chose. He decided to stay away from high-profile cases in the news, and find another way to select his targets. Perhaps old news stories would be ripe for the picking.

The morning's events were on the news as well. Somehow, they'd connected the killing of Wendell Hatfield and his secretary to him. He wasn't sure how they'd done that and didn't really care. He was more than willing to take credit for what he'd accomplished.

The police seemed to be making assumptions. He'd been careful not to be seen, but somehow they knew he was also responsible for the demise of Jackson Badger. Perhaps it was because the targets of the justice he meted out were thieves.

Either way, being the subject of the lead story didn't bother him. He'd expected that, and would've been disappointed if it were otherwise. But what he didn't expect, and what worried him, was to see Moe's face all over the news.

He looked at his friend, who sat at the table, turned toward the blackened screen of the television.

Moe frowned as he caught Jeremy's gaze. "How did they get my picture?" he asked.

"Either the storeowner identified you in the mug books, or they had a video. You're an ex-con, Moe. It wouldn't be hard to find out who you are."

"Maybe we should leave town," Moe said. "Find another city or small town where they don't know us." He paused, his frown deepening. "I don't want to go back to prison."

They were in a predicament. Jeremy didn't want to leave Richmond Hill. Not only did he love the city, but he had a lot of unfinished business here, and he was determined to find his parents' killer. But he felt responsible for Moe. The lug couldn't take care of himself and he couldn't stay out of trouble.

"We can't leave yet," Jeremy said. "You'll have to stay inside the apartment. No offense, Moe, but your face is too easy to recognize."

Not only was Jeremy worried about Moe getting picked up, but he knew with the big lug's level of intelligence, it wouldn't take the cops long to get him to talk. If Moe got caught, Jeremy would have to go elsewhere and leave his friend in the lurch, something he was loath to do.

Uriah had mentioned earlier that, while Jeremy was out, the police had come to his door showing around photos of Moe. It looked like they might be getting dangerously close, but when Uriah had said he didn't know the guy in the photo, they'd left him alone. Perhaps they were canvassing the whole neighborhood, and once they'd covered this area, they wouldn't be back.

He knew the police weren't in this district because of his phone call to Annie. He'd expected they would trace the call, and he'd moved well out of the area, staying on the move during their conversation. And certainly, it wasn't because of the building he'd burned down. They had no way to connect him to it; that was something he wouldn't normally have considered doing, its purpose only to ease his tortured mind—and maybe a little retribution for the burning of his precious barn.

Jeremy had another concern. He didn't know Uriah all that well and wasn't sure how solid he and Moe were as friends. Uriah seemed like a decent enough guy, but if the police offered a reward, Uriah might turn on his friend. Now that the police had connected Moe with Jeremy, offering a reward wasn't out of the question. And if so, it meant his association with Moe would threaten the big guy.

They would have to look into finding a new place, but it would be difficult with no money, and both of them wanted men.

Moe looked worried. Jeremy knew his friend would do what he told him to, but sometimes the knucklehead did stuff without thinking. Moe needed Jeremy to help keep him on the straight and narrow, as it were.

Moe's face brightened slightly. "Jeremy, you gave the money back to the man at the store, so maybe they'll leave me alone."

Jeremy hadn't told Moe what he'd actually done with the money. "That won't help, Moe," he said. "What's done is done and they don't care about the money. They want you and they want me."

"I have some other friends downtown," Moe said, his face still showing signs of hope. "Maybe we can go there?"

"Moe, those are the guys who landed you in prison last time. You can't trust them." Jeremy paused. "Don't worry, I'll come up with something."

He went to the fridge and scrounged around inside. There wasn't a whole lot to eat, but he managed to find a slab of ham behind a loaf of bread. The meat still smelled okay, so he made two sandwiches, plastered them with mustard, and brought one to Moe. They ate in silence, Moe enjoying the snack, Jeremy deep in thought.

He wondered if perhaps he could return to his house, but no, the cops would be keeping an eye on it for quite some time. Maybe they could hide out in a farmer's barn somewhere and help themselves to the crops in the field. He hated to steal from the farmers, but it was now a matter of survival.

And he would have no transportation. He wouldn't have access to Uriah's motorcycle anymore. He could use that old bicycle; it was still in the hallway, but that bike would be hard pressed to hold Moe's weight.

Problems. Problems. Problems. If only they understood his mission. Perhaps one day the police would leave him alone and allow him to do their job for them.

After all, didn't telling them about Joey count for anything? Didn't it show he was repentant for that, and wasn't interested in harming innocent people?

Perhaps it was too much to hope for.

His one wish was that Annie would spend more time on finding his parents' killer, like she promised. He had a lot of faith in the Lincolns' expertise—he'd witnessed that firsthand in the past—and right now, more than anything else, he was dying to know who killed Mother and Father. And the more time she spent on that, the less she would be looking for him.

He had a short window of opportunity at the moment. Right now, Detective Corning and the others would be looking into finding Joey's body. That might take some time and attention away from them, and perhaps give Moe and him a little breathing space—some time to find a new place to stay. He had to make that his top priority at the moment—maybe put further episodes of justice on hold until they got firmly settled.

CHAPTER 43

Thursday, 5:21 p.m.

JAKE WAS EAGER TO BE present when the forensic geophysicist conducted the subsurface scan for the body of Joey Benitto. Annie was enthusiastic about adding to her forensic knowledge, but her main concern was in a successful search, as well as bringing a small measure of closure to the Benitto family.

When Matty had gotten wind of the expedition, he'd begged to be taken along. Jake had agreed immediately, and since there would be no danger involved, Annie had relented somewhat later, realizing the value it could bring to her son's already burgeoning interest in his parents' investigative venture.

They'd agreed to meet Hank at the Spencer property and move into the forest directly west of the house to the spot Jeremy indicated. The cop was already there when they arrived, and a van along with two cruisers pulled up moments later.

Out on the road, a flatbed truck carrying a small backhoe idled. Directly behind, the forensic geophysicist, along with his team who would conduct the exhumation, waited in a van containing the ground-penetrating radar equipment.

Further down the lane, the place where the barn had once stood was strangely silent. All that could be seen were a few of the larger beams that had escaped the inferno, protruding upward at awkward angles.

The small group of searchers gathered around and Hank gave a basic rundown on the area they were looking for. "If we're all ready, we'll spread out and move in."

They walked as a line into the forest, parallel with the road. The fertile ground had produced a rich mixture of vegetation mixed among a variety of evergreens and maples. In less than ten minutes, the group came together at a small clearing, where three maple trees, perhaps fifteen feet apart, made a perfect triangle.

"This has to be the spot," Hank said, heading off to his left. "I'll notify the GPR and excavation teams."

Jake crouched down and surveyed the ground with his eye. There was a slight indentation where the soil settled over the suspected grave, but not enough to be sure it was anything other than a natural dip in the terrain.

The backhoe's treads crunched over fallen branches and small shrubs as it wormed its way a hundred yards from the road to the site. The GPR technician followed behind, wheeling his equipment. The nondestructive method to find evidence or locate subsurface bodies had become an important forensic archaeology tool, used by many law enforcement agencies.

Annie and Matty stood back, out of the way, watching the proceedings.

A ten-foot-square area was laid out in a tight grid pattern, spaced in such a way as to ensure the survey was accurate and complete.

The GPR equipment, looking suspiciously like a small lawnmower, transmitted its high-frequency radio signal into the ground as the equipment was rolled systematically over the grid.

Jake approached the technician monitoring an LCD display. He leaned in and looked at the monitor as the reflected signals were returned to the receiver, interpreted by the computer system and displayed as an image on the unit's panel.

"We have something," the technician finally said, pointing to the display. "It looks like human remains. The computer measures the time it takes for a pulse to travel to and from the target, and it indicates its depth to be just under six feet."

Jake pumped a fist and went over to Annie.

"Did they find the boy who was buried?" Matty asked.

"It looks like it," Jake said. "We'll soon find out."

The excavation began as the backhoe moved in and scooped up the dirt. It continued to a depth of five feet, and then the forensic archaeology team took over, using small shovels, scoops, pails, and brushes, until finally a skeleton was completely uncovered.

Jake moved over and joined Hank, who was gazing down into the grave. The detective let out a long sigh. "Now we have to confirm it's Joey Benitto."

Annie ordered Matty to stay put while she went to the excavation and looked down briefly into the crude grave. She shuddered. "I had to see it for myself." Then she turned and went back to her son.

The somber group left the exhumation to the experts and made their way back to the Spencer property.

"It's exciting to finally bring an end to this, but nonetheless, it's sad," Annie said. "I don't know whether to celebrate or mourn."

Hank nodded. "It's going to be hard to tell Joey's parents. I remember an interview they did about five years ago. They still held out hope their son ran off somewhere and would eventually be located."

"I don't envy you that job," Jake said.

"It's one of my most uncomfortable tasks," Hank said. "Sometimes I think I'd sooner face a killer with a machine gun." He sighed and added, "We have to catch Spencer. Once Nancy takes a DNA sample and confirms it's Joey's remains, I would love to be able to tell the parents we've caught their son's murderer."

"It's only a matter of time," Annie said. "We'll get him." She paused. "I've been working on a few ideas, and I still want to find out who killed Jeremy's parents, but after seeing … what we just saw, I'd rather give my attention to catching Joey's killer. At least for now."

On the way back home, the conversation in the Firebird was limited. Matty was silent in the backseat, looking out the side window as they drove. Jake wondered what the thoughts of an eight-year-old would be on an occasion like this.

Jake's own thoughts were sobering. He'd seen much worse on television and movies, but to view the grisly sight firsthand was a chilling experience.

~*~

AS SOON AS THEY arrived home, Annie went directly to the office and called Callaway.

"I didn't see any information about Jeremy Spencer on the printout of Moses Thacker," she explained to him. "I doubt if anyone at the prison would talk to me. Would you call to see what they have on Jeremy and Moses during their incarceration?"

Callaway agreed and said he would call her back as soon as possible.

Annie hung up thoughtfully. She assumed the two must've become friends in prison and met up again on the outside. The dilemma she was faced with was their current location. Finding either one would help in finding the other.

She studied the printout of Thacker's rap sheet further, memorizing dates and times, as well as the variety of offenses and corresponding sentences. There was no known family listed for Thacker, and Hank's earlier visit to his last known address prior to his incarceration netted nothing.

Jake came into the office and sunk into a chair. He watched her study the papers and notes. Finally, he said, "Except for robbing convenience stores, neither one of our fugitives has any means of support. It appears to me Spencer and Thacker are being aided by a third party."

"Someone either one of them knows," Annie added. "The police have already checked out anyone Thacker was involved with before his arrest and came up empty. Ex-cons who either one of them might know, and are living in the city, have also been questioned and investigated."

"What're we missing?" Jake asked.

Annie shook her head, looking at her notes. She leaned forward. "I can't get the building that burned down out of my mind. It's too much of a coincidence Jeremy's barn burned on the same day, as well …" She paused, turned her notes around so Jake could see them, and pointed. "Look at these addresses."

"The burnt building and the convenience store are only separated by three blocks," Jake said, leaning forward. "I know that area."

Annie produced a map she'd printed out a few minutes ago. She found a red marker in her top drawer and made two circles on the map. She flipped the paper around, pushed it toward Jake, and pointed to one circle. "There's where the fire was." She moved her finger. "That's the store."

"Let's speculate for a minute," Annie said. "We already know Thacker robbed the store. Let's assume either Thacker or Jeremy started the building fire." She sat back. "It stands to reason their hideout may be in the same neighborhood."

Jake sprang to his feet. "There's one more little item. Jeremy was on the move when he made the call to you, but they got his exact location once." He grabbed the marker, added a circle to the map, and stabbed at it with his finger. "That's the spot."

Annie looked at the map. The three circles encompassed a four-block area.

"They're in that immediate vicinity somewhere," Jake said, a grin spreading across his face.

Annie sat back. They might be on to something. Now all they had to do was find a way to cover that four-block neighborhood. It would be a daunting task, but there had to be a way.

"First thing tomorrow," she said. "We'll canvass the area and see what we can find out. I'll work on a plan of action."

CHAPTER 44

Thursday, 7:39 p.m.

MOSES THACKER WAS SICK and tired of staying in the apartment, hour after hour, day after day. Jeremy wouldn't even let him go out to the hallway for a little walk, and he'd had enough of watching television.

He stretched out on the couch and turned his head toward his friend. "Jeremy, I need to go outside for a little while. Can't you disguise me somehow?"

Jeremy twisted in his chair. "Moe, you saw the news. Everyone in the city will be looking for you. We can't chance it."

Moe sighed, put his hands behind his head, and closed his eyes. Jeremy always knew best. He should've listened to his friend before and they wouldn't have these problems now.

He blinked and turned his head when the apartment door squeaked open. It was Uriah. What was he doing here? He should be at work.

Uriah closed the door, pulled off his cap, tossed it onto a hook, and walked into the living room. He dropped into his easy chair and put his feet up.

"You're home early," Jeremy said.

Uriah was silent. "I got laid off," he said at last.

Moe sat up. "What happened?"

"Not enough work to keep us going," Uriah answered with a shrug. "The factory laid off almost half of us."

That wasn't good. Uriah was the only one around here who made any money. "Can you find another job?" Moe asked.

Uriah's face darkened. "Why? So you two can eat all my food?"

Moe didn't know what to say to that. He'd tried to help out by robbing that store, but it'd only gotten him into more trouble. He wouldn't be able to find a job, and for sure Jeremy couldn't either.

"You know we'd help if we could," Jeremy said.

Uriah sat forward and glared at the little man. "I don't owe you two nothing and it don't help having you here. If they find out two wanted guys are living with me, I'm back in the joint for sure."

"We'll find another place soon," Jeremy said.

Uriah stood and came to the table, swung a chair around and sat down, his face a few inches from Jeremy's. He spoke sharply, in a raised voice. "I want you guys out of here by tomorrow. You can stay one more night, but then …" He pointed toward the door. "You gotta go."

"Both of us?" Moe asked.

Uriah spun around to face Moe and spoke firmly. "Both of you."

"But we have no place to go."

"I don't care. It ain't my problem." Uriah stood and paced. "I was good enough to give you guys a bed for a while, but now, it's too dangerous, and in case you haven't heard …" He stopped pacing, glared at Moe, and shouted, "I lost my job."

Moe shrunk back, closed his eyes, and stuck his oversized fingers in his ears. He didn't like it when Uriah was in this kind of mood. It made him afraid. Not afraid of Uriah, just afraid of everything.

His old man used to yell at him like that all the time, just before he beat him. That always made him afraid too. He didn't want to get hit anymore, and sometimes when he got too scared, he would go crazy. He didn't want to hurt Uriah. His friend was good to him.

Moe removed his fingers and looked up when Uriah shook him by the shoulders.

"Did you hear me?" Uriah was still shouting.

"I … I heard you."

Jeremy stood and placed a hand on Uriah's arm. "Please, Uriah. He doesn't understand."

Uriah straightened, looked down at the little man, and spoke in a softer tone. "Yeah, I know. He's a big dud and can't help it he's so stupid."

"I'm not stupid, Uriah," Moe said defensively and stuck his chin in the air. "I'm just slow. That's what my mother always told me."

Uriah rolled his eyes, sighed deeply, and dropped back into his chair. “Whatever.”

Moe felt himself getting angry and he didn’t like the feeling. When he got angry he did bad things. Uriah had called him stupid. He knew that was wrong, and now he couldn’t stop his anger from escaping.

He jumped up, leaned over Uriah, and bellowed, “You’re stupid.”

Jeremy grabbed Moe’s arm and tugged at him. “Moe, forget it.”

Moe pulled his arm away from Jeremy’s grasp, then reached down and took a handful of Uriah’s shirt. He lifted the now-frightened man off the chair and stepped back, bringing Uriah’s face in close to his. “You’re the stupid one.”

Uriah’s feet kicked at the air and he swung wildly at his attacker with his hands. “Let me go.”

Moe threw Uriah on the floor and raised a foot, ready to crush his throat. Jeremy sprang forward and hurled himself into Moe, knocking the big man to one side. “Stop it, Moe. Don’t do it.”

Moe caught his balance and glared down at Jeremy. His friend was holding his hands out in an attempt to prevent him from killing Uriah.

“No more,” Jeremy screamed. “Leave him alone.”

Uriah scurried backward on all fours, rolled over, and sprang to his feet. He ran into the kitchen, pulled open a drawer, and came up with a long knife. He held the weapon out, pointing the tip at Moe. “Stay back,” he growled.

"Relax, Moe," Jeremy was saying. "He didn't mean anything."

Moe stood still and glared at Uriah, his breath coming short and quick. As Jeremy continued his calming words, Moe felt himself relaxing; suddenly, he didn't want to kill Uriah anymore. "I have to go out," he said and sprinted for the door. Jeremy called his name as the big man ran out into the hallway and down the steps.

He almost knocked over a decrepit old man who was entering the building. He mumbled an apology and dashed outside, leaving the man staring after him.

He didn't want to listen to Jeremy right now. He had to walk. That had always helped him when his father was so mean to him. Sometimes he would walk for hours and he felt much better by the time he returned home. By then, his father had cooled off as well.

He flipped up the collar of his shirt, trying to hide his face, keeping his head down when he passed anyone on the sidewalk. He walked for a couple of blocks and turned down a side street.

He knew now, he only had one friend in the world, and that was Jeremy. Even Uriah had turned his back on him, just like his father. But good friends were hard to find and he was willing to do all he could to make it up to Uriah.

Once when he was a boy at school, he'd beat up three other kids who'd made fun of him. They'd used the same word Uriah had—stupid. After a while, he'd felt sorry he'd hurt the other boys, and when the teacher had made him apologize, they didn't call him names anymore.

Maybe he would go back to Uriah and apologize. The word "sorry" seemed to do wonders. If it worked again this time, then everything would be okay.

He circled around the block, ending up at the apartment. He looked forward to getting Uriah back as a friend again.

CHAPTER 45

Friday, 9:02 a.m.

JAKE DROPPED MATTY and Kyle at school and watched them until they were safely inside the building. He didn't suspect they were in danger, but the unexpected happened on occasion, and when dealing with psychopaths, he preferred to be cautious.

The school had been locked down during the day since all this started three days ago, students not allowed out during school hours, and no one let in without passing a security check. Officials were being vigilant, and Matty understood he was to wait inside the building after school until either of his parents picked him up. Other families made similar arrangements, the memory of Spencer's prior killing spree still fresh in their minds.

When Jake arrived home, Annie met him at the door, eager to get started, her handbag over her shoulder, a plastic grocery bag in one hand, a manila envelope in the other. She handed him the bag and he peeked inside. She'd put together some sandwiches and tucked them into the bag along with a few bottles of water, probably anticipating a long day ahead.

Most of the canvassing would be done on foot, but they decided to take Annie's nondescript Escort—not likely to be recognized should their quarry be nearby.

Annie drove to somewhere near the midpoint of the neighborhood, parked on a side street, and shut off the engine. She removed the map from the envelope and studied it.

Jake leaned over and looked at the paper. "It's only a four-block area, but it seems like a daunting task," he said.

"It's not as bad as it looks," Annie said. "Three quarters of it may be houses and apartments, but the rest are stores, offices, and restaurants. If they're in this area, then it stands to reason they may have frequented one or more of these businesses."

Jake brushed a finger down one side of the map. "This part is a middle-class neighborhood, so I think we can eliminate that, as well as any single-family homes. I can't see any homeowners sheltering fugitives."

Annie looked through the windshield and pointed. "Two streets that way are government housing and tenements. If they're here at all, that's the most likely place we'll find them."

"I expect you're right," Jake said. "But it's easy for them to hide, and we can't force our way in. The police already canvassed this whole area and were faced with the same problem."

Annie pointed to the map. "We could stake out one of these streets?"

"That may take all day and we may be on the wrong street."

"Let's start with the shops, then."

Jake nodded and they stepped from the vehicle and walked out to the main street, lined on both sides by a host of businesses. Annie opened the envelope and drew out a pair of photos, one of Moe, and one of Jeremy.

They worked their way up one side of the street, showing the pictures in the shops and to everyone they met. A few recalled hearing about them on the television, or in the newspaper, but no one had seen either of them.

They'd reached the boundary of their target area, so they crossed the street and began their way back. A woman in one of the shops thought she'd seen Jeremy around somewhere, and then changed her mind, supposing she'd only recognized him from the television news.

They continued relentlessly, with person after person shaking their head, or shrugging, before moving on.

Jake stopped in front of a convenience store. A sign read, "Morningstar Convenience." It was the place Moe had robbed. He looked in the window. An old Chinese man stood behind the counter, undeterred by the robbery, making a living the best way he knew how.

A homeless man sat next to the store at the entranceway to a narrow alley. The man looked up at Jake through tired eyes, his wrinkled and darkened features showing the years he'd spent on the streets. His matted hair was covered by a filthy baseball cap, his beard shaggy, his clothes in tatters. He held a paper cup in one shaky hand.

Jake crouched down, dropped some coins in the cup, and held out the photos. "Have you seen either of these guys?"

The destitute man dropped his eyes and peered into the cup, then raised his head and squinted at the photos. A hint of recognition appeared on his face. He lifted the cup, then held it out and shook it, making the coins jingle.

Jake slipped out his wallet, removed a five, folded it, and held it over the cup. "Did you see him?"

The man snatched the bill with his free hand and jammed it into his shirt pocket. He looked back at Jake and poked a twisted finger at the shot of Moses Thacker. "Saw that one yesterday."

"Where did you see him?"

The man waved his hand to one side. "On the sidewalk."

"Walking?"

A nod. "Just walking fast."

"Which way did he come from?"

The man pointed down the sidewalk.

"Was he alone?"

He nodded, lowered his head, drew his feet up, and wrapped his arms around his knees. Jake dropped another five in the cup and straightened up.

Annie was looking down the street in the direction the man indicated. "I'm more convinced than ever," she said. "He's in this neighborhood somewhere. Both of them are."

"And it's somewhere that way," Jake added.

"Not necessarily. He might've been returning home when this man saw him."

Jake shook his head. "I don't think so. The government

housing is the next street over." He pointed back over his shoulder. "There're mostly houses and upscale businesses the other way."

Annie unfolded the map and glanced at it, nodding slowly. "I think you're right."

The public housing came in all sizes and types, from scattered single-family houses to low-rise apartments for the elderly, low-income families, and individuals. The buildings in the area had been erected some forty or more years ago, and the forgotten street was long overdue for a makeover.

Jake frowned at a group of four boys playing street hockey. They should be in school, their best chance for a way out of this crumbling neighborhood. He wondered where their parents were. Without some type of supervision, they might be destined to continue on the same hopeless path.

The boys eyed him curiously as he approached and held up the photos. "Have you seen either of these guys?" Jake asked.

One boy came over, peered at the pictures, and shook his head. The other three hung back. Jake went over to them. "Seen these guys?"

A small boy indicated the picture of Moe. "Think I saw him around yesterday," he said, squinting at Jake. "What'd he do? Are you a cop or something?"

Jake chuckled. "Something like that." He leaned down and looked the boy in the eye. "Do you know where he lives?"

The boy pointed to a group of three low-rise apartments at the far end of the street. "Down there. In one of those buildings."

Jake straightened his back and looked where the boy pointed. "Which building?"

A shrug. "Don't know," he said and scurried after the puck.

"Anyone else?" Jake said, waving the photos.

No one answered, the game now back underway.

Jake returned to where Annie stood watching. He saw the mother in her, concerned about the young boys. She sighed and said nothing.

Jake pointed to the group of buildings. "Thacker may live in one of those. And I'm betting, if we find him, we find Spencer too."

CHAPTER 46

Friday, 9:41 a.m.

JEREMY SPENCER SAT at the kitchen table pondering his and Moe's future. He missed the old days—the days when he could go about his mission without worrying about where to live, or money, or a warm bed. He missed the old house, and his heart ached when he thought about the destroyed barn, the farm, and the surrounding forest. It was home, and reminded him of Mother and better days, and yet, he was unable to safely return.

He shook his head, took a deep breath, and sat back. Those days were in the past, Mother was gone, and the future was now all that mattered.

The mood in the apartment was still one of subdued hostility. Jeremy looked over at Moe, sitting quietly on the couch, his arms crossed, a sad and sullen look on his face as he stared at the far wall. The big man didn't dare open his mouth for fear of starting another war.

The only sound in the small room was Uriah, rattling drawers and utensils, making himself some breakfast from the sparse amount of food left in the fridge. Jeremy supposed Uriah's quietness came from his fear of being a repeat target of Moe's unbridled wrath.

The three had barely said a word to each other the evening before. When Moe apologized, Uriah grunted, and nothing else was said on the matter.

Uriah set his plate of food on the table, sat down, and took a bite, looking at Jeremy while he chewed. "You can keep the gun," he said. "I have no use for it anymore."

"Thanks, Uriah," Jeremy said. "That's very kind of you. We'll be gone out of here today."

"Where you goin'?" Uriah asked in an offhand way.

Jeremy hesitated. "It's not far away, but maybe it's better if I don't tell you."

Uriah shrugged and shoveled in another forkful of eggs. His lips smacked together in an annoying way as he chewed.

"I hope you don't lose your apartment, Uriah. I expect you'll find another job before long. You surely will."

"They won't kick me outta here real quick. It's government housing. Takes 'em a long time to evict anybody, but I gotta pay the rent eventually." Uriah sat back and took a long breath. "Hope you understand. It ain't nothin' personal, but I can't have you guys here. It's not just the money, it's too dangerous for me."

Jeremy nodded in understanding.

Uriah reached into his pocket. "Look, I feel lousy about all this. Here's a hundred bucks before you go. It'll get you started." He peeled off some bills and tossed them over. "I'd give you more, but I ain't got a job."

Jeremy hesitated, then picked up the bills. They had to eat. "I appreciate this, Uriah, and I'll pay you back. I surely will."

Uriah waved it off. "Don't mention it."

Jeremy stood and approached Moe. "We'd better go."

Moe stood, tucked his hands in his pockets, and looked at Uriah with a downcast expression. "Bye, Uriah."

Uriah waved a hand without looking up from his plate. "Take care, guys."

"We'll pick the bicycle up later," Jeremy said to Uriah.

"Whatever."

They had little to take with them, only a bag containing Jeremy's old clothes. He pulled his cap on, retrieved the revolver from under the couch cushion, and stuffed it behind his belt, and they left the apartment without another word to Uriah.

Out in the hallway, Moe turned to his friend. "Where we goin', little buddy?"

Jeremy grinned. "I was up early this morning, before dawn, while you guys were still snoring. I found us a temporary place up the street. I surely did."

Moe's eyes lit up and he followed Jeremy down the steps, and then toward the fire exit at the rear of the lobby. Jeremy pulled his old shirt from the bag and handed it to Moe. "Put this over your head, sort of like a shawl, and cover your face if you see anyone."

Moe took the shirt and did as he was told, and they stepped out the door to the back of the building. Week-old garbage ripened in a big blue bin, papers blowing around the lot. A cat scurried away with a whine and scrambled over the rear fence.

Jeremy glanced at Uriah's motorcycle. It was too bad he wouldn't have its use anymore. It'd come in handy. He would have to be sure to come back for the bicycle after they got established.

He turned and strode across the lot as the big man followed. They climbed over fences as they crossed the rear parking lots of two other low-rise apartments, finally approaching the adjoining street. They waited out of sight behind a tree as two women strolled past, one pushing a baby carriage, the other talking incessantly. When the coast was clear, they stepped out onto the sidewalk.

Side by side they walked down the street, watching carefully for pedestrians. Moe kept the shirt over his head, now tied by the sleeves at his throat.

Finally, a half block away, Jeremy stopped in front of an old industrial building. It had been a profitable shop of some kind in times past, but was now abandoned and boarded up, patches of stubborn grass and weeds poking through where the asphalt had cracked and popped from years of weather.

The entire lot was enclosed by a chain-link fence, now rusting and tottering in some places. At one end, a pair of straps that fastened the links to the post had rusted away. Jeremy tugged on the fence and revealed a space large enough for him to squeeze through. He'd found the gap earlier, and it made easy access for him, but Moe was three times his size.

He pointed to a group of weakened straps. "Can you rip that back?"

Moe grabbed the fence in one hand and the post in the other, tensed his muscles, and pulled. One by one the links ripped clear of the straps. Moe curled back the fence and climbed through the space, and Jeremy followed, tucking the fence back in place against the post. It would only be noticeable if someone looked closely.

He led the way to the back of the building and heaved on a shaky metal door, and it swung open. Stepping inside, they were greeted with the smell of stale air along with a faint odor of old oil. A mouse skittered across the floor in an attempt to escape from the intruders.

Light eased through a pair of uncovered windows on one side of the building. The room was littered with castoffs, years of dust covering cardboard boxes, empty shelving, and discarded furniture.

"This is home," Jeremy said. He kicked aside an old soda can, crossed the room, and opened a door leading into what might've once been the office of a thriving business. "This is where we'll stay."

The big man looked around the dim room, the windows covered with cardboard. "It's better than a jail cell."

Moe seemed to be in a much better mood. The big lug trusted him implicitly, and Jeremy didn't want to let his friend down. He only wished Moe hadn't robbed that store. Then he would be free to move about, and they could depend on each other.

Sure, they had a place to stay for now, but with only a hundred bucks to last them, and difficulty moving around the city without being recognized, the situation was far from ideal.

He had only the weapon behind his belt and Moe's friendship to comfort him. He was determined to find better accommodations as soon as possible, but this building would do for now; it would serve as his base of operations, and he was anxious to get his mission back underway.

CHAPTER 47

Friday, 10:02 a.m.

ANNIE STOOD BESIDE JAKE and looked at the three buildings arrayed in front of them, each a carbon copy of the others. They all had two floors, with three separate apartments on each floor. She could only make a guess as to which building Thacker and Jeremy might be holed up in.

"We'll start at this one," she said, pointing to the closest building.

They entered the premises, and one by one, knocked on each door. There was no answer at two and Annie made a note of those. The inhabitants in the rest of the dingy apartments claimed never to have seen either of the men in the photos. As she showed the pictures, she knew Jake was scanning the apartment with his eyes, looking for any indication the fugitives might be inside.

Annie had made small talk with each tenant, trying to gauge their response to the questions, attempting to get a feel for each person. She was satisfied the wanted men weren't in the first building.

At the front of the next building, a couple of women had brought lawn chairs out to the concrete slab serving as a patio. They were lounged back, sipping on beer and discussing the indiscretions of another tenant when the Lincolns approached.

Annie showed the photos. Neither of them had seen the fugitives, but one woman cocked a thumb over her shoulder. "Landlord's on the first floor. You might ask him if maybe he rented the place to anyone shady."

"They're all shady 'round here, Millie," the other woman said, looking at her friend. "I reckon could be any of 'em."

The other woman nodded her agreement. "That's so, could be." She looked at Jake, her smile revealing a missing tooth. "Don't bother knockin' on 202 or 203 'cause we're out here."

Annie smiled and thanked them, and they went inside. Jake knocked on the first door under a sign reading, "Landlord." There was no answer.

The next door was eventually opened a crack by a leather-faced old man, a few days' growth of beard, a cane in one hand. He peered past the doorframe, poked up his glasses, and squinted at them. "Whatever you're selling, I don't need it."

Jake chuckled and held up the photos. "Have you seen either of these two around?"

The old man opened the door a little further, poked a hand out, and pointed a boney finger. "Lemme see that one."

Jake handed him the picture of Thacker. The old man narrowed his eyes and nodded. "Yup." He pointed at the ceiling. "Upstairs."

Annie's heart jumped. "What about the other man?"

The old man shook his head. "Nope."

"Thank you," Jake said, and the man closed the door.

Annie moved to the foot of the stairs and looked up, her heart thumping. It had to be apartment 201, directly at the top of the steps, and the door was opening. "Wait. Someone's coming from the apartment." She stepped aside and prodded Jake toward the back of the lobby, out of sight of the stairs.

Running shoes squeaked on the steps, and footsteps grew louder as the unseen person descended. A pair of legs appeared. "It's neither one of them," Annie whispered.

Jake took a step closer, waited, and then strode to the bottom of the stairs. The man froze on the last step, his mouth open, his eyes wide.

"I'm looking for Moses Thacker," Jake said.

The guy continued to stare, his eyes directly in line with Jake's as the frightened man stood on the last step. "Never heard of him," he said at last.

Jake moved in a few inches. "I think you have."

"Never heard the name before." The sloppy man shrank back.

"Then what're you afraid of?"

A shrug, then, "Who says I'm afraid?"

Jake laughed. "Aren't you?"

"Let me go." His voice shook, and he tried to move around Jake, but his path was blocked by a hand on his chest.

"What's your name?" Jake asked.

The man frowned. "Uriah. Uriah Hubert."

"Well, Uriah, is he in the apartment?" Jake asked.

"No. I told you, I don't know him."

"Let's go up and see."

Uriah held up his hands, chest high in surrender, then turned and trudged up the stairs, keeping a close eye over his shoulder as Jake followed. He unlocked his apartment and pushed the door open. "See for yourself. I … I live alone."

"Inside," Jake said, giving the trembling man a push from behind.

Annie followed them inside and glanced around the filthy apartment. A bicycle leaned against the wall to one side of the doorway. A blanket and pillow lay on the worn-out couch. In the kitchen, there was one plate in the sink, one cup on the counter.

Jake went into the bedroom, checked the bathroom, then came back and glanced around the living room. He looked at Annie and shrugged.

Annie's attention was drawn by a newspaper that lay on a shelf by the kitchen counter. She looked closer; it was Wednesday's paper. She leafed through it, and her eyes narrowed at page four. An article was missing—ripped out. If she recalled correctly, that was the story on Jackson Badger.

She showed the paper to Jake. A faint smile crossed his lips and he turned to Uriah. "Now, Uriah, you're going to tell me where they are."

Annie held up the paper for the man to see. She pointed to the missing article. "This is Jeremy Spencer's work."

Uriah glanced at the paper, sighed, and dropped onto the couch.

Jake moved in closer, spread his legs, and crossed his arms. "They're staying with you," he said. It was a statement, not a question.

Uriah slouched back, took a deep breath, and let it out slowly. Finally, he said, "They're gone. They were here but I kicked 'em out."

"Gone where?"

Uriah shrugged one shoulder, his neck at an awkward angle as he stared up at Jake. "I … I don't know. They left this morning. They didn't say where they were going."

"Don't you know it's illegal to harbor fugitives?" Annie asked, her hands on her hips.

Uriah frowned, his eyes darting back and forth between his questioners. "Who are you people, anyway? Are you cops?"

Annie laughed. "We're not cops. We're private investigators."

Uriah crossed his arms and looked up defiantly. "I don't have to talk to you."

"Actually, you do," Jake said. He leaned over and grasped the shaking man by the shirt and pulled him forward, almost out of his seat. "Because if you don't, I might get angry. And I'm betting you're an ex-con." He pushed Uriah back into the couch, straightened his back, and shrugged. "If you get hurt, who're they going to believe?"

Uriah held up a hand and stated flatly, "They're gone and I don't know where."

"He's telling the truth," Annie said.

Jake thought about that a moment, then took a step back and pointed at the frightened man. "You'd better be telling the truth."

Uriah jutted his chin. "I told you all I know."

Jake gave the man one last look of warning as he and Annie left the apartment, closing the door behind them.

"We're getting closer," Annie said. "But where do we go from here?" It was a rhetorical question, a question neither one of them could answer.

CHAPTER 48

Friday, 10:18 a.m.

JEREMY AND MOE RIPPED apart some of the cardboard boxes and laid them out on the floor to serve as a makeshift bed. Jeremy lay down and stretched out. It seemed comfortable enough, but he realized it would get cold in the night. Perhaps he should've asked Uriah if they could borrow that extra blanket.

Eventually, they would be able to find some cushions for pillows from people's castoffs on garbage day, and perhaps a mattress, but nobody seemed to throw out blankets.

They would need some form of transportation soon, so he decided to drop back by Uriah's and pick up the bicycle. While they were there, he would ask about the blanket.

Moe had dragged a set of shelves into the office and climbed up toward the high ceiling, and now he was removing the cardboard from the window, ten feet from the floor. The sun would make it a lot homier in here by day, and not so dark at night. They were used to that from their time in prison.

Jeremy watched Moe rip off the last piece of cardboard, toss it to the floor, and climb down. The morning sun gave the room a whole different feel as it splayed across the tiled flooring of the office.

"I'm going back to Uriah's to get the bike, and maybe a blanket," Jeremy said. "You can come if you want."

Moe grinned and moved out to the main room of the building, like a dog waiting for its master, eager to get going.

They left the building, moved to the front, and dipped through the fence to the deserted sidewalk. When they reached the apartment building, they entered through the rear door to avoid a pair of gossiping women out front.

"Somebody's looking for you two guys." Jeremy turned to see a crotchety old man, his head stuck out through his apartment doorway. "Some big, good-looking guy with a woman." He pointed a finger at Moe. "They were showing around pictures of you. Told him you were staying upstairs. Hope it's okay."

Jeremy hadn't wanted to be seen and the old man had caught him unawares. It was too late now; any damage had already been done. He looked up the stairs and then turned back to the old man. "Are they still up there?"

"Nah. Your friend came down and talked to them. They went up for a minute, then came back down, and left a few minutes ago."

"Did they say if they'd be back?"

"Didn't hear."

That wasn't good news. He'd better have a quick conversation with Uriah and then get out of here. Chances were, whoever it was, they might return.

The man disappeared from sight and his door closed. Jeremy beckoned to Moe and they went up the steps and knocked on Uriah's door. It opened a crack and Uriah's face appeared, his eyes darting up and down the hallway, finally settling on Jeremy. "What do you want?"

"We came for the bike."

Uriah swung the door open. "You better hurry and get out of here. Some PIs are snooping around."

Jeremy stopped halfway through the door. PIs? It might be the Lincolns. If so, they were relentless. "Who was it, Uriah?" he asked.

"They didn't give any names. Said they was looking for you two."

"What did you tell them?" Moe demanded, pushing his way past Jeremy.

Uriah looked up at Moe and took a quick step back against the wall. "Told them I didn't know you. Then they left."

Moe moved forward, a low growl coming from his throat. "You're lying, Uriah. You talked. The man downstairs told us."

Uriah put his hands on Moe's chest as if to hold him back, but the big guy pressed forward, his nose a few inches away from Uriah's.

"Take it easy, Moe," Jeremy said, putting a hand on his friend's arm.

Moe paid no attention. He pressed Uriah into the wall

with one big hand and swung a fist. His quarry ducked and escaped into the living room, the fist mashing into the wall where Uriah's head used to be.

"Moe. Stop," Jeremy demanded.

The big lug didn't hear, his anger rising as he spun toward Uriah, his teeth bared, his fists in the air. He growled again and lumbered toward his prey, who now attempted to hide behind the easy chair.

"Moe," Jeremy screamed.

The angry man reached down and pushed the chair aside with one sweep of his massive arm. Uriah dove, barely avoiding a crushing fist. He hit the floor, rolled toward the hallway, made it to his feet, and dashed into the bedroom. The door slammed.

Moe followed, huffing and puffing. His tiny eyes, sunk into a crimson face, burned with anger.

Jeremy pulled out the revolver from behind his belt. "Moe, stop or I'll shoot you."

The big lug stopped and turned slowly. "You won't shoot me, Jeremy." He turned back to face the door and wrapped his huge fists together into a giant battering ram, and with one swing, the door crashed forward and slammed against the inner wall.

Jeremy raced down the hallway, tucking the weapon away as he ran, and tugged at Moe from behind. He found himself being dragged forward as the angry lunk shuffled across the room toward a terrified Uriah.

The frightened man had his back to the wall, a baseball bat

poised in his hands. "Don't come any closer, Moe, or I swear, I'll kill you."

Moe snarled and moved in.

The bat whistled through the air as Uriah swung it in warning. "Stay back."

Moe didn't listen. As he stepped forward, the swinging bat whacked his upraised arm and slipped from Uriah's hands. The bat spun across the room, struck the wall, and clattered to the floor.

"Moe. No. Let him go."

An enormous hand reached out and wrapped itself around Uriah's throat. Moe squeezed as Uriah sputtered and fought for air. His eyes bugged out, and his tongue flapped around in his open mouth.

Jeremy grabbed Moe's arm and pulled, but the big man held on to the throat, squeezing and growling until finally Uriah sunk to the floor, his lifeless body no longer trying to breathe, no longer a care in the world.

Moe glared at the body, then turned, brushed past Jeremy, and lumbered from the room. Jeremy watched him go. It was too bad about Uriah, but he'd done his best to stop his friend.

He sighed and went to the living room. Moe was sitting on the couch, his hands in his lap, his head back and his eyes closed.

Jeremy stood in front of him and spoke softly. "We'd better get out of here, Moe."

The lunk opened his eyes. The anger was gone and he looked like the old Moe again. The big man nodded and clambered to his feet.

Jeremy went back to the bedroom, took one last look at Uriah, then grabbed a blanket from the bed and went back to Moe. "You carry this. I'll take the bike."

Moe took the blanket as Jeremy wheeled the bicycle out into the hallway and down the stairs. They went out the back door where Jeremy stopped and turned to his friend. "I'll ride the bike. It won't hold you. You'll have to walk, okay?"

Moe nodded.

"I have to go to the street," Jeremy said, pointing across the adjoining, fenced-off parking lots. "I won't be able to get through there with the bike. Can I trust you to go straight back to our new home?"

Moe nodded again.

Jeremy watched him amble across the lot, climb over the fence, and continue on. He sighed, long and deep, before wheeling the bicycle toward the street.

CHAPTER 49

Friday, 10:36 a.m.

JAKE SAT ON THE GRASSY slope beside the sidewalk and leaned back against a tree. Annie sat and faced him, her knees up, her arms wrapped around her legs.

"It's impossible to say if they're still in this area," Jake said. "They've got a good head start out of here."

"They could be anywhere by now, but I think they'll soon run out of places to hide."

Jake looked over as a bicycle rattled past, less than ten feet from where they sat. It came from the apartment building. The young man had his baseball cap pulled low, and as he glanced at Jake, the rider's face took on a look of recognition, his eyes widening.

"It's Spencer," Jake said as he sprang to his feet. He dove for the bike and missed, his hand brushing the back of the rider as the bicycle spun away and wheeled down the sidewalk.

Jeremy peddled furiously, taking a sharp turn into the street as Jake sprinted behind. The rider swerved into the path of an oncoming car, and then veered back at the last second as the driver leaned on the horn and touched the brakes. Jake felt a breeze from the vehicle as it zipped past. The driver shouted something through an open window, picked up speed, and shot away.

Jeremy was gaining ground, his short legs pumping like pistons as he leaned over the handlebars. Jake sprinted after the bike but the distance between him and his quarry was growing. He wasn't going to make it.

A hundred feet away now, the bike tore through a stop sign and took a sharp left, down a residential street.

Jake stopped in the middle of the road, glanced back at Annie, and shook his head in disgust. She was on her feet, waving frantically and pointing. Jake caught her signal and he streaked across the street, over the sidewalk, and dashed up the side of a small clapboard house.

He vaulted over a low fence dividing the dwelling from the one behind it, and raced down the side of the second house, to the street beyond.

Annie's suggestion was dead on. Jeremy had circled back and was coming around the block, heading directly toward him. Jake stepped into the middle of the street. Brakes squealed, tires hopped, and the bike spun halfway around, ten feet away. Jeremy lost control, hit the ground heavily, and the bicycle clattered to the pavement, its front tire still spinning freely. He rolled once, struggled to rise, and when he came to his knees, he had a pistol in his hand.

"Stop right there," Jeremy said through gritted teeth. "I'll shoot you right where you stand. Yes, I surely will."

Jake stopped. What were his odds of grabbing the revolver? Not so good. He held out a hand. "Give me the gun, Jeremy."

"Not on your life." Spencer stood, careful to keep the weapon pointed at his target. "Don't come any closer, Jake. I don't want to shoot you, but I will if I have to. Yes, I surely will."

Jake didn't move. He'd been shot once before by the little creep, and he wasn't too keen on a repeat performance.

Jeremy's face contorted, his voice manic as he said, "I'm not going back to prison, and I'll kill anyone who gets in my way."

Jake crossed his arms. "You're free to go."

Jeremy looked at him sideways as if trying to decide whether or not Jake was serious. Finally, he crouched down and picked up the bicycle with one hand while holding the gun steady in the other.

Jake stood rooted to his spot and glared as the cold-blooded killer backed the bike up a few feet, keeping his eyes glued on Jake. Then with one motion, he twisted around, hopped on the bike, and leaned on the pedals.

Jake sprung forward. His hand brushed against the spinning rear wheel, leaving a black mark across his palm as the bike picked up speed. He followed, continually losing ground, until finally he stopped, stood still, and watched the bicycle disappear from sight.

He'd almost had the little creep. So close, but now he was as far away as ever.

~*~

ANNIE HAD WATCHED as her husband raced along the side of the house to the street beyond. She wasn't so sure Jake would catch Jeremy, but it was worth a shot.

The obvious thing was, the bicycle Jeremy had ridden was the same one she'd seen in Uriah's apartment. They must've missed him by a few minutes. She assumed Uriah had mentioned their visit. It might be a long shot, but she had to have another conversation with Uriah Hubert.

Annie walked across the lawn toward the front door of the apartment building. The women were still there, still sipping on beer, and still prattling on endlessly. She forced a smile as one of them waved a hand.

She went cautiously toward the front door. There was a possibility Moses Thacker might be lurking nearby and she had no desire to run into him. He was more than a match for her, and even Jake would be hard pressed to deal with the huge ex-con.

The lobby was empty, so she stepped inside, went to the foot of the stairs, looked up, and frowned. Uriah's door was open. She waited in case someone was leaving the apartment. She didn't hear any voices, the door stayed ajar, and all was quiet except for a muffled hum coming from an air register over her head.

She crept up the stairs, a step at a time, stopping on each

tread to listen. Finally, she reached the top and peered into the apartment, then poked her head around the frame. The bicycle was gone. A clock ticked on the wall. She breathed carefully, slowly, constantly listening for any sound indicating the presence of someone inside.

The living room was empty, no one in the kitchen. That left the bathroom and the bedroom. She took a careful step forward. She could see the bathroom, and the light was off. No one there. Now, for the bedroom.

She tiptoed down the hallway and stopped. She could she a rumpled bed, a clock on a small nightstand, bare walls above. One more step and she breathed a sigh of relief. The room was empty. She moved inside the doorway and looked around.

She gasped and her heart pounded. The room was not empty; there was a body on the floor. It was Uriah, and he lay in an unnatural position, one leg curled under, his eyes staring at the ceiling.

Dead. He had to be dead.

Annie crept a little closer, her body trembling, her breath quickening. Two more steps and she stood over him, staring down through unbelieving eyes.

He was dead. There was no doubt.

She immediately realized Jeremy couldn't have been the killer. Uriah appeared to have been strangled, with darkening bruises on his throat, his mouth halfway open as if gasping for air. Jeremy wasn't big enough or strong enough to do this. The little man would've shot him, not choked him to death with his bare hands.

A baseball bat lay against one wall. Uriah must have tried unsuccessfully to defend himself. Only a huge bundle of bone and muscle could've wrestled it from his grasp.

It had to have been Moses Thacker.

And he might be close by.

She spun around and listened, ready to dive under the bed or into the closet. There was no sound, and she held her breath as she stole silently from the room, down the hallway to the living room, and then to the doorway. She looked up and down the empty corridor before easing downstairs and out the back door.

She called 9-1-1, gave her name, and reported the murder of Uriah Hubert. She would give her statement later, but first, she was anxious to see if Jake caught Jeremy.

She hurried to the sidewalk where they'd parted and was disappointed to see Jake coming across the street, empty-handed.

Jeremy had eluded them again.

CHAPTER 50

Friday, 11:04 a.m.

JEREMY SQUEEZED THROUGH the gap in the fence, dragged the bicycle in behind him, and wheeled it around to the back door of the shop where he and Moe were hiding out.

It was a close call but he evaded Jake. He subconsciously touched the revolver behind his belt and glanced around. They hadn't often seen anyone on the streets in this area, but he was determined to be careful as they came and went from their hideout.

He pushed the bike inside the building, leaned it against an inner wall, and called, "Moe? Are you here?" He was relieved to hear an answer, coming from the office.

"In here, little buddy."

Jeremy hurried to join Moe. His friend had spread out the blanket on the improvised cardboard bed and lay flat on his back, staring at the ceiling. He sat up and crossed his legs at the ankles when Jeremy entered the room.

"We may be in trouble, Moe. I had a run-in with Jake Lincoln."

"But you got away," Moe said.

"Yes, Moe, I got away, but if I didn't have the gun he would've caught me. He surely would've."

Moe tilted his head slightly to one side. "Maybe we should leave this area. Go somewhere safe."

Jeremy sat on the end of the bed and looked at his friend. "I had a spill on the bike and I think the frame is bent. It doesn't ride very smooth now. It might not last much longer and won't support both of us."

Moe squinted as if trying to absorb that information. Then his tiny eyes brightened and he sat up. "We could get Uriah's motorcycle. He won't need it anymore."

"No, he surely won't, but it might be dangerous to go there again. We would have to go into the apartment to get the keys."

"I can stay outside," Moe said. "Make sure nobody comes while you go in." He shrugged. "Nobody knows he's dead anyway. Uriah doesn't have any other friends and no one ever came to see him while we were there."

Jeremy thought about Moe's suggestion. They needed some form of transportation, and the motorcycle would be perfect. The Lincolns, however, were a problem. They might be still hanging about. If they went to get the bike, they would have to be doubly careful. No doubt.

He knew if he were to continue with his mission, the police, as well as the Lincolns, were always going to pursue them no matter where they went.

Yes, the motorcycle would be ideal, and perhaps he could see if Uriah had any more money in his wallet, and grab some food from the fridge. After all, it wasn't wrong to steal from dead people. He'd done it before and his conscience hadn't bothered him.

Moe fidgeted with his hands, a troubled look on his face. He opened his mouth to speak but no words came out as he rocked slowly back and forth.

"What is it, Moe?" Jeremy asked. "What's troubling you?"

Moe looked away a moment, then dropped his eyes, staring at his hands. "Jeremy, I'm sorry I killed Uriah. I don't know why. Sometimes I can't control what happens when I get angry." He raised his eyes, pleading, "I'm sorry. I did a wrong thing."

Jeremy took a deep breath and leaned in. He spoke softly. "Moe, saying sorry isn't going to help this time. He's dead and sorry won't bring him back."

Moe dropped his head and nodded slowly. "Yeah, I know that."

Jeremy touched his friend's knee. "It's all right, Moe. It really is. It wasn't your fault."

Moe's face brightened. "Then you forgive me?"

"I forgive you."

Moe really was getting hard to control, but Jeremy was determined to stick it out. His friend needed someone to keep him on the straight and narrow, and Jeremy was the only one who cared enough to watch over the big lug. The problem was, they were both wanted men, the hounds hard on their heels, and he didn't see things getting any easier.

It didn't appear Annie Lincoln was doing much by way of finding out who'd killed his parents. Instead, she was spending her time searching for Moe and him. He'd kept his promise and told her where Joey was buried, and he was severely disappointed she hadn't honored her word. He'd trusted her.

Maybe she was a liar and no better than the rest.

He considered Moe's suggestion they move to another city—one where they weren't known, and where people would leave them alone.

He decided that might be the answer.

He stood and beckoned to Moe. "Let's go get the motorcycle before it's too late." After they returned with the bike he would be able to relax and figure out their plans.

Moe made it to his feet and lumbered from the room, following his friend's lead. Jeremy stopped at the door, removed the pistol from his waist, and spun the cylinder. It was still fully loaded, with lots of ammunition in his pocket. The revolver was a trusted friend now—it had saved him from getting caught by Jake Lincoln, and he wouldn't hesitate to use it if necessary.

He pointed to a length of chain, about four feet long, tossed up against one wall. He'd noticed it earlier and never thought much about it until now. "Grab that chain, Moe. I only have one gun, and that may help protect you."

Moe moved to the wall and picked up the chain, examined it a moment, wrapped one end in a big fist, and swung it over his head. He grinned. "This should stop anybody."

Jeremy watched Moe ball up the chain and work it into his

pocket. He turned toward the door. He felt much safer inside the building, but they needed the bike. He pulled his cap low, opened the door, and peeked outside, surprised now he was getting so paranoid.

No one was in sight. They walked carefully to the front of the building and moved to the gap in the fence. He looked up and down the sidewalk, then prodded Moe back out of sight as a pickup truck rolled past.

Moe followed him through the fence and they hurried up the sidewalk toward Uriah's apartment, watching carefully on all sides lest they be seen. The chain in Moe's pocket gave a rattle with each step.

They crossed the parking lots, hopped the fences behind the buildings, and approached the back door. Uriah's old Suzuki was still in place, chained to a post by the rear door.

"Stay here, Moe," Jeremy directed. "Keep out of sight while I go in." He pointed to the big blue bin. "If anyone comes, hide behind there."

Moe nodded eagerly.

Jeremy continued, "If it's anyone you don't know, don't try to stop them. But if it's Jake or Annie Lincoln, you have to do whatever you can to keep them out."

Moe nodded again and pulled the chain from his pocket. He swung it in the air a couple of times and then stood beside the door, ready to keep guard.

Jeremy pulled open the fire escape door and peered inside. "I'll be back right away," he said as he stepped inside the building. The door scraped closed behind him, and he hurried up the stairs to Uriah's apartment.

CHAPTER 51

Friday, 11:19 a.m.

JAKE LOOKED AT HIS WATCH, expecting the police and emergency vehicles would arrive soon. This wasn't exactly an emergency; Uriah Hubert was already dead and beyond human help, but what concerned him most was the presence of Jeremy Spencer in the neighborhood. If the bicycle was all he had for transportation, he wouldn't get far, but time was wasting. The sooner the police got on his trail, the better.

Jake had called Hank and given him a rundown on what they discovered. The detective was on the other side of the city at the time, but was now on his way. A massive roadblock would be set up shortly, encompassing a multiblock perimeter surrounding the neighborhood, watching all possible escape routes.

An extensive and thorough search would then commence. Vehicles would be stopped, the drivers questioned and examined, door-to-door canvassing would begin, and any conceivable hiding places would be scrutinized.

Jake turned to Annie, who was pacing up and down the sidewalk. He could almost see her mind at work as she walked, her head down, her brow in an intense line.

She stopped pacing and looked at Jake. "He's close by," she said. "I'm sure Moses Thacker killed Hubert, yet you ran into Jeremy and he was alone. Unless they went their separate ways—which is doubtful—they have to meet up eventually." She made a sweeping motion with one arm. "They're around here somewhere."

"Perhaps we should get the car and patrol the streets until the police come," Jake said with a shrug. "It's only a couple of blocks away, and it's better than standing around doing nothing."

Annie agreed. "I'll get the car," she said. "You can stay here and wait until the police arrive." Without pausing for an answer, she set off on a quick march in the direction of the vehicle, digging in her handbag for the car keys as she went.

Jake watched Annie leave before heading toward the apartment building. She'd said Uriah Hubert had been strangled, and if the killer was indeed Moses Thacker, then they were looking for not one, but two cold-blooded murderers. He knew Spencer was armed, but wasn't sure about Thacker. The big thug had used Jeremy's weapon for the robbery, so it seemed unlikely.

Jake crossed the lawn and nodded at one of the two women lounged outside the building. She waved a hand and leered at him as he walked by. The second one was taking a siesta, her head flopped sideways at an awkward angle. Probably passed out, and by the looks of it, the other one would soon follow.

He pulled open the door and went inside the small lobby in time to see the rear door swinging closed. Someone was just leaving and from what little he could see of the person's back, he recognized who he saw.

It was that little creep, Jeremy Spencer, and he wasn't going to get away this time.

With half a dozen long strides, Jake made it to the door, pulled it open, and leaped out to the rear parking lot. Spencer was ten feet away and must've seen him from the corner of his eye. Jeremy's hand reached to his belt as Jake dove forward and bore him to the ground.

Spencer landed heavily on his back, struggling uselessly under Jake's full weight as Jake straddled him and pinned his arms.

And then the slimeball smiled. At first, a hint of humor appeared on his face, and then a full smile, and then finally, a laugh—crazy, like a lunatic.

In the next moment, a pair of massive hands were around Jake's throat and he was dragged bodily to one side, and then yanked upright. He struggled to breathe and brought his hands up as huge fingers dug into his neck, his unknown assailant emitting a deep, maniacal growl in his ear.

Jake's head felt light. Through dimming eyes, he saw Spencer clamber to his feet, brush himself off, and then cross his arms and smirk as Jake worked at the powerful hands cutting off his life.

With a final effort, Jake was able to wrap a fist around one of the viselike fingers. He brought his hands together and, summoning his remaining strength, he gritted his teeth, pulled, twisted, and prayed. His biceps bulged and he heard a sickening snap.

His assailant's growl turned to a screech of agony, the death grip was released, and Jake gasped for air.

Spencer screamed, "Hang onto him, Moe."

Jake spun around. The face of his attacker looked even uglier in person than in the mug shot. From five feet away, small eyes glared at him with a burning hatred. The killer had a torso like a wooden barrel, legs like pillars of stone, and except for the broken finger, hands that looked like they could crush solid rock.

The giant of a man was eye to eye with Jake, but his massive proportions made him seem a foot taller. The monster leaned forward, gauging his opponent, ready to pounce at the first sign of an opening. His muscled arms hung out to his sides like an ape, the broken finger seemingly forgotten as he huffed, puffed, and panted.

Spencer hopped around eagerly, still screaming, "Get him, Moe. Break his spine."

Jake took a step forward and swung an arm toward his adversary. The action was not intended to strike a blow, but rather to gauge the reaction of the ugly stack of flesh and bones standing in front of him. The ape's response time was slow.

"Use the chain, Moe." It was Spencer again.

Moe grinned and reached his right hand to his side. He

raised it a moment later, his fist wrapped around the end of a chain, the links rattling as the weapon uncoiled from his pocket.

It whistled through the air, singing a deadly song as Moe swung it over his head, around and around.

"Move in, Moe. Wrap it around his neck."

Moe stepped forward. The weapon sang, and Jake ducked.

As the chain circled again, Jake straightened and took a step back. He spun around, looking for a weapon of any kind—anything that would protect him from the deadly swinging chain. Nothing seemed to fit the purpose. He turned back to face his opponent, keeping a safe distance. If that chain connected once, Jake would be finished.

The deadly weapon stopped whirling and now hung limp from the monster's raised fist, ready to be brought into play again at a moment's notice.

As Jake slowly circled his opponent, Jeremy stayed behind his friend, well out of danger. With his peripheral vision, Jake saw the little man reach to his waist and pull out a revolver. He held it up and screamed, "Move, Moe. I'll shoot him."

Moe turned his head in reaction to the voice and Jake stepped in. He wrapped his fist around the chain and whipped it backwards. The ape held on. A tug of war began as biceps bulged, leg muscles rooting each combatant in place.

It was a test of strength, will, and wit.

Intelligence won the battle.

Jake released the chain and Moe went sprawling, landing on his back with a whump, still holding the chain.

Jake kept his distance. He didn't want to physically tangle with the muscle-bound giant. If he could manage to hold him off until the police arrived, they would take care of him.

The big lunk lumbered to his feet, his eyes spewing hatred, his face contorted and twisted with rage. He raised his hands, clenching and unclenching his fists in front of his bared teeth. Jake stayed well back—one careless move could be his last.

A motorcycle roared to life and Spencer shouted, "Moe, get on the bike."

The raging maniac glanced toward his friend and his face calmed somewhat. Jeremy eased the bike backwards, the revolver poised in one hand. Jake kept the monster between him and the gun as Moe climbed on the back of the motorcycle, the chain wrapped in his huge fist.

Jeremy touched the gas. The bike hopped forward, wobbled, and labored under the heavy load as it gained ground.

Jake stood helpless and watched as the madmen rode out the driveway and spun onto the road.

He heard the faint sound of sirens in the distance.

CHAPTER 52

Friday, 11:27 a.m.

ANNIE PULLED HER VEHICLE to the curb in front of Uriah Hubert's apartment building and shut off the engine. It didn't appear the police had arrived yet, but she was sure she heard sirens coming from somewhere far away.

Hank should be here before long as well, and she was anxious to get the search underway before it was too late. They couldn't afford to let Jeremy slip from their grasp this time. Too many lives were at stake. She knew from past experience, Jeremy was impulsive at times, but he was intelligent enough to be more careful after such a close call.

She spun her head, startled to hear Jake's bellowing voice. "Start the car." He dashed across the lawn toward her, waving his arms.

She reached over and swung open the passenger door and then turned the key. The engine came back to life as Jake hopped in the vehicle.

He twisted in the seat and pointed ahead. "That way. Quick. Spencer and Thacker just took off on a bike."

Annie pulled the transmission into drive. "Both of them? On a bike?"

"Not a bicycle. A motorcycle."

Annie touched the gas and the car sprung ahead. They headed down a side street, away from the government housing, deeper into the suburbs.

"Are you sure you don't want to drive?" Annie asked, as the car careened down the road. She'd never been a fast driver, even on the highway. Speed was more Jake's thing, and he usually pushed the Firebird to the limit whenever he had the chance.

"You'll do fine," Jake said. "Just give it a little more gas."

Annie pressed the pedal a little closer to the floor.

Jake leaned forward and peered through the windshield. "They can't be far ahead. There's a lot of weight on that little bike."

Annie slowed at a stop sign, rolled through, then touched the gas.

"Back there," Jake said, poking a thumb over his shoulder. "They went to the right."

Annie hit the brakes. Tires squealed. She made a three-point turn as Jake urged her to hurry. Finally, she got the vehicle headed the other way.

"Forget about the stop sign," Jake said. "Just go. There's no traffic."

She barreled through the stop sign, made a turn, and pressed the pedal to the floor. "My Escort isn't really made for this," she said.

Jake pointed ahead. "I can see them. Just keep going."

The car hit a speed bump. It jolted them in their seat, the shocks taking a beating as the vehicle bounced and rebounded. Annie struggled to hold the car on the road.

"We're gaining on them," Jake said.

Annie chanced a glance at her husband. He was enjoying this—a lot more than she was. "What happens if we catch up to them?" she asked.

"I'm not sure. We'll worry about that when it happens."

"You're not wearing a seat belt," she said.

"I trust your driving."

"That makes one of us."

Jake chuckled. "Welcome to Jake's Driving School."

"They're turning again," Annie said, peering through the windshield.

They were twenty seconds behind their quarry, slowly gaining. Annie touched the brakes as she neared the spot where the motorcycle turned. It was a sidewalk leading from the main road into a residential area.

"You can make it," Jake said.

"On the sidewalk?"

"Yup. It's wide enough."

Annie hit the brakes hard and spun the wheel. The vehicle hopped onto the sidewalk and zoomed ahead, a handful of spare inches between a pair of light posts.

"You're a natural," Jake said.

Five seconds later they were on the next street, safely off the narrow sidewalk, and the motorcycle was dead ahead.

They were close enough to see an expression of anger and

determination on Jeremy's face as he twisted his head toward his pursuers. He knew they were chasing him. She heard the roar of the engine as the bike wobbled dangerously and then righted itself.

Jake pulled out his iPhone and called RHPD. As he waited for an answer, he said to Annie, "We need to get a roadblock set up."

Someone answered the phone. "RHPD. How can I help you?"

"It's Jake Lincoln. Patch me through to dispatch immediately."

It was Yappy. "Sorry, Jake. I can't do that. You're a civilian."

"Yappy, this is an emergency. We're chasing a serial killer here. I think Diego will be pretty upset if you don't put me through."

A pause on the line, and then, "Hold on, Jake. I'll put you through."

The motorcycle continued on. The street took twists and turns through the otherwise quiet residential neighborhood. Annie hung on to the wheel. They were close enough now she could run them off the road if she wanted to.

Jake got through to dispatch, gave his name and location, and requested any cruisers in the area to aid in the chase. After dispatch checked with Captain Diego to get his okay, Jake was hastily informed it might be several minutes, and to stay on the line.

"They're turning again," Annie announced.

The car tires squealed as she slowed abruptly, then twisted

the wheel and spun expertly onto a wide street. The motorcycle passed a car ahead, swerving into the oncoming lane and back again. Annie followed, well over the speed limit. The driver of the car gave a hand gesture and shook his head. She didn't pay any attention. The unsuspecting driver would likely find out more on the evening news.

They had reached the boundary of the subdivision and would soon be entering a commercial area. Not far ahead, factories and warehouses made up much of the terrain. It would be easy for a motorcycle to weave in and around the buildings and through places a car wouldn't be able to go.

Jake continued to give their location and drummed his fingers on the dashboard.

Annie checked her fuel gauge. No problem there. If one of them ran out of fuel, she bet it would be the bike.

The motorcycle wobbled again and straightened itself as it made another turn, this time into a warehouse area. It sped to the rear of a large steel-framed building, poking up two stories high. They whipped by parked trucks, garbage bins, and loading docks. The bike maneuvered around a tractor-trailer, Annie following, as she relentlessly continued the chase.

Jake still held the phone to his ear—waiting for something or someone—but his attention was on the pursuit.

"You're doing great," he said. "Hang in there and we're gonna get them."

The fugitives reached the end of the building and the bike slowed, about to make a sharp turn into a narrow alleyway between two buildings. The car would never make it through there.

Annie hit the brakes hard. The vehicle spun halfway around and came to a jolting stop. She stared through the windshield as the bike turned into the alley, wobbled, righted itself, wobbled again, and then hit the concrete wall of the adjoining building.

She heard the sickening sound of metal on concrete as the motorcycle scraped along the wall, then went down, spinning across the asphalt. Its riders were thrown clear, the big one in a heap against the rock-hard wall of the building, the small one on his back, resting awkwardly against the rear wheel of the mangled motorcycle.

The chase was over.

As she sprang from the vehicle she heard Jake's impatient voice. "Trace the location of my phone and send a cruiser. Now."

CHAPTER 53

Friday, 11:41 p.m.

FROM WHERE JAKE SAT, it appeared Moses Thacker was badly hurt. His left pant leg was tattered and nearly ripped clean off. His leg must have taken a good beating as it scraped along the concrete wall. That was a good thing; he was no longer a threat.

Jake left his phone on, his call to dispatch still connected, and shoved it into his pocket as he jumped from the car and ran to the alleyway behind Annie.

Jeremy groaned and leaned forward, resting on one elbow. His other hand reached for his waist, and in a moment, a revolver was gripped in his hand. He raised the weapon, his face twisted in pain as he struggled to a sitting position.

Annie came to a quick stop and brought her hands up halfway, palms out, an involuntary motion as if to protect her from being shot.

With one more stride, Jake reached her side and stopped.

Spencer was ten feet away and the look on his face showed he was willing to use the weapon. The little creep was down, but not out, and Jake's odds in disarming him before he squeezed the trigger weren't ones he wanted to test. Cornering Jeremy would only antagonize him further, forcing him to shoot his way out.

Jake reached out a hand. "It's over, Jeremy. Give me the gun."

Jeremy waved the pistol, his teeth gritted. "Never."

"The police are on their way."

"Doesn't matter."

Moe groaned, worked his way to a sitting position, and examined the lacerations on his leg. His face contorted with anger as he looked at Jake. A growl escaped from his throat and he tried to stand, then winced in pain and fell back heavily. He leaned against the concrete wall, half-twisted to face Jake and Annie. His small eyes flared as he raised a clenched fist and bared his teeth.

"I'm going to break your neck," the monster of a man said and growled again, a sound mixed with anger and pain.

Jake crossed his arms and glared back. "It really doesn't look like you're in any position to do that right now, but feel free to look me up again if you ever get out of prison."

"Shut your mouth, Jake Lincoln," Jeremy screamed. "He's not going to prison and neither am I."

Annie put a hand on Jake's arm and spoke softly to Jeremy. "If you shoot either one of us you'll only make things worse."

"How can things get any worse?" Jeremy looked at the

bike, kicked at the wheel, and cursed. "The bike's ruined, my friend is in pain, and so am I."

"You can't blame us for that."

Jeremy kept one eye on Jake and struggled to his feet. He held the gun high, aimed down the barrel, and limped forward one step. He winced in pain, then stopped and glanced at his leg, testing his weight. He was obviously in pain, perhaps a cracked bone.

"Neither of you can escape in your condition," Annie said calmly, holding out a hand. "Give me the gun."

Spencer's face contorted. "No. Never. Never." He glared a moment and looked at his bandaged thumb. He tried to move it, his mouth twisting into a grimace. He dropped the arm to his side and let it hang loose.

Moe shook his head violently. "Don't give them the gun, Jeremy."

Jeremy looked at his friend. "I don't intend to." He turned his gaze toward Jake and sneered. "I'm going to kill both of them soon if they don't leave." He brandished the gun. "I didn't want to kill you but I have no choice."

"If you kill us, Jeremy, you'll never find out who murdered your parents," Annie said and shrugged. "The police don't care. Nobody cares but us."

Jeremy frowned deeply, his lips tight as he considered Annie's comment. Finally he spoke, his voice calmer but skeptical. "Did you find out anything?"

"Maybe."

Moe clenched his teeth and made another unsuccessful attempt to stand. "Shoot them both," he said as he fell back against the wall. "They're lying to you."

Annie raised her chin. "Why would we lie, Moe?"

Moe licked his lips. "Because you're liars."

Jake rolled his eyes and held back a smile. He leaned in. "What're you afraid of, you big ape?"

Jeremy glanced at Moe with a confused look. "Moe, what makes you think they'd lie about it?"

Moe didn't answer.

Annie spoke softly, pleading. "If you put the gun down, Jeremy, I'll tell you who killed your parents."

Jeremy looked at the weapon in his hand a moment, then gave a deep sigh and looked at Annie.

"Shoot them, Jeremy," Moe said. "They're trying to trick you."

Jeremy focused his eyes on Moe, a confused look on his face. "Do you know something you're not telling me, Moe? Do you know who killed Father?"

Moe avoided Jeremy's eyes and growled. "I didn't know him."

Jeremy continued to glare thoughtfully for a few moments, his eyes narrowed. Finally, he asked, "Were you in prison when my father was there?"

"It wasn't me," Moe said, keeping his head down. "It wasn't me. It was another guy killed him."

Jeremy's body stiffened. "I thought you didn't know him?"

Moe was silent as Jeremy crouched down and looked at his friend, bewildered. "Moe? Did you know him? Are you lying to me?"

Moe looked up, pain in his eyes, and he reached out a trembling hand toward his friend.

Jeremy's eyes bulged, he leaned forward, and his voice grew in intensity. "Moe? You didn't kill Father, did you?" His head moved back and forth between Annie and Moe. "Tell me it's not true."

Moe dropped his head, fidgeting with his hands in his lap.

"Did you kill my father, Moe?" Jeremy screamed.

Moe swallowed hard and took a deep breath, then looked up, avoiding his friend's eyes. "I'm sorry, Jeremy. I didn't mean to do it."

"Do what?" Jeremy screamed.

"Didn't mean to kill your father. I'm not good at secrets and this was the only one I ever kept." Moe shrunk back. "I . . . I was ashamed."

Jeremy looked at Annie, open-mouthed, confused.

"Jeremy, please put the gun down," Annie said, pleading.

Jeremy's stood again, his eyes narrowed, his breathing rapid and shallow as he dropped the revolver to his side and looked at Moe. He tried to speak, his mouth opening and closing, but no sound came out.

Moe held his hands out toward Jeremy, tears now escaping from his eyes, his voice a deep, gasping whine. "I'm sorry, little buddy. I didn't want to kill your parents. Things happen when I get angry."

Jeremy limped toward Moe, the revolver now pointed toward the monster on the ground. "My parents?" he screamed. "You killed Mother too?"

"I didn't want to hurt her. I only wanted to say sorry for killing your father." Moe was hysterical, panting, and he pleaded with his lips, his eyes, his hands. "She wouldn't listen to me. I told her I was sorry and she wouldn't listen. Then I hung her in the barn to make it look like she did it herself."

Jeremy gripped the gun tighter, his screaming voice increasing in intensity. "Why didn't you tell me this before?"

"I … I was ashamed … and afraid. We were friends before I realized who you were, and then … I was afraid to tell you. Afraid you wouldn't forgive me."

Jeremy trembled all over. His hand shook as he held the revolver six inches from Moe's frightened eyes. "What about my barn?"

Moe kept his eyes on Jeremy, his body shaking, his voice trembling. "I burned it because they might find evidence. When you were inside talking to the reporter lady." He clasped his hands together and looked up at Jeremy.

The gun moved two inches closer to Moe's forehead as Jeremy shrieked, "I thought you were my friend. I took care of you, watched out for you, protected you."

"Don't do it, Jeremy," Annie screamed.

Jake took a slow step forward, unsure what to do.

Moe shrunk back as the tears continued to flow down his face, dripping onto the front of his tattered shirt. "I'm sorry, Jeremy. Please forgive me. I'm sorry."

Jeremy dropped his head back and emitted a roar of anger, pain, and disappointment, then abruptly brought his head forward, wrapped his hands together, and squeezed the trigger.

Moe's head shot forward. Blood, body tissue, and brain matter painted the wall behind him. The blowback of scarlet spattered the gun, the killer's hands, his arms, his face.

Jeremy howled and pulled the trigger again. And again and again …

The hammer smacked the firing pin over and over—click, click, click—as the angry young man poured years of pent-up wrath into the empty weapon.

The Lincolns watched quietly as Jeremy lowered his head, physically exhausted, emotionally broken, his spirit consumed. His shoulders slumped as the now useless weapon slipped from his hand and clattered to the asphalt at his feet.

EPILOGUE

ANNIE STOOD QUIETLY and observed the pair of cold-blooded killers, one dead, covered with his own treacherous blood, the other reduced to a quivering, pathetic creature, moaning with emotional torment, heartbreak, and utter despair.

Jake stepped forward and retrieved the blood-spattered revolver as the whine of sirens sounded in the distance. Officers would be here shortly, in time to pick up the pieces.

Three or four people were gathered at the far end of the alleyway, drawn by the sound of the shots. They leaned against the wall, or stood with hands in pockets, or folded arms, each with a different opinion about what took place.

Annie turned as a brown Chevy pulled up beside her car. Hank got out from behind the steering wheel, King from the other side. The detectives moved into the alley and stood beside the Lincolns.

Hank observed the scene, shaking his head slowly. "I wasn't sure if I could get here in time," he said. "Looks like I didn't need to."

Annie motioned toward Jeremy, sunken to his knees, his head still down. "He's all yours."

"Cuff him, King."

Detective King slipped a pair of cuffs from his belt as he moved toward Jeremy. "Stand up. Hands behind your back."

The defeated killer stumbled quietly to his feet and King slipped the handcuffs on. The prisoner winced in pain as the restraints were tightened about his wrists.

Hank was on his cell phone, calling for an ambulance. Soon, the scene would be processed—documented, photographed, and analyzed, the body of the dead killer taken to the city morgue.

A cruiser's siren died as it pulled up at an awkward angle outside the alleyway. King prodded the despondent murderer past them and pushed him into the backseat of the waiting vehicle. The door slammed—the prisoner secured.

"I was at Uriah Hubert's apartment when I got the call from dispatch," Hank said. "They're still processing it. Looks like our forensic team's going to have a busy day."

"Hopefully, they can all take a vacation after this," Jake said. "That little creep's killing spree is over."

An officer urged onlookers to step back and both ends of the alleyway were secured with yellow tape. Another cruiser pulled up, then a third.

Hank stood speechless as Annie related Moses Thacker's confession to the killing of Jeremy's parents. "You have three witnesses to what he admitted," she said. "According to the warden, they knew it was him, and, not surprisingly, the other inmates said they saw nothing." Annie shrugged. "Without a witness, they couldn't prove it."

Annie continued, "The unofficial story is that Moe got in a fight with another inmate and thought Quinton Spencer snitched on him. The truth is, he didn't snitch, but Moe was convinced he did and so he killed him."

"We can't convict a dead man," Hank said. "But a hearing, with both of you testifying as to the statements of the deceased, will clean up a pair of cold cases and at least set the record straight."

"We'll fill out complete statements later," Jake said, then glanced at Annie. "But right now we just want to go home."

Hank smiled and nodded in understanding. "I'll talk to you soon."

Annie turned and followed Jake, and they ducked under the tape and went to their vehicle. She glanced over to the backseat of the cruiser holding the subdued killer. Jeremy sat quietly, his head down as a torrent of tears washed away the blood of his former friend.

Annie watched the cruiser pull away and disappear from sight. She was torn between absolute abhorrence and an inexplicable sympathy for the wretched young man.

The Lincolns turned their back on the scene, got into their car, and drove away quietly.

It had been a long week.

###

Made in the USA
Columbia, SC
23 September 2023